TEMPTATION
A Robin Covington New Adult Romance

Giving in never felt so good.

She needs to be good.

At sixteen, Kit ditched her crappy life and moved to Nashville with only $200, her guitar, and a notebook full of songs. She hit it big, but five years of living like a rock star plus a stint in rehab has killed any good will she had with her label. The suits have ordered Kit to shape up or ship out of the limelight. The last thing she needs is a hot, sexy distraction with a sinful smile.

He doesn't know the meaning of the word.

Max Butler is as far from a celebrity as you can get and he likes it that way. A Nashville firefighter, he's living the single life with a revolving door of parties, friends, and a different woman in his bed every night. When his normal life suddenly collides with the girl on his favorite Rolling Stone cover, he sees the perfect chance to fulfill his ultimate fantasy and see just how bad Kit can be.

Sometimes bad is so very good.

With three weeks until Kit leaves for her big tour, Max promises to give her a break from being the good girl--no strings attached. But when hot days lead to sultry nights, the lines get blurred and suddenly three weeks of bad might not be   good   enough.

What others are saying about TEMPTATION

TEMPTATION

BY

ROBIN COVINGTON

Giving In Never Felt So Good

Copyright © 2014 by Robin Covington d/b/a Burning Up the Sheets, LLC. All rights reserved, including the right to reproduce, distribute, or transmit in any form or by any means. For information regarding subsidiary rights, please contact the Publisher.

Burning Up the Sheets, LLC
23139 Laurel Way
Hollywood, MD 20636

Visit my website at
 www.robincovingtonromance.com.
Edited by Kristin Anders, The Romantic Editor
Copy edited by Kim VanDerwerker,
        Wordsmith Proofreading Services and Nicole Bailey at Proof Before You Publish, Inc.
Cover design by Babski Creative Studios.
Cover Photo Credit: Jenn LeBlanc/Illustrated Romance
Formatting by Anessa Books

E-book ISBN: 978-0-9905432-0-6
Paperback ISBN: 978-0-9905432-1-3

Manufactured in the United States of America
First Edition August 2014

DEDICATION

For my father, who gave me the gift of music at an early age and taught me the power of a great lyric delivered with heart.

I love you.

CHAPTER ONE
Kit

I was going to die in a bathroom.

Just like Elvis.

The thought that I might end up as one half of a morbid trivia question—I'll take "name the music stars who died in the bathroom" for $400, Alex"—did not stop the panic from rising in my throat as I struggled to focus my thoughts over the God–awful shrieking of the fire alarms. In the restroom of my record label's rehearsal studio, the emergency lights gave off just enough light to let me see the smoke creeping under the edge of the door. I was no expert on the ideal smoke–to–actual–fire ratio before you died of smoke inhalation, but I knew I had to get out of here and make it to safety. Now.

Physically shaking off my dark thoughts, I stumbled over to the row of sinks, grabbed several lengths of paper towels, ran them under water and squeezed out the excess just like they'd taught me in school many years ago. *Hey, Mrs. Midkiff; I really was paying attention!*

I caught my dim reflection in the mirror and it wasn't pretty. Terror was not a good look for me. My long curly hair was in snarls and sticking to my face and neck with sweat, the crimson streaks that were my trademark looked Halloween–costume creepy when paired with my runny mascara and eyeliner and the smeared red of my lip gloss. I hadn't looked this bad since I'd checked my ass into rehab.

Coughing at the smoke irritating my throat, I slapped the towels over my nose and mouth, my hands shaking as I desperately tried to get my nerves under control.

I didn't want to die. I was only twenty–one years old.

Succumbing to panic was not an option.

I took another look at the smoke creeping under the door.

And neither was staying here any longer.

The smoke was definitely getting thicker now and I had to force my wobbly legs to take me to the door. I reached out with the back of my hand and touched the metal door to see if it was hot and I almost wept when it wasn't. I might have a clear path to safety once I got out of the restroom.

Dropping to my knees, I covered my mouth and eased the door open with my free hand. The alarm was even louder in the hallway and the smoke so heavy the emergency lighting was useless out here. I was now virtually blind and deaf because of the noise. Not a good combination.

I picked the direction that I thought led to the stairwell, briefly considering going back to the studio for my beloved Martin guitar, Jolene. I loved that instrument more than anything in the world but I couldn't risk trying to find my way back through the twisty hallways of the One More Song Entertainment studios. The thought of never holding it again made me want to lie down on the floor and bawl like a baby, but I couldn't do it. I'd worked too hard to get clean and bounce back from all the stupid decisions I'd made eighteen months ago. I was just starting to see the future that I could have—one where I called the shots and where I figured just who the hell Kit Landry really was in and out of the spotlight.

It wasn't going to be easy—there were so many people who didn't want me to rock the successful, money–making boat that they'd all ridden on for years. They wanted me to be the same girl—America's country–music sweetheart— and I was just figuring out that I was more; that I *could* be more. More than the image I'd hidden behind for the last five years. I was determined to have the chance to find a balance between the old and new Kit and that desire kept me crawling on this floor. It kept me from lying down and giving in to the exhaustion that was weighing me down.

The top of my head hit an immobile object with a brain–scrambling thud and I reached up, feeling the emergency door under my fingertips. *Thank you, baby Jesus!* With the excitement of potentially avoiding death giving me an extra jolt of energy, I lifted up and pushed on the release bar.

It wouldn't budge.

Shit.

Overcome with the urge to take a deep breath, I dropped to the ground and re–covered my mouth with the cloth. Panic hovered on the edge of reason as I frantically searched my brain for what to do next. I was running out of all the stuff I'd learned in the few years I'd attended school regularly.

Okay... just staying here sounds like a bad idea, but I can't see down the hall...maybe I should just stay here... the fire department will see me signed in on this floor... the smoke is getting really thick... don't cough... makes it worse... damn, I really don't want to die like this... this will be on one of those awful "How did they die?" documentary shows... I'm just getting my life back...

Huddled closer to the ground, I tried to breathe in shallow bursts but the smoke was so thick I couldn't stop coughing, and inhaled more and more smoke. I couldn't go forward. I couldn't see enough to go back.

I was so screwed.

Paralyzed with fear and only shitty options, I re–covered my face with the towels and listened for any sounds of rescue.

I was dizzy and disoriented, a heaviness settling in my arms and legs—making it hard to keep my mouth covered. I tried to focus, but my mind was drifting, memories moving through like the way sunlight skated across my eyelids when I was a kid lying on the soft grass near my house—my Daddy and Mama, being on my own way too soon, coming to Nashville alone and broke at sixteen, selling my first record... touring... Jake when he was my first love and the first one to break my heart... my months at Spring Ridge Rehab... the fans... performing....

Fuck; they were right. It really does pass before your eyes...

But what killed me were the things I didn't see. A normal life. A real date with a guy I hadn't met through my publicists. An end to all the lying and secrets. A family. Marriage. Kids. A home.

Hell, yeah, to the minivan. Bring it on—at least someday. I wasn't going to judge something I'd never had.

And if someone didn't find me quick... I never would.

I heard noises in the distance, relief kicking up the adrenaline again and giving me enough energy to raise myself up on my knees. I tried to see if anyone was coming down the hall but the smoke had thickened, the smell of burning plastic, commercial carpet, and electronics getting stronger by the second. Hot tears fell from my burning eyes and down my face, and I knew I was about three seconds from losing my shit. I was a tough girl. Life had knocked me around, but this blow had come from left field and I zigged when I should have zagged.

Too fucking bad.

I removed the towels from my mouth and yelled as loudly as I could. Which wasn't loud at all.

I sucked in another breath through the towel filter and coughed before trying again. "Help!"

Oh, shit. That took it all out of me and I collapsed on the floor, ignoring the pain that shot through my chin when my head landed with a THUNK! on the nasty commercial carpet. I hoped to God that someone heard me because I had just blown my entire wad with that stunt. My eyes were sliding shut and there wasn't a damn thing I could do about it.

A voice, distant and muffled, filtered into my consciousness. "Hey, Dean! I found someone over here!"

Through the fog in my brain, I registered a pair of rough gloves yanking on my arms and hauling me close to a large body. A mask was placed over my mouth and I sucked in big gulps of smoke–free air. It was delicious. Better than chocolate, I swear.

"Hang on. I've got you. Just hang on." The smooth, deep voice of my rescuer rushed over me, calming me until I suddenly remembered Isaac, the security guard on duty.

Pushing off the mask, I croaked, "You've got to get..." I wasn't able to finish the warning because I started coughing, so much that I expected to see my toenails go flying across the room with the next big hack.

"Is there someone else in the building?" He looked down at me, up close and definitely space–invading because of the thick smoke, but he was able to see me nod. He pressed a button on his uniform and spoke into a walkie–talkie mounted on his shoulder. "Dean, we've got a second vic in the building."

"Get yours outta here. I'm on it."

"My guitar." I knew it was stupid and selfish to mention an object, but she was like a person to me.

"Your guitar?" he asked and when I nodded he immediately shook his head. "Sorry, I'm not going back for a guitar. My captain would have my ass in a sling for that one."

My rescuer lifted me up, murmuring into my ear as he moved down the hallway, "Let's get you safe and checked out. Just hang on, ma'am."

Shifting his hold on me, he shoved against the emergency door several times. It still wouldn't budge even with his ginormous body ramming against it. That fucking door was really messing with my need to get out of the blazing inferno. Mr. Rescue wasn't happy either.

He let out a creative curse and spoke into the walkie–talkie again. "Unit Three. I have a female victim on the third floor. Emergency exit blocked. I'm headed to the windows on the northeast side of the building. Going to the fire escape. Over."

Fire escape. Heights. Rickety stairs.

I pushed down the panic that surged up from my

stomach and threatened to splatter all over his nice fireman's uniform. I hated heights. When my team had suggested my adding some of that Cirque Du Soleil stuff that P!nk did in her shows to my concert, I told them that I was all for it as long as they issued raincoats to all the seats under me. I would hurl. Everywhere. I've seen me do it.

But now, I could do nothing but cling to him as he carried me into an office, shut the door, and walked over to the expanse of windows.

Placing me on the floor, he eyeballed me through the safety glass of his mask. "I have to break out this window." He positioned my mask more firmly on my face. "Stay here and keep this on."

I started to nod my head in agreement but moving made me feel sick all over again, so I slumped against the wall and waited for him. Glass shattered and a clean rush of evening air cooled my cheeks. My rescuer knelt down, lifted me up, and propped me up close to the new opening.

"Let's get you outside for a little fresh air."

Let's not. Let's get out of the building in a way that doesn't require me to suspend myself three stories above the very hard concrete on nothing but a rusty metal staircase.

I kept my death grip on the wall as he stepped onto the escape and kicked at the ladder release with a booted foot several times. It shuddered and squealed and made noises that did not assure me of its stability. If he suggested that we jump, I would kill him.

He swore and turned on his walkie–talkie. "Unit Three. Fire escape on northeast side is broken. We need a bucket."

Oh, great. I've seen this on TV. I've watched "Backdraft". We were going to leave the fire escape and get into a container suspended on top of the fire ladder. Why was I here on a Friday night?

That's right; I was being a good girl these days.

After confirmation squawked back into his device, he reached inside and lifted me through the open window and over the windowsill. I had shut my eyes tightly the minute it looked like he was going to take me out on the suspended death trap, but when he stopped I couldn't help myself. I opened my eyes and immediately, involuntarily, looked down. On instinct, I jumped back away from the ledge, grabbing the fireman standing next to me.

"Whoa, whoa. You okay?"

Heart pounding, I hid my face against his chest like a little kid. "I'm afraid of heights."

He chuckled. "Well, we could go back inside..." When I grabbed him and lurched towards the opening that led back inside, he held me tighter and stroked my back soothingly. "Hey, we can't go back in there. Sorry. Fireman humor."

I whimpered. Honest-to-God whined like a puppy but I couldn't stop it. I now understood the whole "rock and a hard place" thing. I knew in my head that I couldn't go back inside, but standing out on this tiny fire escape with smoke around us and the wind blowing was like someone had reached inside my head and arranged my worst–case scenario. But when I rubbed two of my oxygen–deprived brain cells together, I knew this was better.

Still clinging to him with one hand, I moved the mask off my face. "I really didn't want to die in the bathroom."

His chest rumbled with low laughter. "Most people aren't real particular about the location. Just the *not dying* part."

I peered up at him in the dark but couldn't clearly see his face with all the safety gear on. "Are you making fun of me?"

"No, ma'am; just trying to distract you."

"Oh..." I huddled closer to him, shaking uncontrollably. "I can't stop sh–sh–aking."

He chafed my arms with his hands, the rough texture of the gloves causing enough friction to warm me up a little bit. He grabbed the oxygen mask and put it back over my nose and mouth, tightening the strap to make sure it stayed on. "It's shock. They'll fix you up once we get you to the bus. Just hang on."

Nodding, I took a deep, shuddering breath to steady my nerves. *Don't cry. Don't you dare cry.*

His voice broke across the silence. "What were you doing here on a Friday night? No hot date?"

I coughed again and shook my head, moving the mask to the side in order to overshare. I babbled when I was nervous. Not a good trait when you had to give interviews to rapid–fire, story–hungry reporters all the time.

"I haven't had a date in over a year."

"The men you know must be stupid or blind."

My head was starting to do that swimmy–thing again, but I squinted up at him. "Are you hitting on me?"

He shrugged, placing the mask back on my face. It was becoming a game. Yay.

"Maybe. Is it working?"

"Oh... you're distracting me again." I leaned against him as the coughing resumed. The lights from the fire truck that had pulled in below us hurt my eyes as he spoke to his co–workers on the walkie–talkie. My head felt like it was floating—I couldn't focus. Bone–deep exhaustion was seeping into my muscles. *I just want to go to sleep.*

"Hey!" He shook me gently and spoke into my ear, "Stay with me; your ride's here. Don't pass out on me now—you haven't agreed to go out with me yet."

I tried to laugh, but the heaviness was pressing down again and it took all of my effort to stay awake. Through the fog in my brain, I was aware of my fireman securing a belt around my waist and moving me into the metal cage at the top of the ladder. I thought about going into a full–blown panic attack at this new level of craptastic fun, but I just couldn't muster the energy. The rollercoaster lurch in my stomach as we made our way to the ground was minimized by my epic level of tiredness.

Once it landed on the ground, I was instantly surrounded by a mob of people tugging on me, putting me on a stretcher, and checking my vital signs. I forced my eyes open and looked up into the face of the man who had saved my life.

His mask was pushed completely off his face now and I could see his features clearly. His skin was smudged with black soot that emphasized his strong, angular jaw. His eyes were a deep topaz fringed by thick, black eyelashes.

He was fucking gorgeous. Not movie–star or prettied–up male model good–looking, but real man, works–for–a–living, has–women–falling–all–over–him at the grocery store smokin' hot. If I could have custom–ordered a man, this is what he would look like.

I slumped against him and groaned. "Oh, no. I'm dead."

Concern clouded his perfect features as he leaned down to me. "No, ma'am; you're okay. You'll be fine."

"Nope. I'm dead." I pointed at him with a shaky finger. "Because anybody as beautiful as you must be an angel."

I thought I heard laughter as everything went black.

CHAPTER TWO
Max

Let's be clear. I'm no angel.

I've been called many things. Some of the people I rescue call me a hero but I hate that word. I'm just doing my job, but it did make me feel like all my hard work and the risking–my–life thing was appreciated by those I serve. The women in my life called me the name of the Almighty when they were under me and then a son–of–a–bitch when I left—but those were both exaggerations made in the heat of the moment. In truth, I was somewhere in between.

But I have *never* been called an angel.

When the tiny brunette had uttered those words at the scene, it was cool. But, when Bobby Lane, the firefighter manning the bucket, told the other guys on the A–Shift team, the warm glow of the moment turned into burning irritation.

In the face of the ration of shit they gave me, I wore an expression of nonchalance—as my mom always said, "Don't give that dog something to chase." But two weeks of finding little halos and wings in my locker had grated on my last fucking nerve. Add to that the almost constant "411" commentary from the assholes on my celebrity victim and I was about to go out of my ever–lovin' mind.

I didn't need the "411" anyway.

I was Kit's biggest fan.

Now two weeks later, I'm trying to hide my six–foot–three–inch frame behind a fake plant in a random municipal conference room, still unable to believe that I'm going to meet her again. In fact, I'm going to be seeing a lot more of her since her label and my boss decided that the joint-positive PR from a few events was a good idea.

I wasn't complaining.

In less than an hour, I would walk over to the makeshift stage situated on the other end of the room and receive a letter of commendation—delivered by Kit Landry herself. She was probably one of the few things that could have enticed me to get decked out in my dress uniform and endure the formal ceremony. I love the job, but I can't stand the press–the–flesh crap that comes with the territory since we got our new director—Paul Bates. He never passed up an opportunity to rub shoulders with the celebrities in Music City, especially if it got him a photo op and some good press for the department.

He was totally in love with me right now. Saving the "Sweetheart of Country Music" had saved my bacon with the brass. According to my captain, they were prepared to overlook some of my less–than–stellar off–duty activities—specifically my "chasing tail, drinking and fighting".

And I got to spend some quality time with my favorite fantasy girl.

"I can't believe you didn't recognize her."

I glanced over at Dean, my best friend, and shrugged. "Man, it was smoky and my mind was on the job."

"Uh-huh." Dean rubbed his lower back. "My back is still out of whack. How did I get stuck with the security guard built like a linebacker and you got the hottie who weighs about a buck ten?"

"Righteous living, my friend."

Laughing, as Dean gave me the one–finger salute, we both turned as Bobby Lane sidled up to us. Bobby is an okay firefighter. So far, he's managed not to get my ass killed at a scene but he's also the world's biggest douchebag.

He fucks anything that moves and brags about it even though none of us wants to hear it. Don't get me wrong; I'm all about getting laid as often as possible but I don't have to brag about it. The fact that my partners usually end up coming back for seconds and thirds says it all for me. Truth be told, a third date is about the limit for the women I typically meet. Once they realize that moving in and buying a new comforter and throw pillows isn't ever going to be on the agenda with me, they move on, unless they like to keep it hot and casual.

"Is she here yet?" Bobby smoothed a hand over his short blonde hair. "I can't believe you had the balls to ask her out."

I groaned. "I told you, I was just trying..."

"Yeah, yeah; you were just trying to distract her." Bobby waved me off. "Just let me know if you actually plan to follow through with nailing your dream–girl, because if you don't..." He leaned in a little closer and I took a step back. Did I mention that he's a douchebag and a close talker? "...I plan to."

Dean choked out a laugh and Bobby looked like he wanted to knock him on his ass. "Why do you think she'd go out with you? If she's gonna go out with anyone, it would be Max. He's the one who saved her life."

"I know." Bobby placed his hand over his heart and flashed a leering smile. "God bless women at the scene— they're always *so* grateful."

"Bobby, you need help," I said.

"Hey! Don't act like you've never done it." Bobby was offended and then accusatory. "You've done your share of cashing in on badge–bunny adoration."

Okay, he was right. I wasn't one to pass up the best perk from the job—appreciative hot women who wanted to deliver their thanks up close and personally. I just didn't want to talk about it with Bobby. And I definitely wasn't talking about Kit with him.

Dean was the first to speak. "Kit Landry is no badge–bunny."

"And, I'm not *you*," I said. And, this was Kit Landry we were talking about. Famous people were a whole other species in this town and I wasn't interested in dipping my dick or anything else into that gene pool. I'd grown up in Nashville and the celebrity around here was served with a side of fake and a dab of crazy. No thanks.

But for Kit, I would make an exception. At least one night; one *very long* night.

"Yeah, I know." Bobby snorted. "You think because you don't talk about all the fucking you do that it makes you better than me. How many times have I had to deal with one of your women who didn't get the memo about how quickly you turn them in for the next model?" He had the balls to lean over and poke me in the chest. "And you're going to do the same thing with your favorite jerk–off fantasy girl, so save the angel act."

His comment pissed me off and only Dean's hand on my arm kept me from taking a swing. It wouldn't surprise anyone around here if I got into a fight—just another one of the things they overlooked because I was good at my job. "Shut the fuck up."

Bobby had apparently eaten his Wheaties this morning, because he barely glanced down to where my fist was clenched at my side before he kept talking. "Look, we all know you have a thing for her. You have *all* of her music."

I shrugged. "So do lots of people."

Bobby wiggled his eyebrows. "Yeah, but everyone doesn't have that issue of *Rolling Stone* with her centerfold in those little Daisy Duke's and halter top stashed under their bunk."

I bit back a curse and looked away. Crap. He wasn't wrong.

I looked around the room, wondering when this was ever going to get started so I could get out of this uniform and away from Bobby. I hate being trussed up like a turkey on Thanksgiving even more than I hate Bobby and his childish attitude, which on a good day puts him on the same level of maturity as a fourteen–year–old.

I needed to walk away before I also acted like a high–schooler and gave him a swirlie in the bathroom.

But still, Bobby kept talking. "I'll bet you a hundred bucks you can't hook up with her."

Okay, make that a twelve–year–old.

I turned my gaze towards Bobby as Dean mumbled something that sounded a lot like "what an ass".

"Are you kidding me? I'm not going to bet that I can fuck a woman—Kit Landry or anyone else. Were you born a dick? In what universe is that cool?"

"Since your dream girl can't get you motivated, I'll throw in a little money to sweeten the pot."

I rounded on Bobby, the effort to keep my voice down in this crowd of bigwigs making my throat hurt. "I'm not crazy enough to take your sucker bet. Kit Landry is a world–famous country music star. She dates movie stars, football players, rock stars—do you see a pattern here?"

"We all know she's got a bad girl inside who loves to come out and play, and I'm betting that even rehab didn't calm down Miss Kitty."

I would never admit it, but I think he's right. Until a year and a half ago, she'd been the poster child for the kind of girl you took home to your parents and then put a ring on it. But then, she'd taken a turn—a sexy, bad girl turn—and then a nosedive. I hadn't liked watching her spiral into rehab but I hoped that the new, improved Kit kept some of the edge from her walk on the wild side. While she hadn't been hitting the party scene lately, she'd kept the crimson red streaks in her long brown hair, added a new tattoo on her arm and the bootleg versions of her new music circulating the local scene showed an entirely different sound. They weren't the carefully executed songs that stayed with the good girl image, but raw and honest—with maybe a glimpse at the real girl behind the guitar.

And that was a girl I would love to meet up close and personal, and preferably naked.

Bobby moved my finger off his chest and flashed a smile that didn't quite reach his eyes. That's the thing about Bobby—deep down he had a streak of mean and I wanted no part of it. "I'll make it five hundred."

The crowd behind us started getting loud, the buzz of excitement rumbling through the small space. I turned around just in time to see Kit come through the door. Flashbulbs were going off all around her, but they were completely unnecessary—she lit up the room all by herself.

Today she was dressed in a modest black dress instead of her usual jeans, sexy top and boots. With her glossy black curls trailing down her back and her petite frame, she was the living and breathing version of my dream girl. And, as usual, my dreams were definitely drifting into the X–rated section of the mental video store.

Bobby leaned over to me and stuck out his hand. "Five hundred. Are you in?"

"Fuck off."

"Gentlemen."

I turned to look down at the man who'd slipped up behind us without our noticing. The press pass hanging around his neck was the last thing I wanted to see. *Fuck me. What had he heard?*

The newcomer glanced around the group, but his eyes finally settled on me. His eyes were hard and assessing and, although I didn't know exactly what the guy was selling, I knew I wasn't buying.

"Firefighter Butler." His lips pulled back in a smile but it didn't quite reach his eyes. "Congratulations on your commendation."

"Thanks." I crossed my arms over my chest and waited him out.

The stranger chuckled softly, reached into his pocket, and fished out a business card which he held out to me. I didn't take it, didn't even look at it. This dude was the worst judge of body language, otherwise he'd be long gone.

"I'm Earle Foster with the Daily Scoop and I'm prepared to offer you one thousand dollars for an exclusive interview with you about Kit Landry."

"It isn't much of a story. Everyone knows I rescued her

from the fire. No big deal."

I was done. I turned my back on him. The reporter reeked of sleaze and lies and suddenly I needed a shower.

"I don't want a story about the rescue. I want an exclusive on the time you're going to spend with her during these PR events your boss and her handlers have cooked up."

I looked down into the shorter man's face. "You need to go. I'm not interested."

The guy smiled, as persistent as he was butt–fuck ugly. "I can go up to five thousand dollars if you get me a story that will put her on the front page again." He looked over his shoulder to where Kit was standing on the stage before turning back to me. "She's been such a good girl lately, we haven't had any juicy stories to report."

"And you won't get any from me."

I felt his hand dip into the pocket of my uniform and withdraw without the business card. When I fished it out and tried to hand it back to him, he backed up and shoved his hands in his own pockets.

"Mr. Butler. Don't worry. If you call me I'll be discreet. Ms. Landry is extremely touchy about her friends talking to the press."

"I said no."

"I'm a good reporter. Maybe I'll just poke around and find out what will persuade you to cooperate."

"Knock yourself out."

I was now officially over this conversation. I shoved him aside and walked towards the stage. I was within a few feet of Kit when another man decided to block my way— my boss, Captain Price. He was the only guy who was going to stop my progress right now.

"Butler."

"Captain."

He looked me over and I stood at attention, holding my breath until he gave the nod that said I'd passed inspection.

"Congratulations on your commendation."

"Thank you, sir."

"Saving Ms. Landry pulled your ass out of the fire with the Department." I looked at him to see if he was cracking a fireman joke, but his hard glare told me he wasn't. "This is your shot to erase all the bar fights and the Christmas party incident from their minds when they review your application for promotion."

Holy shit. Were they ever going to stop bringing up last year's Christmas party? It was like no one had ever had sex in a supply closet before.

"I understand, sir—"

"Let me be clear. There's lots of press here today, people with video cameras. The whole goddamn city will see this on the news as they eat dinner tonight." He nodded at someone across the room. "Don't fuck this up."

"Yes, sir."

He barely looked at me before he walked away. I was a good firefighter, but when you were trying to get promoted, your extra–firehouse activities mattered—especially when they landed you in jail and in between the wrong woman's thighs.

I shoved all that to the back of my mind and looked back to where Kit sat on the stage. I had a few moments before the ceremony started and I had a surprise for our special guest up my sleeve.

But first, I needed to properly introduce myself to Kit Landry.

CHAPTER THREE
Kit

"You didn't tell me he was hot."

I didn't even pretend to misunderstand who Bridget was talking about. Max was the hottest thing going in this room and we both knew it. Examining the hem of my dress, I shifted in the uncomfortable folding chair on the dais and rolled my eyes. I knew better than to encourage Bridget when she got on the subject of men... it never ended well. In fact, men in general never ended well for me. "I told you he was handsome."

"No, you said he was good–looking." Bridget elbowed me in the side. "Now, just so we're clear for future conversations—'good–looking' is between 'not ugly' and 'I could lick him all over'." She jerked her thumb in the direction of where Max stood with the other firefighters. "Max is clearly lickable."

I felt the rush of blood to my cheeks and neck, knowing that she'd made me go all red and splotchy. I grabbed Bridget's hand and leaned in closer to whisper, "Could you please stop pointing? I was almost a crispy critter. I didn't notice his looks all that much."

I was a big fat liar. The minute I'd walked in the door, I'd picked Max out of the crowd. He stood a good two inches taller than his friends and his broad shoulders reminded me of how safe I'd felt when he'd held me out on the fire escape. Thankfully, much of that frightening night was fuzzy, but I remembered Max. He was very hard to forget.

Bridget laughed out loud—a belly laugh that had several people looking in their direction. Shaking her head, she dabbed at her eyes dramatically. "You're a terrible liar."

I glared, knowing it wouldn't do any good. "I'm going to fire you."

"No, you won't. You love me. Besides, I'm trying to get you laid as your best friend—not your personal assistant."

"Who said anything about getting laid?"

"I did. Since you seem to have given up on that part of your life entirely, *someone* needs to worry about getting you some action." Bridget reached down to grab her PDA, which was buzzing like a bumblebee. Glancing at the screen, she groaned, "Ugh, it's Ron. I'll take care of this and you can go over and talk to Max and see if he'll help you out with your little dry spell."

"The last thing I need is a little action." Out of the corner of my eye, I spied the director of the fire department and Liam Connor, my record label president, headed over towards the stage. "I *need* to behave myself until my new contract is signed."

I had a lot of people who depended on my not fucking this up and I owed it to them. Romance—temporary or otherwise—shouldn't be on my agenda. And I had other shit to figure out. Life for me was complicated and I didn't have the energy or time to figure out how to fit someone new into the mix.

In spite of my best efforts, my eyes wandered over to where Max was standing by the stage. *Was he waiting for me?* Our eyes connected and suddenly my skin was tingly, hot, and too tight. Needing to move and break the tension, I stood up next to Bridget, rubbed my damp hands on my dress, and averted my eyes. Hell, I'd played two sold-out shows at Madison Square Garden—I could handle the hot local firefighter.

"The label is breathing down my neck to prove that I'm not going to go off the deep-end again. I've got a shit-load of my own money invested in a tour that starts in a month and a number of people who depend upon me for their paycheck." I eyeballed my best friend and drove my point home. "I don't have time for a relationship."

Bridget scoffed and gave me a slow, knowing smile. "Who said anything about a relationship? I was just talking about sex."

I stood there as Bridget sauntered away, unable to get in the last word unless I yelled or chased her down. I wasn't running in these heels. "Damn. I *hate i*t when she does that."

"Does what?"

Startled, I whirled around too quickly and lost my balance, but a strong hand grabbed my arm just in time to keep me from falling over. My hands grasped the torso in front of me—a hard, muscular, male torso. I knew who it was before I looked up.

"Whoa. Steady there." Max's voice was filled with concern and I bit my lip at the sexy, deep tone. If he ever gave up firefighting, he could do phone sex. Just for me. I would pay a lot of money for that.

I was staring at him and couldn't stop. His face was finely chiseled along the cheekbones—the skin a golden olive tone. His black hair was cut short and stubble shadowed his strong jaw. I wondered how it would feel against the tender skin of my face, my breasts....

"You okay?" His brows were scrunched together in worry, his hands tightening their grip on my arms.

I was... lusting... ogling... wondering what you look like under that uniform... "Fine." Once again, the telltale hot flash crawled up my skin and I knew I was blushing. I eased his hands off my body, bit back a groan at the loss of his touch, and stepped back. I laughed and gestured towards my shoes. "I'm okay. These shoes..."

He looked down at my high–heeled sandals and back up at me—a smile tugging at his mouth. Damn, this man was so fine and I know what I'm talking about. Prince Harry, George Clooney, Johnny Depp—I've met them all—and they'd never made me feel like this.

"So, you hate when who does what?" he asked.

"That was..." *About you having sex with me.* "Um... nothing."

He shrugged his shoulders and glanced over at the director finalizing all the stuff on the podium. Turning back to me, he offered me his hand with a full, sexy smile that curled my toes. "We haven't *actually* met. I'm Max Butler."

His accent was movie–star southern, thick but not country–twangy like mine and I responded in my best "Scarlett O'Hara" impression as I took his hand, "My hero!" and giggled as a blush crept up his neck. Jesus, he needed to stop being so damn cute.

"Yeah. Something like that."

"I'm Kit." I tugged at my hand but he held it fast. My pulse was thrumming underneath his fingers and I wondered if he could feel it.

His voice was soft. "I know."

I looked around the room and noticed that we were starting to attract attention and, while I liked holding hands with the big, hot guy, this was not the focus I needed right now. The "good girl" plan required by my label didn't encourage public displays of affection—unless they were arranged by my publicist. I tugged a little harder and he dropped it, raising his own to rake it through his hair, giving it a slightly tousled effect. *Probably what he would look like when he first woke in the morning—all drowsy and rumpled.*

Damn Bridget and her suggestions. Now that I had it in my head, I couldn't stop my mind from drifting to X–rated fantasies of Max.

His voice pulled me back to the present. "...I have something for you."

I blinked several times, trying to focus on his words and not the way his jaw was covered by the beginning of the sexiest dark stubble. "I'm sorry. What?"

Max's eyes twinkled mischievously and I wondered if he knew where my thoughts had drifted.

"I have something for you. The brass wanted me to present it to you at the ceremony but I get the feeling that you wouldn't want an audience for your reunion."

I was now thoroughly confused, craning my neck to watch him as he walked behind the stage, leaned over and picked something off the floor. When he straightened, I saw what he had in his hand and my heart did a somersault, the bottom fell out of my stomach and the tears that would ruin my hour–long makeup job threatened to do their worst.

My guitar case. Jolene.

"Oh!" I slapped my shaking hand over my mouth and resisted the urge to knock over the three people in between me and Max and my baby. He sauntered over, holding her as gently as you would a baby, before placing the case on a chair.

"The case got a little wet from the sprinklers, but I checked her out and she sounds fine. No signs of warping or any damage."

I couldn't speak. What the hell could I say to even touch what I was feeling at the moment? This instrument was more than a bunch of wood and wire. It was the one link I had to my life before Nashville and the girl who existed back then.

"Oh, my God. Thank you," I managed to whisper over the tightness that had overtaken my throat. I blinked hard and fast, willing myself not to give in to the tears that this moment probably deserved. But I was a professional pretender and, while I didn't think I would mind showing my hand to the man who'd witnessed my panic attack four floors above the ground, I wouldn't do it in front of all these people. All these strangers. "This is the kindest thing..."

I leaned over and opened the case and hovered over her. I always did this, savored the moment just before I touched her for the first time. This guitar was more important to me than any lover, our connection elemental, and I respected the hell out of it. She'd gotten my ass off the street and made it possible for me to take care of the people important to me.

And with the songs I'd been writing lately, she was

going to help me get back on top.

"We were told that the building and its contents were a total loss. We already filed a claim for the insurance," I said, finding my voice. I closed my fingers around her neck, cradled her body, and lifted her out of the case. The wood was cool but it would soon warm up to my body temperature, an extension of me in every way. I threw the strap over my neck and felt myself exhale down to my marrow. "I never thought I'd see her again. Jolene belonged to my grandpa."

"A Martin 1944 D–28."

I looked up at Max, not even trying to hide the surprise on my face. "You know guitars?"

"A little. My Grandpa Butler loves them and I absorbed a little over the years."

I experimented with a soft strum, testing the sound. She sounded wonderful. "You play?"

"Doesn't everybody who was raised in this town?" He was quick to add, "Not well enough to do justice to this beautiful lady."

He reached out to touch her his long fingers stroking the neck with a reverence that told me he understood how special she was. He brushed my hand and I closed my fingers over his, giving them a squeeze that didn't even come close to expressing my thanks.

Max raised his eyes from my guitar to look at me and I caught my breath at the connection that arced between us. It was like Jolene was a conduit for all the untapped, raw interest we had in each other. I knew then that my attraction wasn't one–sided. If I wanted it, all I had to do was reach out and take it. Max would meet me more than half way.

Someone bumped into me from behind and I snapped back to the present. The room was even more crowded than before and people were watching us. I closed my eyes, centering my emotions and putting on my game face. When I opened them again, Max was staring at me, confusion clouding his eyes.

He started to speak, but the sight of the director taking the podium signaled that the ceremony was about to begin. I reluctantly put Jolene away and tucked her case behind the stage. We took our seats next to each other on the dais and listened while Director Bates praised his firefighters for their bravery and dedication to the people of Nashville. I wholeheartedly agreed; their bravery had saved me from an untimely death, but I couldn't focus because right now I felt really, really alive.

Max was sitting close enough for me to feel the heat pouring off his body and it kept my senses on high alert. I shifted in my seat to ease the tension building in my belly.

Maybe Bridget was right. It *had* been too long.

Finally, we stood up so I could present Max with his commendation. Next to me, he stood at attention as the director read aloud the account of his brave actions the night he'd saved me from the fire. Max looked tense, uncomfortable; as if he disliked all of the attention. I put it in the column of one more thing I liked about him.

The director finished his recitation and turned to me, handing over the ribbon to pin on Max's chest. I reached up to do my duty, but hit a snag right away—he was too tall for me to reach comfortably without having my skirt ride up and show the whole world my assets. He looked confused by the delay until I motioned for him to lean down a little— a move that caused a ripple of laughter in the crowd and a small smile to form on Max's lips that softened his features.

Tearing my eyes away from his face, I focused on the task at hand and murmured so only he could hear, "Thank you for saving my life." My hands were shaky with emotion as I struggled to get the ribbon pinned on his chest.

"Well, I couldn't let you die in a bathroom, now could I?"

I laughed softly. "No, I guess you couldn't."

Finished with his ribbon, I rested my hands on his chest and leaned up to kiss his cheek.

Under my hands, his chest constricted with his swift

intake of breath at the moment my lips touched his skin. I inhaled deeply, soaking in his scent of cedar wood, citrus, and warm male, while the blood pounded in my ears and my skin grew warmer. Pulling away, we both exhaled slowly as our eyes locked in a heated exchange of shock and desire.

There was no mistaking the look of desire in his eyes, and I'm sure it matched the one in my own. I wanted him with jaw–clenching intensity and the part of me that was all woman unfurled after being packed away for so long. I might as well have been back on that fire escape, because this felt just as dangerous. More dangerous.

Behind me, the gathered paparazzi began to call out above the murmuring of the crowd.

"Give him a real kiss, Kit!"

"Is that how you thank a hero?"

"Kiss him!"

At the sound of their voices, I glanced over my shoulder. Everyone was smiling encouragingly; the press wanted the photo, the other firefighters were cheering on their boy.

I looked back at Max for his opinion.

A smirk pulled at the edge of his lips. "I *did* save your life."

I narrowed my eyes, not really mad at the suggestion. "That's not fair."

He shrugged his shoulders the slightest bit and grinned. "Chicken?"

Oh. Hell. No.

Determined and rising to the bait, I lifted my face, slowly closing the distance between our mouths. This would be quick, fun and flirty, and over before it began.

I had no fucking clue what I was talking about.

The first press of our mouths was like being hooked up to a live wire. We both broke contact in surprise but quickly began again, the lure of such intense pleasure already addictive.

I was the one who took it deeper, running my tongue

along his, dipping inside to taste him. I couldn't help myself; it was like putting my favorite dessert in front of me and saying that I could only have a sample. Good luck trying to stop me.

Max groaned and grabbed my hips, his fingers lightly digging into my flesh—tugging me closer and turning the kiss hotter, wetter. His mouth slanted over mine and his tongue stroked past my lips, taking what he wanted and what I freely gave. My knees went weak, and I clutched the fabric of his uniform, holding him close as the kiss went on and on.

The sound of whooping and clapping startled me and snapped me back to reality. This wasn't good.

I distanced myself from Max, only far enough away to end the kiss but not far enough to lose the physical contact of his hands on me. I was breathing hard, my breasts swollen under the tight dress, my lips tender and tingly. Max was panting, his face hard and eyes hot.

Painfully aware of our audience and my management and label president glaring at me from the other end of the room, I tried to pull back further but Max shook his head, holding me in his grip.

"We shouldn't have done that," I said.

"Maybe not, but I want to do it again," he answered, his smile intimate and naughty enough to make me shiver. "And I want to do more."

I sucked in a breath. I had thought the fire was dangerous, but I was wrong. Max was the thing I needed to worry about.

"You're no angel," I whispered.

"I'm glad you finally figured it out."

CHAPTER FOUR
Max

"I still can't believe you kissed her."

I paused in my inventory of the truck equipment and shot a look over my shoulder towards Dean, who was leaning against the threshold of the open bay doors of the firehouse. It was a gorgeous early summer day and I was happy to take on a duty that let me enjoy the outdoors for a while. Turning back to my task, I replied. "Actually, *she* kissed me."

Dean scoffed. "Technically."

"No, *not* technically, asshole."

Dean laughed in my face, ignoring my shitty tone. "Well, you *did* kiss her back and I know I saw a little tongue action."

The sight of his waggling eyebrows made me laugh out loud. He wasn't wrong. I'd seen the video of the kiss over and over, and sure enough, it was clear that the kiss was way more than a TV kiss peck of the lips. In fact, some commenters on YouTube said that it should be marked as inappropriate for people under eighteen. My mother had even called and lectured me on the types of kisses that were appropriate in a public forum.

The director had flagged me down after the press conference and chewed my ass about proper conduct in uniform, but it rolled right off my back since I could still taste Kit on my lips.

I turned, crossed my arms, and leaned against the truck. "I wish everyone would stop talking about it. It was a little publicity stunt and it'll never happen again."

"Frustrated much? Wishing that Kit would take that kiss a lot further?"

"Fuck, yeah." I wasn't going to deny it. I wanted her and now that I'd gotten a sample of just how sweetly hot she was, my bad mood was directly related to the lack of opportunity to pursue it. "I haven't heard from her since she was swept away by her management team right after the press conference. I don't have her number to call her."

"You could call her manager," Dean suggested. "I'm sure he'd be happy to organize your booty call."

"Fuck off." I didn't want to do that, but it looked like the joint PR events might not be happening after all. If I wanted my shot with Kit, calling her handler might be my only option. I'd give it another day. "At least the press stopped following me around."

"Is that one reporter still calling you?"

"The guy from the Daily Scoop?"

"That the douchebag from the ceremony?"

"Yeah. He somehow got my cell phone number and he's even approached my mom at work. There's no way in hell I'm going to give him a story, but he still keeps calling." I curled my hands into fists; I'd made sure he'd gotten the message the last time he'd shown up in person. That dude could haul ass when he needed to and my six–feet–three–inches in his face was good motivation. "He threatened me the last phone call; told me that if I wasn't part of the solution then he'd make it my problem and get the scoop on me, as well."

"You? What could he possibly have on you?" Dean asked.

"Nothing. Even the last time I was hauled into the captain's office for fighting in a bar was old news. But, we both know the director wouldn't like any kind of bad publicity and it could screw up my chance at promotion." I squinted into the sun shining into the firehouse, and counted down the six weeks until I could put in my request for a team leader position. At twenty–three, I was still junior to lots of the guys who would apply, and my chances weren't great, but I needed to send a message that I wanted it. My interest would lead them to offer me lesser opportunities and that would make me more competitive the next time I applied. The politics of the job were not my strong point, but I was learning. Moving up in the ranks was determined by more than running into burning buildings. "All he wants is some dirt on her so he can get a byline, and he doesn't care who he hurts to get it."

I'd lived in Nashville my whole life and it didn't take long to notice how the press constantly hounded the local celebrities. Yeah, they'd chosen a career in the public eye and it wasn't as bad as what people talked about in Hollywood or New York, but there had to be limits. Being a fan, I'd followed Kit's stories this past year and rooted for her to pull out of her tailspin. Her crash and burn had rivaled Britney—minus the extreme haircut—but she was clearly trying to get beyond that and all this guy wanted to do was tear her down for the price of a daily tabloid cover price.

And truth be told, I'd saved Kit's life and that created a bond of sorts between us—at least one that required some degree of loyalty. But, even if I didn't feel that connection with her, I possessed a highly developed sense of self-preservation. If I gave a story, then the possibility existed that *I* would become the story as well—at least for a short time.

No. Thank. You.

I'd keep my mouth shut, figure out a way to get in touch with Kit, and get her in my bed for at least one night. As it was, I was thankful my fifteen minutes of fame was over.

Dean's voice interrupted my train of thought. "Are you going to tell Kit about that guy?"

"No. Why should I? She's got a whole team of people keeping an eye on him, I'm sure. Soon I'll no longer be worth his interest."

Dean stepped into the bay and leaned up against the truck. Oh, shit. He had his serious face on and that meant I was getting a lecture about my lack of a committed relationship at the ripe old age of twenty–three. "The heat between you two was pretty clear to YouTube viewers worldwide. Maybe you want to think about trying to get beyond casual with Kit."

"Dean, I'm glad that you've got your happily–ever–after with Shannon, but that's not gonna happen for me. I don't want that. I'd suck at that two kids and minivan thing." I pushed off from the truck and walked over to the open bay, gazing out onto the street. "I tried that once and it blew up in my face."

"Yep. I remember." Dean pointed at his chest. "Front row seat, remember? I'm not saying you'll live happily ever after, but what's wrong with living in the moment? Just having fun and seeing where it goes with no restrictions in your head about the shelf–life? You plan the end before you've even got the condom on the first time. Maybe you just see how it goes for once." He smiled and patted me on the back as he headed towards the residential part of the station. Now he could answer my mother truthfully when she asked him to help me "find a nice girl and settle down".

I turned back to my task as I mulled over what Dean had said. Have a little fun with Kit Landry? Sure thing. Over and over, and all night long.

Anything more than casual? Not going to happen.

But, I couldn't stop thinking about that kiss. How she'd tasted, how she'd felt in my arms. Despite the difference in our size, she fit perfectly against me—like she was made to be there. We had chemistry, alright. But that was all it was or would ever be.

"Excuse me, can you tell me where I can find Shannon Jones?"

The voice came out of nowhere and I lurched up, banging the top of my head on the edge of the truck door. Biting back the "fuck me" that could get me written up, I straightened, turned, and found myself looking right into the eyes of the woman I'd just been obsessing over.

Kit was standing there in my station, an expression of surprise and then concern on her face as she glanced to where I'd clonked the living shit out of myself just seconds before. She was wearing a low–cut, little blue sundress and cowboy boots and everything else was miles of bare skin and dark curls. My brain went mushy. Maybe I'd hit my head harder than I'd thought.

Her voice was full of concern as she moved closer. "Max, are you okay? I didn't mean to sneak up behind you."

I stared at her like an idiot. In person, I was reminded again of just how gorgeous she was. She walked towards me and I couldn't move, couldn't take my eyes off of her. If you looked up "dumbstruck" in the dictionary, you'd see my goofy–ass face pasted right next to it.

I still hadn't answered when she stopped in front of me. Standing on tiptoe she touched my recent injury. "Are you sure you're okay?"

Her voice was feminine, with a whiskey–edge that tied my gut up in knots. Her hand was cool on my over–heated skin and, as she moved closer, I could smell her sweet, summery, honeysuckle scent. All I wanted to do was pull her lush curves against my body, take her mouth, and find out exactly where this crazy chemistry would take us.

I definitely had a head injury because suddenly I realized that I had her close enough to do all those things and I wasn't doing anything about it.

Get your shit together, Butler. Carpe the fucking diem.

I grabbed her by the waist and pulled her towards me, turning us so she was backed up against the door of the fire truck. She still held her packages in her hands and I missed the feel of her touch on my body, but I could work with what I had.

She stared up at me, her big, blue eyes wide with shock but mostly what I saw there was curiosity. She licked her lips and that was all the invitation I needed. I leaned into her, bypassing the prize of her mouth to press a kiss to her throat, just above the place where her pulse pounded against her skin. She was delicious all over, sweet and warm, and I wanted to drag her down to the floor and bury my cock inside her body for hours.

I looked down and realized that my hands were shaking, my breath as quick as hers—and I hadn't even kissed her yet.

"When we fuck, it's probably going to kill me." It came out as a growl, as I tipped her face up to mine and wasted no more time in taking what I wanted.

Kit didn't play games, no pretending that she didn't want this, too. She opened to me, meeting my tongue more than halfway when I dove inside. She was as hungry as I was and the kiss was anything but the usual finesse I used on women. There was no slow seduction here. It wasn't in my power to play games. I was at the mercy of whatever she would give me.

I slanted my mouth over hers, barely giving her a chance to take a breath before I went at her again like I was starving.

And I was famished. For her. It was the craziest thing I'd ever experienced, but I wasn't going to let a little insanity stop me. It never had before.

I wrapped my arms around her waist, inserting my body in between her legs. The skirt of her dress rode up high on her thighs as I pressed my hard–on against the hot cleft of her pussy. I rolled my hips against her and she dropped the bags in her hands with a thud against the concrete, weaving her fingers into my hair with a pressure that brought a little pain with the pleasure.

I didn't care. She could do whatever she wanted to my body as long as I got to do exactly what I was doing right now. As long as she let me do this and so much more.

The blast of my lieutenant's voice over the station intercom was the biggest cock block of my short life. He wasn't looking for me, but it made Kit pull back from the kiss and that was tragic. I held on tight, brushing my lips against her, light as a feather but as intense as bungee jumping.

"What are you doing here?" I asked, pressing a soft kiss against the side of her mouth.

"I was looking for the paramedic, Shannon Jones." One of her hands left the spot where they were looped around my neck to point at the floor by our feet. "I've got the T–shirts and tickets that I promised. She told me she would be around today."

"You could have sent somebody else with those things. No need to come down here yourself," I teased, taking a chance that she'd shown up in my house without her entourage because she couldn't forget the kiss either. My gamble was rewarded by a soft laugh and an embarrassed flush on her cheeks. Busted.

"I wanted to see you." She pulled back, ending our kiss and replacing her smile with a frown. "To make sure you were okay."

"I'm fine. Why wouldn't I be?"

"I know the press was following you after we..."

"After we kissed." I leaned back in and reminded her of what we were talking about. She sighed the minute our lips touched and I decided that the feel of her fingers in my hair was just about the best thing ever. I knew that standing here like this was insane in a busy firehouse, and it was only a miracle that we hadn't been found yet. Time to cut to the chase. "It *was* a little crazy. It's over. Thanks for asking, but that isn't what we should be talking about right now."

"It isn't?" She picked up on my tone and her lips curled up in smile. "Then what should we be talking about?"

"Our date."

"Oh? Do we have a date to talk about?"

"We will, once you say yes."

"I'm not supposed to be dating," she bit her lip, her eyes losing some of their glow from a few minutes earlier. She was a grown woman, twenty–one and independent—

who could tell her not to date? "The label, my management. Part of my deal was to concentrate on getting ready for the tour, writing music for the new album. Not dating."

Oh, the mile–wide loophole her team had left for me to plow through. I'd been getting around parental restrictions since I realized what fun girls could be when their mamas weren't looking and how easy it was to get them out of their panties.

"Don't call it a date—an outing. Community outreach. No press. No pressure. Just you and me hanging out."

"I don't know."

That wasn't a yes, but I could hear her excuses crumbling like an old brick wall. It was time for the big guns.

"I *did* save your life."

Kit narrowed her eyes. "What exactly is the shelf–life on you using that to your advantage?"

I sensed that the prize was almost mine and I worked hard to repress my grin. That grin always got me in trouble. "I don't know. Until I get what I want."

"And what do you want?"

"I want you."

"You're very direct."

"I don't see any point in skirting the issue, since all I want is to get under yours."

She laughed, a small hand with black and silver fingernails clapping over her mouth to stop the giggle. I didn't know if that was a good sign or not, especially when she wiggled out of my arms, removed her phone from a bag at her feet and held it out to me.

"Give me your phone. Program in your number."

I did as she asked, wondering if she was ever going to give me that 'yes' I was looking for. When we were done, she bent back down and gathered her bags from the floor.

"Okay. One not–a–date." She walked past me towards the door to the main part of the firehouse. When she got to the door, she turned around and gave me a look that said that I was in for a wild fucking ride with this girl. "But if you

want another one—you'll have to rescue me again."
"Lucky for me, I have my own fire truck."

CHAPTER FIVE
Kit

"I can't believe you eat that stuff."

I shoved the last piece of the sugar–covered funnel cake into my mouth and licked my fingers. Max watched in slack–jawed awe as I smiled up at him. "What? You bring me to a carnival and I'm going to eat carnival food."

"Come to think of it, I'm not as concerned about *what* you're eating as in *how much* you're eating." He raised a hand and counted off on his fingers—as if I needed reminding. "A corn dog, cotton candy, ice cream, and now a funnel cake." He waved in the general direction of my body. "Where do you put it all?"

I looked down and checked out my outfit—jeans, a tank top, and flip–flops. None of it screamed "country music star" and that is exactly what I wanted; a low profile. Max had called that morning and I'd taken twenty minutes to throw on some clothes and sneak out of the house. With my hair pulled up in a ponytail, a baseball hat shoved on top of my head, and only mascara and lip gloss on my face, I was not what people would be looking for, even in Music City. I couldn't be expected to walk around like I was performing at the Grand Ole Opry all the time, could I?

"I run three miles every day, and do yoga. I don't think my figure suffers for it." I waved my hand along my body, inviting comment and ogling.

Max didn't disappoint. His eyes followed my lead, and lingered.

The impact of his gaze was as powerful as a touch and my body reacted with a slow spiral of desire. No part of me had forgotten our kiss yesterday and all of me wanted another chance to feel that good again. Max was like a drug and I was seriously considering getting another fix as soon as possible. But we needed to get some ground rules established first—I couldn't afford to proceed without making sure we were on the same page. My career might depend on it.

And I had lots of people depending on me.

He shifted closer until he brushed against me from breast to thigh. His height forced me to look upward to meet his gaze, as his hand lightly caressed my arm with a sensual touch that created a series of shivers under my skin.

He smiled down at me, his grin telling me that he knew exactly what he was doing to me. "I think you," his eyes moved back down my body and back up to my eyes in one long sweep, "look more beautiful today than you've ever looked before."

I stared at him, my mouth suddenly as dry as the desert, my brain cells scrambled. Now, I knew that Max was a sweet–talker and probably used it to get a new woman in his bed every night, but his look told me that he was looking at the girl and not the star and, damn, was that sexy.

And scary.

I could handle men looking at me as a conquest, a trophy for their arm, but I was unnerved by the way that Max treated me like something more. I knew he was a fan, but that had never been a thing between us. So, it often took a while for a guy to see me as just a regular person—if they even wanted to see me that way. Too many times I was just a meal ticket, a way to get their foot in the door to the music business or a chance to get more face time with the press by being seen with me. Many of my so–called friends and former lovers dove for cover when I detonated last year. It was a tough lesson to learn, but one I would never forget.

But Max felt different and I was still trying to decide if this was a sign to stick around or run for it. He made me feel normal and this was unfamiliar territory for me. I was both thrilled and terrified. It was why I had agreed to go out with him in the first place—other than the crazy sexual heat between us. I had a shot at having something normal for at least a little while and it made me want to lean into him, wrap my arms around him, and just be Kit. What a concept.

As if he could read my thoughts, Max's large hand tugged at my waist, pulling me closer to him. My breasts pressed against his chest, my nipples tightening in response to his touch and residual lust he'd left me with since that crazy kiss at the firehouse. I wasn't the only one feeling the effect of proximity. Max's cock was heavy where his jean–clad body pressed into mine and I would have given anything to pull that zipper down and see if he could deliver on the promise he made with his every touch.

Heavy lidded with desire, his eyes darkened and I licked my lips as he lowered his head to kiss me.

"Oooph. Sorry, buddy." I heard the apology from whoever it was that bumped into Max, jostling him and breaking us apart before I succumbed to the sexual lobotomy that happened whenever Max was near.

I didn't know what I was thinking. Anybody with a cell phone could grab a photo of us kissing and I'd have my label on my ass so fast they'd break the sound barrier. This man made me sloppy.

Max was nothing but pure, unadulterated, yummy distraction and I really couldn't afford a distraction right now. I needed to be good. I needed to rehearse my tour and write songs and give radio and TV interviews and whatever else I was told to do until they agreed to keep me on the label.

When he returned his gaze to mine, I cleared my throat and attempted to sound casual, to ignore the way my fingers itched to reach up and touch his hair. "Beautiful, huh? Makes me wonder why I spend money on all those stylists and make–up people if you think I look better now."

He shoved his hands in his pockets and flashed a sheepish grin. "Don't get me wrong, you look amazing on stage." His gaze lingered over me once again. "But I like this Kit. You look like a normal girl."

I smiled at that and sauntered over to the arcade area. I was intrigued by this turn in the conversation. "A normal girl? I'm not what you expected?"

"No." He shook his head. "Fuck, no."

"Why?"

"I guess I expected the party girl who goes to fancy Nashville parties." He glanced over at me and then around the small, local carnival. "I mean, I had no idea if you would like this sort of thing, but you've been awesome." Max chuckled. "I can't remember when I had such a great time hoping my date wouldn't throw up on me on the Tilt–a– Whirl."

I punched him in the arm and Max hammed it up by rubbing the place where I'd made impact, as if I'd really done some damage. The guy had a good foot on me in height and one hundred pounds in weight and was built like a Mack truck. If he decided to take me right then and there, all I'd be able to do is hang on for the ride.

It wasn't lost on me that I wouldn't mind taking that ride.

Laughing, we walked down the row of stalls containing various cheap stuffed animals and carnival employees hawking their game as a sure–winner. One guy with a shaved head and goatee caught Max's eye and cajoled him into winning a prize for me.

I learned something about him at that stall—Max never backed down from a challenge and he had a killer arm. When I wasn't distracting him.

Thirty minutes later, we were walking back to the firehouse and I was carrying the largest stuffed frog I'd ever seen.

"I can't believe how rigged those games are." Max frowned as he glanced over at me. "I think the only reason that guy let me win is because he thought you were pretty."

"Thank goodness! We might have been there all night

if we'd waited for your aim to improve."

"Hey!" Max replied in a wounded tone. "I know what you were doing with all the touching and blowing in my ear. No fair distracting the pitcher."

Laughing, I stumbled on the sidewalk and the grip on my frog slipped. Max reached out to grab him but I resisted. "Hands off! I can carry Merle all by myself."

Max snickered. "Merle? Merle Haggard? You *aren't* naming that frog after one of the greatest country music stars of all time?"

I sniffed. I thought the name was perfect. "Merle will have a place of honor on my tour bus this summer. It's only fitting that he has a name fit for a country music frog."

He sounded unconvinced. "If you say so."

Laughing easily, we walked along in a comfortable silence and I thought about the afternoon with Max. It had been the most fun I'd had in... forever.

"Thank you."

Max looked over at me, his expression puzzled. "For what?"

"For today." I stopped next to my truck, dropped Merle onto the hood, and turned to face Max. "Thank you for giving me a break. For letting me be a 'normal' girl for the afternoon. I don't get a whole lot of normal in my life."

He shook his head. "You know there's something wrong with a girl who has the world at her feet, but can't do what she wants once in a while."

"I did what I wanted for a while and it got me in a lot of trouble. Now, I'm paying for it. I have to be a good girl now."

"I get that, but when do you stop paying?" He stepped forward and tipped my chin up with his finger and leaned down so that I could almost look him in the eye. "It sounds to me like you need to take your life back."

"That's the plan."

"So, what's stopping you?"

Me. The answer was right there but I clamped my lips

together, unwilling to spill my guts in the Harris Teeter parking lot.

He moved closer to me—so close I could smell him, feel his body heat. Like a magnet, my body swayed forward slightly and I grabbed what little control I had left and backed up against my truck. Not a smart move. Max took a couple of steps forward and caged me in between his body and the truck.

Max leaned in and nuzzled my cheek, murmuring into my ear, "I'm going to end this non–date by kissing you."

I normally didn't like bossy men who crowded me with their bodies, but Max was breaking all the rules for me. I got off on it; he made me hot, wet, and itching to find a horizontal place with a door where we could get naked and sweaty.

Swallowing hard, I was breathless when I answered. "This probably isn't a good idea."

My body involuntarily arched into his and I exercised restraint I didn't know I had in order to resist reaching up to run my hands over the hard muscles covering his chest.

And then he did that bossy, sexually aggressive Max– thing and broke down one more barrier. He reached down and hooked his fingers in my belt loops, pulling my lower body close and nudging a hard thigh between my legs. Deliberately, he shifted his leg up and pressed against my core, and the pleasure was so good I moaned low and deep in my throat. He responded by rocking his cock into me again, his eyes hot and aggressive.

"Fuck. I love that sound. It makes me hard." Max touched a curl lying across my shoulder. "Even if this is the worst idea ever, I don't care."

His hand grazed my collarbone and his eyes drifted down to where my nipples poked out against the thin cotton of my tank top. The slight lift of his mouth assured me that he knew exactly what he was doing.

It pissed me off. Not in a bad way, but in the totally sexy, arousing way that led to long sweaty nights in a big bed where we worked out the power dynamic.

I let my own gaze wander up and down the length of his body. So big, strong—I took another peek at the bulge in his jeans—and definitely interested. For the past year, I'd been out on dates with slick, phony, musicians or Brad Pitt–wannabes—all arranged by my label's publicity team. It had been a long time since I'd indulged in what it felt like to be young, healthy, and sexy. Part of my treatment had focused on reclaiming who I was and this was a part of myself that I had yet to bring back online. At my core, I was a steady–relationship kind of girl, not the fling kind of chick, but maybe Max was the guy to help with my first step back into the land of the sexually living.

It didn't have to be anything serious. That was definitely in my plans, but Max would be a very enjoyable detour.

I trailed my hands up his chest, caressing the hardness underneath his T–shirt. He shuddered as I scraped a nail over his nipple. Smiling, I wrapped my arms around his neck, caressing the smooth skin of his nape and tangling in his hair. He pushed against my hand, silently begging for more, like a big cat.

His big hands trailed down my body, grazing the sides of my breasts and momentarily cupping their fullness before drifting lower to pull my hips even closer. He leaned in, his nose tracing a path of fire across my jaw, my neck, and landing just behind my ear. "I'm going to kiss you now. Last chance to object."

Rubbing my body against his, I had nothing. My head told me that this was a really bad idea—why tempt myself with something that couldn't go anywhere? I was sure one word from me and Max would let me go.

But I wasn't going to say it and he knew it. I wanted this. Wanted him. It was time for me to rejoin the world of sexually active twenty–somethings and to enjoy myself. Just for the sake of sex. Just for the sake of feeling good.

Moving my face to the side, I found his lips with mine

and murmured, "Stop talking about it and do it already."

The kiss was not what I expected. He'd been fast and frantic before, but this joining was slow and sweet; just a gentle brushing of lips against lips. But it still burned me alive. The heat from his touch started at my mouth and caught fire as it raged through my system. My fingertips were glowing, my toes curling, and fire surged low in my belly. I pulled back a second to catch my breath and found myself looking into his eyes.

I didn't think it could get any hotter but Max knew how to play me better than any Nashville musician I'd ever worked with. He cupped my jaw with one hand to hold me in place and that little gesture flipped my switch and I spontaneously combusted, leaning up to take his mouth for my own. He tasted of mint, spicy male, and pure pleasure. His teeth nibbled on my lower lip before soothing the sting with a warm lick of his tongue. I gasped and he took full advantage, invading my mouth with a slow, teasing thrust.

I *really* needed to write a song about this.

Linking both arms around his neck, I drowned in the kiss, pressing my body into his hands as they roamed my back, over my hips, and down my thighs. Groaning against my skin, Max covered my neck with hot, open-mouthed kisses and the skin exposed by my skimpy tank top. I felt him tug on the fabric with his teeth.

"I want to pull this down and suck on your tits until you come for me."

"Yes." I wanted that, too.

I grabbed his head between my hands and forced his lips back to my own and it was my turn to control the mesh of tongue, lips, and teeth.

Max let me have my way for ten seconds before he grabbed my ass and lifted me off my feet. The movement prompted me to wrap my legs around him, bringing my aching pussy into direct contact with the hard length of his cock. Best. Position. Ever.

"Hey, Max! Whoa! Sorry, man!"

The voice rudely ripped through my sexual haze. Panting and flushed, I stared up at Max, his bewildered expression surely mirroring my own. Both of our gazes drifted over in the direction of the voice of the intruder.

Dean, embarrassed, waved his fingers at us while Shannon peeked over his shoulder.

Damn and double damn.

And then it hit me. Anyone—fans, the press—could have seen me wrapped around Max in the middle of this parking lot.

I looked down and realized I was *still* wrapped around Max.

Bad. Bad. Very bad.

Scrambling, I struggled out of Max's arms and hit the pavement, quickly adjusting my clothes. This whole thing was crazy, and I needed to grab my frog and get the hell out of here, before Max worked his voodoo on me again and I actually fucked him in the parking lot of the Harris Teeter.

I just needed some space. I needed to let Max know what this was and wasn't. Set some ground rules.

"I should go."

I turned and grabbed Merle, moving towards the door of my truck. My hands shook and I was cursing the blasted door lock when I heard Dean over my shoulder. "Nice frog."

Resting my forehead on the window glass, I took a few steadying breaths before I turned to face him. He was smiling and I flashed him a grateful look for breaking the ice. "Thanks. His name is Merle."

Dean nodded. "The Hag. Good choice."

I looked at Max and gave him an "I told you so look", that he brushed off with a wave of his hand and roll of his eyes.

Dean cleared his throat. "Sorry about the interruption. We came looking for you two because we need a favor. Shannon, the love of my life, has gotten us involved with a bowling league." His facial expression was classic whipped male and I had to giggle when Shannon punched him in the shoulder. "Anyway, we're short two people tonight and need you to fill in."

Shannon took over, her bouncy delivery making me smile. "No pressure, but we'll have to forfeit if we don't get two more bowlers." She clasped her hands in a pleading manner. "Please?"

"You don't want me," I said. "I can't bowl."

"Don't worry. We just need the bodies."

I looked over at Max. This was totally his call. Hanging out one–on–one was cool, but maybe he didn't want me around his friends.

Max crossed his arms over his chest, his face expressive but hard for me to decipher. He watched me for a few seconds, trying to gauge my reaction, too, I guess. Finally, he gave a quick nod.

"I'm in if you are. You said you didn't get a lot of normal in your life." His lip lifted in a smirk. "There's nothing more normal than bowling."

Yep, I'd said that and I'd meant it. Lately, I was always living cautiously, following the plan with no deviations. I didn't have to be in the studio tonight; no rehearsal, no appearances until early tomorrow morning. Why the hell not?

I closed and locked the door of my truck and turned back to the waiting group. "Okay. I'm in."

Pleased, Dean smiled and nodded. Shannon clapped her hands; talking a mile a minute as her boyfriend led her away.

"You really okay with this?" Max asked.

Was I? Did I want to spend more time with him? Get a chance later to talk about what was and wasn't brewing between us?

"Yep. I'm cool with this."

Max grabbed my hand in his, weaving our fingers. "Good. We'll have fun."

"Yeah, yeah, yeah. But, tell me this." I matched his grin

as we followed the others across the parking lot. "Why does normal have to involve rented shoes?"

CHAPTER SIX
Max

"Holy shit. She really is terrible."

I stood with Dean on the side of the bowling lanes assigned to the league and watched Kit bowl the first ball on her last frame. We both tensed as the ball careened down the lane and finally landed in the gutter—again. I shook my head, as Kit turned to Shannon and lifted her hands in defeat. Shannon stood up and embraced her as they both laughed at something Kit said.

I checked out her scorecard. Straight gutter balls. "Well, she *did* warn us."

"I know, but it usually isn't true." Dean's face was contorted with laughter and disbelief as he raked a hand over his face. "People just say that kind of stuff to be modest."

"She should have let us put up the bumper guards." I watched her as she grabbed the ball for her second roll and lined up on the lane. I leaned forward slightly as she walked forward, swung her arm out, and sent the ball down the lane. She was still bent over at the waist, anxiously watching the ball progress towards the pins and I couldn't help but enjoy the view. Her ass was fine and I vividly remembered what it felt like in my hands when I'd kissed her earlier today.

I could still taste her on my lips and smell her perfume on my clothes. Straightening, I discreetly adjusted my jeans over the permanent hard–on that appeared whenever she was around. What I'd intended to be a light, sexy kiss had blown up into something so hot that I was amazed my lips weren't scorched.

"Sorry about interrupting your make–out session in the parking lot earlier," Dean said.

"No worries; it isn't like I won't get another one."

"Yeah? You going out with her again?"

"It wasn't a date." I'd told Dean all about Kit's reservations to call it an actual date. "I wonder how long her label and manager are going to keep her on such a short leash."

"If you believe the papers, she cost them a shit ton of money. They're just protecting their investment."

"I guess."

"So is this it or are you going to have another non–date?"

"I want to. She's very cool." Truth be told, she was one of the most fun girls I'd ever spent time with and we hadn't even made it to a bed yet. And I wanted to take it that far with her. Over and over again, for at least one entire night. "I think she's into me."

Kit glanced over her shoulder at me with a big smile before returning her attention to Shannon and the fans who had just realized who Kit was.

Eyeing the exchange, Dean commented. "If the look on her face is any evidence as to how she feels, she's into you in a big way. "

I continued to watch her as she laughed and joked with the rest of the bowling team. In the midst of a group full of strangers, she exuded warmth and friendliness—and she was so damn hot.

Yeah, I'd fantasized about her, but the reality was so much better. And the crazy part? If the kiss was any indication, then Dean might be right, and she also felt this wild chemistry between us.

We were going to fuck each other. For one night? For more? I had no idea, but it was something we needed to iron out. I always made sure the women knew where I stood and Kit was no different just because she was a celebrity. As soon as we got that straight, I'd consider it a green light.

I didn't know if she was looking for a picket fence, but I wasn't offering one.

Forget the whole movie–of–the–week bullshit about a regular guy and a celebrity; they had the cold reality of the situation to deal with. I'd brushed up against the life of the rich and famous in this town since I was a kid and had ended up way the worse for wear. Frankly, I didn't know how she dealt with all the lies and bullshit in the music industry, but I did know that my future plans did not involve being in any tabloid.

Kit was smack–dab in the middle of the very public fishbowl in which she had chosen to live her life, and anyone who wanted to be with her had to take that on. Always watching what you did, what you said, what you wore—it was exhausting to think about it. And now she was faced with having to play the part of the good little girl for the court of public opinion.

A good girl. The words reminded me of the Daily Scoop reporter. The guy still called every day and I continued to refuse his offer. It must fucking suck to have assholes like that following you around all the time, buying your secrets from people who went cheap.

After today, I had some secrets to share—at least some insight into her world and what she was really like. For some reason she trusted me, at least enough to let down her guard a little bit. If I was a dick, it would be so easy to use that trust and get her to reveal so much more. And if I got her to give into this attraction, and didn't mind sharing the details? I could be at least five grand richer for the price of an afternoon at the local carnival, a condom, and a cell phone video camera.

"So, what are you gonna do now?" Dean's voice cut into my thoughts, dragging me back to the present.

"I'm going to have the talk with her and then see where it goes."

"Don't."

"Dean, don't start."

"Max, I know I'm starting to sound like a broken record, but why do you set rules that kill any chance of you having more? You don't have to marry her." He leaned in like he had a secret to share. "There's this thing called *dating* and some people think it's a fun way to spend your evenings and weekends. You do it until you want to make it permanent because you love each other or you break up and change your statuses on Facebook. Why don't you just try it and see where it goes?"

"It's not my thing. You know that."

"All I know is that every woman isn't Sarah. You've got to let go of the past."

"I'm not the one who keeps bringing her up." I reined in my temper. He was my best friend and he thought he was doing the right thing, but it was getting old. The disaster with Sarah went down four years ago and I'd learned my lesson and moved on. "Just fucking drop it."

"Hey Max!" Shannon skipped over to us, slinging her arm around Dean's neck. It was hard to maintain the tense atmosphere when she was around. "Kit says she'll be ready to go in a few minutes." Her face beamed with excitement. "I can't believe I got to bowl with Kit Landry! I have to call my mom!" She was practically levitating with excitement as she skipped away, dragging Dean in her wake.

I decided to sit down and observe Kit while she wrapped up the last autographs. She gave each person focused attention, asking questions about them and their families. Her entire vibe was warm and approachable and she seduced them all with her authenticity. It was no wonder she had so many loyal fans.

This afternoon with Kit had rocked my world and I didn't want it to end today. Not yet. But, I wondered if she would be up for what I had to offer.

No strings. A little fun between consenting adults.

It was all I could offer. Ever.

There was only one way to find out.

TEMPTATION

Fifteen minutes later, the last fan walked away, excitedly looking at his photo with Kit now saved on his cell phone. She wandered over to me, smiling apologetically. "Sorry about that. Occupational hazard."

I stood up, letting her lead the way out of the bowling alley and towards my truck. "No worries. I liked watching you work." I gestured towards a few fans still in the lot. "They love you."

She climbed up into the cab and I rounded the truck and was seated before she answered with a heavy tone. "They love the image. They don't know me."

I was surprised at first by the answer, but there was truth in it. Hell, until the past few days, I'd been one of those people and even now I didn't pretend to know her well at all. "If they got to know you, they would find lots to love."

"I wonder." She leaned against the window and sighed. "Getting to know someone means looking beyond the image and taking the good with the bad—including the ugly secrets."

I couldn't disagree with her. "I guess you're right, but that's true even if you aren't famous. How often does anyone really let others see the deepest, darkest parts of their life?" I thought of all the reporters—and one in particular— who circled her like vultures. I turned to face her in the darkened truck cab. "We *all* have secrets."

She sighed and laughed softly. "Ignore me. I'm just tired."

I tried to see her in the gloom of the truck; something in her voice sounded off to me, like she was carrying something heavy. I didn't have the right to pry and I guessed that she wouldn't tell me even if I asked. Why should she?

"Well, I've gotten to know you a little and I like what I see."

I watched Kit, noting how she nervously bit her bottom lip—a move I found entirely adorable. And sexy. She was about to bolt, and I knew this might be my one chance.

Needing to touch her again, I moved closer, pressing my body against her and nudging her back against the seat of the truck. I rested my arms on either side of her tiny frame as she tipped her head back to look into my eyes. Her hands drifted up to rest on my chest, her fingers alternately clenching my T–shirt and petting my chest.

My body jolted with the electric shock from where we connected and, just like that, I was *right there*. Hard as rock and dying for her. In the silent cocoon of my truck, I leaned in close, touching our foreheads together, listening to each other breathe as the seconds ticked by.

Tracing lazy circles along the soft skin of her breast exposed at the top edge of her tank top, I murmured, "I want to fuck you and I think you want me to."

"I do." She laughed softly when I paused. "What? You expected me to play it another way? I don't do games, Max."

"You shocked me a little," I admitted.

"My work life is full of games. Half–truths and strategy. I don't want that in my bed."

Jesus. She was me. Without a penis. Thank God.

"What do you want in your bed?" I leaned in to bury my face in her hair, the warmth of her skin against my cheek and her sweet scent surrounding me.

"You. For three weeks," she murmured, arching her neck when I began pressing a series of soft kisses on her skin. She was melting under me, her body heating up with the fire we had growing between us. "I don't have time for a relationship. I'm three weeks away from the most important tour of my life and I shouldn't be thinking of anything except work."

"But..." I lifted my head to look at her, needing her to say the words to seal the deal.

"I want you and I plan on having you. A lot."

"Any way you want me. Any time. I live to serve."

"Good."

I leaned forward and brushed a kiss across her lips.

When her lips opened slightly, I slipped my tongue inside and leisurely explored her mouth. It was like I had the key to unlock her. She opened up under me, her legs spreading to accommodate me as much as possible in the front seat of my truck. I could take her here. Peel off her jeans and panties and slide in where she was hot, wet, and tight. It would be a fast and hard fuck that would take the edge off and then we could head back to my place.

I broke off the kiss to lay out my plan of action when my phone went off.

Fuck me.

It was the ringtone for the department and I knew I had to answer it. My chances for getting lucky tonight were about as good as winning the actual lottery.

I picked it up and accepted the call. "Yeah?"

Dispatch told me exactly what I didn't want to hear with a hot willing woman in my truck. My plans for Kit Landry were going to have to wait. I hung up and moved back behind the wheel.

I looked over at her and wished I hadn't. A tousled Kit, lips wet from our kisses, her tits on display under that tiny tank top was not a vision I wanted to trade for sweaty guys, smelly fire gear, smoke and flames. "I'm not on duty, but I'm secondary and they need all hands who are fit for duty to report."

"That's cool. You've got to go." She leaned over and kissed me, her hand trailing down my chest to settle on my cock. She stroked me lightly, making my eyes cross with the pleasure of it. I felt like fucking Superman when I managed to keep my hands on the wheel and off her. "We've got three weeks. I'm not going anywhere."

And at that moment, I wondered if I'd gotten in over my head with Kit Landry.

CHAPTER SEVEN
Kit

"He offered to do what?"

I settled back into the chair and glanced around the open, utilitarian warehouse space the label had provided for rehearsals of my upcoming tour. I took a sip of my coffee as Bridget worked through her emotions. I wasn't surprised. My band, my friends and companions for the past five years, stuck by me through the ups and the downs of my crazy career and they worried about me—especially after the train wreck my life had been just a year ago. But Bridget had sat right by me through the whole thing, never once breaking eye contact or dumping me.

I'd been cruel to her at times—coming down from the alcohol and pills hadn't brought out the best in me. She'd taken it like a champ, called me out like a true friend, and forgiven me when I asked for it. She is my sister, my secret keeper, my most trusted companion and she wasn't on board the Max train. Not even a little bit.

Bridget was now looking at me with expectation, so I took a deep breath and plunged right in. "I went over to the fire station to take the photos, T–shirts, and tickets and then he asked me out. We had a good time and then... one thing led to another. "

"Okay, I got it. He's the reason you disappeared the other night." She took a big gulp of her coffee and pointed at me across the table. "Get to the point where he offered the sex."

"Keep your voice down!" I glanced around the rehearsal space, noting with relief that none of my band mates seemed to have overheard this particular conversation. "He didn't offer the sex until I asked for it."

"Oh, that makes me feel *so* much better."

"Bridget, it wasn't like that." I thought about how to ease her mind and explain my reasons for this. "He makes me feel something I haven't felt in a long time. With Max, I feel like 'Kit the woman' and not like..."

"'Kit the merchandise'. 'Kit the paycheck'."

"Exactly." I pulled my hair off my face and into a scrunchie on top of my head.

"He sleeps with a lot of women," she mumbled, suddenly engrossed in the design of her Starbucks cup.

I gave her the hairy eyeball. "Did you check up on him?"

"Ron had your security team do the usual checks. He's a good firefighter on the job, but he's run into some trouble in his personal life."

"Like what?" I instantly regretted asking. This felt invasive. Unfair. Max and I weren't about details. And if I was looking for any semblance of a normal thing with him, I shouldn't act like a paranoid celebrity.

"He's got a hot temper. Won't back down from a fight but he doesn't seem to go looking for them." She paused and I knew the next fact was a whammy. "And he slept with the Fire Department Chief's niece..."

"Was she legal? Married?"

"...in the maintenance closet at the department Christmas party."

"Oh." It wasn't funny but I couldn't help the chuckle that spilled out. "Not a career–enhancing moment."

From the look on her face, it was clear that Bridget didn't find this as funny as I did. What did I care about who he'd slept with before me? His past wasn't any more my business than mine was his. Although, to find out about mine all he had to do was Google me or follow the hashtag #dumbassdecisionsaboutmen on Twitter.

"What the hell, Bridget? You told me to do this."

"Honey, I know I told you to jump his bones, but I didn't think you'd actually do it. You *never* do what I tell you to do. You want something more in your life than tour buses and hotel rooms and I *totally* get that, but this guy—he could just be using you. He could sell his story to the tabloids and ruin all your hard work. The label *would not* be happy with another scandal."

I thought about my life. I'd given up a lot in the pursuit of my career and taking care of my responsibilities. Then I'd fucked the whole thing up when I'd missed concerts and album deadlines because Jake had broken my heart. I understood it now. I knew where the feeling of no control came from, why I'd spent a year watching myself do all the things I did from a distance in my head. In fact, everyone had been briefed by my doctor on why I'd lost it—but emotional breakdowns weren't an acceptable excuse in the music business. Unless they increased your digital download sales.

The label was giving me one last chance to prove that I was still a good investment, and I couldn't afford to blow it. Some of the label management was looking for any excuse to drop my contract and they were all watching me like a hawk. Even at my young age, I wasn't the newest thing to hit this town and I could feel the hot breath of all the new arrivals on the back of my neck.

My head was telling me to stay away from Max—but the way he made me feel was addictive. With him, I felt like I could be myself because that was who he really wanted and this wasn't going to last beyond this brief period in time.

"I'm in a good place. I'm taking care of myself and following the diet and exercise plan put together by the nutritionist. We've built in lots of down time on the tour..."

I looked around to see if anyone else was close by. Bridget was one of the few people who knew why I'd really gone into rehab and that secret would be a gold mine for any reporter who got their hands on it. The label and my management team had told us that market tests showed that "alcoholism trended better than crazy".

Their words. Not mine.

So, I'd come out as a drunk—which wasn't a total lie because I'd had a drinking problem. But my reaction had been extreme because I was also hypomanic—bipolar disorder's manageable, but lesser known, little sister. I understood why it was necessary to pick the more marketable of my personal defects, but it didn't mean that I was thrilled with adding yet another secret skeleton to the pile in my closet.

I was tired of the lies. I was tired of an image that was put on me five years ago. I was ready and strong enough to make the change. If the fans followed—that was great. If they didn't, I would change my course as necessary.

"I've got my illness under control. I respect it and I'm on program."

"I know you are," Bridget said and I didn't miss the worry in her tone. I had scared the shit out of her for a long time and she was still waiting for the other stiletto to drop.

My mother had suffered terribly from bipolar disorder. Actually, we'd all suffered—living with someone suffering from that illness and going untreated was a living hell. And it was hereditary. It had been somewhat inevitable that I was going to have to deal with some emotional issues, but I'd been as shocked as anyone to find out that my mood swings, alcoholic binging, and the disruptive behavior were due to my hypomania. I was learning to live with it, forging ahead, and that meant enjoying every aspect of my life.

"I love what I do and you know how important it is for me to provide for the people I love. But, I've pushed aside having anything for myself for a long time. Not since Jake have I..." I faltered. I wasn't a good enough liar to say that it still didn't get to me. He'd stomped on my heart big time and, even though it had scarred over, it never quite pumped the same again. "Max is here and I want this now."

"We hit the road in three weeks."

"Yeah, we do; and when we go, this fling will end."

"What about finding someone to have a real relationship with?"

"I want that. And I will have it, but we both know now is not the time."

"Look, Kit." Bridget lowered her voice to prevent anyone overhearing. "Your illness isn't the only thing you need to keep under wraps. Are you sure this is the right time to bring someone new into your life? Someone you need to trust not to play 'kiss and tell'?"

She was so right; I had no argument. I could count on one hand the number of people who knew my mother wasn't dead, but living at the Shady Grove Assisted Living home. Years of drug use and drinking due to her mental illness had fried her brain—literally. Now, she lived quite happily with private nursing care in her world of dolls, crayons, and everything a young child would enjoy. Some days she knew who I was, and other days something would trigger a mania and she would slip into the peace the sedative injection would grant her.

I was a young, poor, and hungry kid when I agreed to the lie of her death and that was my only excuse. They agreed to move her out of the state home and I signed the confidentiality agreement. Back then, I'd had no idea how much the secrets and lies would weigh on me and there wasn't a day when I didn't want to go back in time and say no. No matter who came into my life, I was lying to them from day one and that fact always stood in between. Jake had told me that I kept my heart locked up in a room with no door and that, no matter what he did, he was never going to be able to get in. It was why I had fought for him when he left. He was right.

I plopped my head down on the table in frustration. Just yesterday, a blogger had printed the news that the fire in the studio was deemed "suspicious" by the NFD. The information would have eventually been made public, but the article also disclosed the details of the meeting with the label reps and my management, including the fact that I'd been questioned about anyone in my life who would want to hurt me. It was clear that the leak was on the inside and the label was furious.

Hell, I was furious. Whoever it was better hope that someone else got to them before I did.

On some level, I knew Bridget was right. I didn't know Max and I had all this crazy shit going on. I had secrets. Big ones. Now was *not* the time to start expanding my circle of friends—but I wanted Max. And something about him told me that I could trust him.

You want to trust him.

This year of celibacy wasn't by choice. No one had tempted me enough to take the chance of having someone turn on me and spill it to the press.

Background checks really killed the mood.

My head still on the tabletop, I mumbled, "I just want to have sex. Good sex. Up–all–night–sex."

Bridget lifted my hair from where it hid my face, her eyes filled with genuine concern. "Take a breath. Slow down to your usual pace of slower–than–molasses and think about this." Her face lit up with her next idea. "Call Paul!"

No way was I calling Paul. He'd retired from being my manager and I'd bothered him enough during the Jake fiasco. Paul had left his beautiful ranch and come to me when I'd hit the bottom, checked me into rehab and made sure I was fit to face the public again. No, I couldn't bother him with this.

"We have a lot to do before the tour starts."

I jumped at the sound of Ron Harris' voice just over my shoulder and I hoped to God he hadn't heard what we were talking about. The last thing I wanted to discuss with him was sex. Looking up, I groaned at the pile of documents in his hands. Ron was an excellent manager. He organized, planned, and coordinated like the professional that he was, and I knew my recent revival was due in no small part to his hard work on my behalf.

Lately, though, we'd had quite a few differences of

opinion and it had strained our relationship. Ron wanted me to take on more projects and tour longer and farther. He wanted me to record the same kind of music I'd put on my last album. I wanted a little breathing room to explore other options both in my personal and professional life. I wanted to go with the music that had poured out of me since I'd walked through the fire and survived.

Clearly, we needed to talk.

Ron plopped down the tour itinerary on the table and what looked like four million promotional photos for my signature. "We need to discuss some stuff. We have a few new requests for appearances, and the label..."

I cut him off. "Ron, I don't want to add any more appearances to the next three weeks. The band needs to spend some time with their families and I want a little time for myself."

Ron stared at me like I'd sprouted a third eye. "Are you kidding me? You can take time later when you can only get booked at Branson."

Bridget flipped through the papers Ron had placed in front of her. "Australia? New Zealand? A Christmas special? Ron, you really need to loosen up. Kit has to take care of her health, pace herself."

He stopped her with a hand in her face and Bridget looked like she wanted to bite him. I would have paid to see that.

"Look, in the three years since I've taken over Kit's management, she's tripled her income and is now one of the most recognized faces in country music. In spite of her lapses, her smaller arena shows are selling out in a matter of hours and her face is on at least one magazine cover every month. Give me another year and follow my plan, and you'll be back to headlining at the largest concert venues in the country."

"All this," Bridget gestured towards the papers on the table, "doesn't have to happen in the next three weeks. Kit wants a little space..."

TEMPTATION

He interrupted in a voice loud enough to make surrounding conversations come to a halt. "Kit doesn't know what she wants."

Enough was enough.

"Stop!" Silence descended as I took control of the situation. I focused first on Bridget. "I really appreciate you looking out for me, but let me handle this, okay?" Bridget nodded and I turned to Ron.

"I appreciate you keeping my career afloat when I was sick, but I'm back now and I call the shots. I love your ideas, your enthusiasm, but you can't make plans without asking me. You need to get a life. I don't have one and I *know* you don't because you're usually with me."

I reached out and squeezed his hand. "Ron, once we hit the road I am yours one hundred percent, but right now I need some space... time to take care of some personal matters. You got me?"

Ron stared at me for a few seconds, clearly measuring what he was going to say next. His face tensed with determination as he patted my hand and said, "Now, Kit, you're on the verge—"

"'Of something big'. I know." I interrupted the speech I'd heard many times before.

It appeared that taking back control of my life was starting now.

"Ron, I'm serious. No more stuff added to the schedule."

Ron looked at Bridget and gestured towards me in a "you talk to her" motion. Bridget shook her head while I rose from the table and moved towards the band.

The conversation had solidified my decision. I didn't know Max and having an affair with him was a risky proposition—especially for someone in my position. But Max was a delicious opportunity I was not passing up.

CHAPTER EIGHT
Max

"I don't know how you do this all the time."

Flashes were going off all around us as we stood on the sidewalk in front of the Bluebird Café. I could barely hear anything with all the reporters yelling out her name, but I knew she was right there beside me. Normally Kit was a force of nature, but in the spotlight she was a tsunami, a hurricane, and a tornado all at one time and everyone she came across was fighting for the chance to get pulled in.

It was insane and she was the eye of the storm. Calm. Serene.

She fucking owned this place.

Kit leaned into me, grabbing my arm and looking up at me with a smile on her face. "This is one of the fun parts! All you gotta do is smile and look pretty."

"Well, you've got that down."

"You're kind of pretty yourself, Mr. Butler," she teased as the flashes doubled in frequency as they recorded every move we made. "So, on a scale of one to ten... how badly are you hating this right now?"

"I'm ready to have a seizure." According to the press release, I was here as her guest—a thank–you–for–saving–my–life present. I had no choice but to deal with it but it didn't make it any less painful.

"Okay, drama queen; we're done. Come on; I hear there's food inside."

She gave one last wave towards the crowd and pulled me through the front door and into the calm of the Bluebird. I'd been here once or twice with my grandfather before, to listen to someone play and I'd always liked the small, cozy place. No flash; no sparkles—just a place to enjoy great music with nice people.

"I thought big industry parties were all held in expensive hotels," I said as she grabbed my hand and drew me through the crowd towards the bar. Everyone spoke or nodded to her and most of them gave me a curious glance and then a second when they saw us holding hands. I squeezed her fingers before asking, "Is this okay?"

We made it to the bar and she ordered a club soda and a beer before answering my questions.

"This is the number one party for a song I wrote and I got to pick the venue. I didn't want to spend the evening at some stuffy hotel." She squeezed my hand again. "The press inside was hand–picked by me and my label. This is cool."

"Can I kiss you like I want to?"

"No." Kit laughed and nudged me with her elbow. "You'll just have to control yourself for an hour or two."

"That's easier said than done when you look like that."

Kit looked more like a star tonight than anytime since I'd met her, with a short sparkly black dress, hair curly and flowing down her back, and heels that gave her another three inches. She wore makeup, but underneath she was still Kit—right down to the crimson streaks in her hair.

"Uh huh."

"Are you fishing for compliments?" I accepted my beer from the waitress and took a sip, letting the liquid cool me down from the heat that always pounded on Nashville in the summer. Even the A/C in the café was struggling to keep up with the number of bodies in here tonight. I noticed that several of the people were looking at her, clearly judging whether they could interrupt us. She was the party girl and needed to make the rounds. I was just the "plus one". I placed a hand on the small of her back and nudged her towards the crowd. "I refuse to inflate your ego any more than it already is. Go see if one of these people will tell you how gorgeous you look."

She was immediately sucked in by a crowd of people who hugged and kissed her in congratulations. Watching her was becoming one of my favorite activities and I settled back against the bar—the best seat in the house.

I'd surprised no one by calling her first. The emergency call had been a bad one and it took most of the night to clear up but before I hit my rack at the station, I'd called Kit to arrange our next non–date. We'd come to an agreement about what this was and I was anxious to make it happen. She was constantly in my thoughts and those were the kind that had me waking up hard and aching for her.

She told me to pick her up for this party and suspended in the air between us was the knowledge that when I took her home tonight, I wouldn't be leaving.

"Having a good time?"

I turned, surprised to find Ron, Kit's manager, standing beside me. He didn't like me and was really bad at hiding it. I was reserving judgment on him.

Okay, that was a lie. I thought the guy was a dick.

I sat back, waiting to see what he wanted because there was no way he was there to become BFFs.

"Kit said she needed some time before the tour starts to take care of some personal matters," he said, scanning the crowd, smiling and nodding when he made eye contact. "I'm guessing that you're the 'personal' in the 'matters'."

"I hope so." What was I doing? I wasn't playing games with this guy. If he was going to dig into things that were none of his business, then he was just going to have to deal. "I know I am. What's it to you?"

"Everything about Kit concerns me. It's my job."

"And?"

"Kit knows what she needs to do and that isn't a distraction with a slick line, a rubber, and a truck parked off in the woods somewhere."

"Meaning that I should leave her alone." I laughed. This guy had brass balls. "Why are you trying to cock block me, man?"

That got his attention. He turned to eyeball me, his gaze calculating. If this guy was trying to figure me out, he was going to be really disappointed. He didn't even know who the fuck I was.

"I'd like you to keep your dick in your pants and away from Kit, but if you can't, please keep it off the Internet. No sex tapes. No tell–all interviews."

"I think I can guarantee that I have no plans to plaster my ass on YouTube."

"If you need an incentive, I can make it worth your while."

Okay, he'd shocked me. I turned to fully face him because I needed to watch him as he pimped out Kit.

"Are you offering to pay me to sleep with her or not sleep with her?"

"That's up to you," he said.

"This is what is fucked up about this business. If you're who she's got looking out for her, then I feel sorry for her."

He scoffed, "I didn't realize you were trying to play knight in shining armor."

"Anybody who met her would do the same thing." I was done with this douchebag. Kit was getting ready to take the stage and I sure as hell would rather listen to her. "Nice talking to you, Sir–Pimps–A–Lot."

I found a seat next to Bridget in the front, just as the head of her record label took the stage. Kit made her way to the front and I openly ogled her legs. They were spectacular and I'd be lying if I said I couldn't wait to feel them wrapped around my waist later tonight. The view and the fantasy went a long way to lift the bad mood that talking to Ron had started.

Kit caught me and winked, causing several people to turn and look my way. I winked back at her and she laughed, drawing the attention of her label president. She caught his look and immediately toned it down a notch or two in the fun department.

"Don't encourage her," Bridget whispered in my ear,

her smile taking the edge off the scolding. I opened my mouth to respond but never got the chance because the ceremony began.

"Ladies and Gentlemen, I'm Liam Connor, the president of One More Song Records and we are here to celebrate the latest number–one song written by our own Kit Landry." He paused while we all clapped and a couple guys in the back added wolf whistles to the mix. Kit looked embarrassed by the attention, dipping her head and hiding behind her curtain of dark curls. "No one is prouder of how far she's come since she signed with us at the tender age of seventeen." He turned to her, waiting until she looked up at him to continue. "She went from a homeless kid living on the street, to three multi–platinum albums, sold–out arena tours, and twenty number–one songs written and recorded by her or the biggest names in this business. These are just a few of the things I can list that make her a great artist. But what makes her a great person is the way she walked through the fire and came back to us, healthy, happy, and filled with the same, signature Kit Landry country music."

Kit tensed at his last few words. It was hard to see if you weren't looking, but I had my eyes trained on her and she didn't like what he was saying one little bit. The room remained quiet as he reached for a large framed print of the sheet music for the song and turned back to present it to Kit.

"Congratulations, Kit, on your latest number–one song."

The room burst into applause, and flashbulbs went off as the photo opportunity was played out on the stage. And as soon as it started it was over, and Kit was on the stage all by herself, looking out at the crowd with a smile as everyone quieted down. She was poised, everything you expected a star to be, and I remembered that she was only twenty–one. A kid, by most people's standards and she was doing what most people only dreamed about and had survived having the devil on her tail.

TEMPTATION

"I'm never good at speeches, so I'll say thank you the best way I know how."

She nodded at a couple of guys just off stage and they joined her up there, pulling up three chairs. Kit turned and lifted Jolene out of her case and joined them in the intimate circle under the spotlight.

She pulled the microphone closer to her and spoke into it, her low voice weaving a net that caught all of us. You had to stay and listen to every word she uttered; there was no way you'd have the power to walk away. *This* was how she'd sold all those records. This was why she'd get back on top.

"Songs come from inside you. I write because I have all these things—pain, joy, longing, anger—inside me and they have to get out. I've had a lot to say lately as I've been working on the new album and... well... it's different from what I've recorded before." She took a deep breath, making eye contact with people as she scanned the room as if she was looking for allies. "Nobody stays the same. I hope y'all like what I have to say."

The guitars started a slow strum, the three of them playing as one on a melody that could only be described as delicate. The notes paused on a second in time, hung in the air like smoke, and then Kit's voice added the element that I didn't know was missing until I heard it. The lyrics were written to a lover, telling him to change his mind about trying to get her back. It was a plea to leave her alone, between the lines an appeal to come back and push her over the edge and a question of whether she would survive either option.

It was sad and hopeful and raw and gritty and unlike anything I'd ever heard her sing before. It blew me away. I had no idea how she did it and I was in awe of her talent. For her not to do this would be a waste.

She was in her element. I couldn't tell where she ended and the guitar began.

Kit sang in that spotlight, her eyes closed as she laid her heart and soul on the ground for everyone to see. This song

73

was more than a love song; it was a tale of a life hard fought and won against demons. It was Kit's testimony for anyone who looked deep enough to see it.

I ran into burning buildings and *this* was the bravest thing I'd ever seen.

She opened her eyes and the fire that blazed out was even brighter than the spotlight shining down on her. I couldn't have looked away if I'd wanted to and I realized that I didn't, even when she locked her gaze with mine and seared my soul for a few seconds before moving on to brand the next person in the room.

I glanced around, gauging other people's reactions to the song. Most were clearly enjoying it, moving their heads to the beat, tapping fingers idly on the tabletop in time with the rhythm. Everyone, except Liam Connor.

He stood to the side of the stage, mostly in the shadows, his expression dark and disapproving. Hell, the guy looked like he wanted to walk on the stage and rip the guitar out of her hands.

"What's with Liam Connor? Did someone pee in his beer?" I asked Bridget.

She glanced at him and cursed under her breath. She leaned over to me and whispered, "That's what trouble looks like."

"Why? Everyone loves the song."

She grabbed her drink and took a sip before patting my hand like I was four years old. "You'll need to ask Kit about it, but remember: the first rule of the music business is that it has nothing to do with the music."

CHAPTER NINE
Kit

"What the fuck was that supposed to be?"

I didn't have to turn around to know who was behind me or to know what his face looked like. Liam Connor was always in a bad mood around me lately—I'd lost him money and that was *the* cardinal sin, in his book. I'd also deviated from the agreed–upon playlist at the last minute. Spurred on by my recovery, the great progress during tour rehearsal today, and the way Max looked at me, I was feeling good and empowered and in control for the first time in a long while and I'd decided to flex.

"It was material for the new album. Everyone's heard my other stuff and I figured I'd thank them all for their loyalty by giving them an exclusive sneak peek."

I turned to look at him and it was exactly as I expected. Face red and hard with his displeasure, he crowded me into the back staff room of the Bluebird where I'd gone to take a restroom break after my performance. He was a big guy, a former college football semi–star who'd moved into the music business after graduation. He wasn't above using his size to make a statement, but I'd seen it all before. I'd faced shit down in my head that was scarier than Liam.

"I haven't approved that song for the album."

"According to my contract, you don't get approval on content unless it violates the morals clause. I get creative control over my music."

"Yes, but I can refuse to release an album if I'm not happy with the final product."

Shit. He could. The label ultimately had the last word

and it would be difficult for me to force them to release it or to get the rights to take it elsewhere. I wasn't even sure I had the cash to buy out my contract and I didn't want to go down that road unless I had to.

"Liam, did you see the audience? They were eating it up." I deliberately took out any agitation in my voice, hoping to get my way by gently shaking the sugar tree.

"This crowd is all the 'music is art' group, but they aren't a commercial audience. They aren't your demographic, your fan base."

"I'm twenty—one; my fan base is growing up with me. They would love that song." I took a breath and tried to plead my case. "I'm not the girl you signed five years ago. I've changed, grown. My image needs to change, too."

"I think you need to focus on how much you owe this label and how much you cost us with your little detour from your contractual obligations before you decide to change what's been proven to make money."

Ouch. That hurt and I must have shown it on my face because he had the bad manners to look like a smug dickhead. I knew I'd lost them money, but they'd also recouped a bunch of it by releasing a "greatest hits" album while I was in rehab. But my alternative was to tell them to shove it up their bottom line and see if some other label would buy out my contract. Nothing was guaranteed with my track record. I was hoping to get back on top with this tour and a successful next album, and then I'd have more options.

"Fine, Liam. Obviously we have a lot to discuss about the new album."

"I think you need to be prepared to do some listening." He nodded at me, spun on his heel and walked back into the café to navigate the danger zone of having his mistress and his wife in the same room at the same time. I'd taken no end of happiness by adding them both to the guest list. It was petty and mean and I was not sorry.

I walked over to the staff lockers, slamming a door in

frustration. I knew I had to make good on my promise to apologize for my failures, but having to kiss his ass was a whole other story. I needed to talk to my legal team about my power over this album. I wouldn't go to Ron; he sided with Liam and thought the status quo was the way to go. Once I knew where the lines were, I'd figure out which ones I wanted to cross and which ones needed to go entirely.

"Hey, you okay?"

I turned to find Max standing in the doorway, partially blocking the noise and people in the Bluebird. He took one look at me, glanced behind him at the crowd and shut the door. He stalked over to me, eyes locked on my face, and even though I wanted to look away, I couldn't. Instead I did what I did best. I hid.

"Don't do that," he said.

"Do what?"

"That thing where you shut down." He reached up to brush a curl off my face and I leaned into the touch in spite of myself. "You did it the other day when I gave you your guitar. For a couple of minutes you were real and then it was like you flipped a switch and this mask came down."

I just stared at him. I knew exactly what he was describing. I'd started doing it when I had come to Nashville on my own at sixteen. It was self–preservation to keep people at a distance and it had stuck once I'd become a celebrity.

"It's Super Kit," I mumbled, wishing I had a better way to describe it.

"Super Kit?"

"Yeah, that's what Bridget calls my alter ego. The make–up, the costumes, the band behind me—they're usually a dead give–away." I flexed my arms and struck a pose like a cartoon superhero. It was lame, but Bridget and I had done it so often when I needed a laugh that it was second nature. "Super Kit! Able to fill arenas in a single night!"

Max didn't laugh. Instead he cupped my face with his

large, calloused hand and looked me right in the eyes, his own searching for something I wasn't sure if I wanted him to see or miss. He was warm and I was freezing in the A/C, and it took super human strength not to latch on to him just to steal his body heat.

And cop a feel. I could be honest with myself about wanting to grope his ass at the first available opportunity.

"I could use one of those costumes," he said.

"Sorry. It's one–of–a–kind. I made it myself."

He pulled me close and I rested my head on his chest and wrapped my arms around his waist. We couldn't stay in here forever. The rumble of the crowd was just beyond the door but I would take this moment for an opportunity for calm before launching back into the fray. It was nice to have someone on my side. Really nice.

I inhaled deeply, indulging in the amazing combination of hot male and spicy aftershave. Yum. His body was hard beneath the cotton of his shirt and his muscles bunched and rippled when I touched him. His hand caressed the skin exposed on my shoulders and back and the sensation from the touch raced under my skin, lighting me up and starting a slow burn deep inside.

His voice rumbled in his chest, just under my cheek. "A job that requires all that armor doesn't sound like much fun."

I rolled my eyes and poked him in the side. "Says the man who wears a ton of protective gear every time he goes out on a call."

"Point taken." Max pulled back and smoothed the hair back from my face. "But that's a physical danger. Your costume sounds more like it's designed to protect your feelings."

Uncomfortable with the turn of the conversation, I pulled out of his embrace, turning to trace the name on the locker closest to me. "I love what I do." I tried to play it cool but, even to my ears, my voice sounded defensive so I paused to collect my thoughts. "Dolly Parton said that those of us in the music business have the same problems as everybody else. Money, fame—nothing changes that—we just get to do it in public." I smiled to myself, the rightness of my new music bubbling up in spite of the smack–down from Liam. "The music makes it worth it for me. It always comes back to the music."

Max's arms looped around my waist, his front pressed against my back, head resting on my shoulder. His voice rumbled in my ear and I felt it down in my bones. "But you still need the costume?"

I sighed and leaned into the warmth of his touch. "You meet people and they have expectations of you because of the image. The trick is figuring out who you can trust enough to let them see behind the costume."

"And people you know?"

Somehow he'd zeroed in on what had put me in this funk. Smart, nosy bastard.

"My label, my management—they don't want me to change anything about the costume."

"And now it doesn't fit."

I turned around then, staying within the circle of his arms, and eyeballed him, wondering how he'd gotten all of this so right. He didn't wait for me to finish.

"That song... it was amazing, but Liam Connor was the only one not thrilled about it. Then Bridget said some cryptic shit about the music not being about the music and Liam left you back here in a mood and slamming doors." I let the shock show on my face. I was impressed. His lip tilted up in a sexy grin. "I'm more than just a pretty face and big dick."

While I desperately hoped the second part was true, he'd accomplished what he'd sought to do. Make me laugh and shake off the fun–killing mood.

We stood like that for a few moments while his words settled between us. I was more comfortable with Max, almost a stranger, than I was with people who surrounded me every day. He'd been real since the first time we'd met and he treated me like a normal girl, even though my life was anything but ordinary. I liked him and I ignored the whisper that said I could do a lot more than like him if our timing was different.

Curious about him, I turned the tables. "So, your turn. Do you love what you do?"

Max backed us up until my back was pressed against the cool metal of the lockers, the sharp contrast causing me to give an involuntary shiver. He placed one hand against the lockers, tracing the line of the skinny strap on my dress with his fingers. That gave me the shivers, too—for an entirely different reason.

He broke eye contact with me, instead focusing on the movement of his hands, his face losing some of its usual playfulness.

"Yeah. After high school someone close to me died and I wanted a job that helped people."

"Because you couldn't help your friend?"

He nodded. "I considered teaching like my folks, but the thought of a job stuck in a building all day didn't appeal to me. I signed on with the NFD and I have no regrets. I'd like to get promoted, be a shift leader someday, but I still love it."

I gazed up at him, struck by his simple sincerity. Max seemed like such a *real* guy underneath all the swagger. I didn't doubt that he would deliver on everything his body and sexy mouth promised, but there was more to him. I'd met lots of people and I think I'm a good judge of when I'm being fed a load of crap. I hadn't always been adept at figuring it out and that had led to lots of heartache, broken promises, feeling used, and dating losers.

Lots of losers.

Losers who used me for rides. Losers who used me for a place to crash. Losers who used me for music connections. Losers who used me so they could sell the story to the tabloids.

I was pretty sure Max wasn't a loser. But I had to be

sure.

I already knew he had a truck.

"Do you have a home, a place to sleep?"

He was amused and baffled. "Yep. And I have a mortgage to prove it."

"Do you want to be in the music business?"

"No, I can definitely say that I have *no* desire to be in the music business."

"Are you going to sleep with me and sell the story to the papers?"

I cringed at how awful the question sounded actually spoken aloud. A quick peek to check his reaction and his thunderous expression told me that I'd definitely pissed him off.

Max grabbed me and dragged me against him. His eyes were almost black as he loomed over me, trapping my body between his long, hard legs.

He claimed my mouth in a kiss that was dominating, full of anger at my question, and the pent–up sexual heat that had simmered between us since we first met. Suddenly ravenous for him, I nipped at his lips and he plunged his hands into my hair, holding me still while he reclaimed possession of my mouth.

I gasped when he pulled away and held my face in between his hands. Max's voice was rough and edgy. "I want you. I want to do things to you that might be illegal in a few states. I want you in my bed, my truck, on a blanket by my favorite lake..." He moved even closer, grinding his cock against me and making my toes curl from the combination of his hard arousal and his words. "I want to lift up this skirt, push aside your panties and fuck you hard against this wall, but I *do not* want to tell any reporter about it."

His face was hard and intense and so damn sexy that I wanted to kiss him. So I did.

I licked his bottom lip and kissed the corner of his mouth. My hands wandered; I couldn't touch enough of him and I cursed the clothes that kept me from feeling the direct warmth of his skin. Max read my body like a book and he zeroed in on my neck, pressing kisses on the sensitive skin behind my ear, at the place where my pulse pounded under my skin. His hand returned to the strap of my dress and then drifted lower to cover my breast.

I squirmed against his body, needing more of him than I could take here with a roomful of people just five feet away. I pulled back and soaked in the delicious sight of a spun–up, on–the edge–of–control Max and I knew what I needed to say.

"Take me home, Max."

***

Max

"You live *here*?"

I heard Kit laugh softly from the passenger seat of my truck. The directions she'd given me didn't lead to the fancy, celebrity neighborhoods and farm–mansions that surrounded Nashville. Instead, she directed me to a part of downtown that wasn't trendy, hip—or totally safe. A few blocks off Music Row, I pulled into an alley behind a building that housed an all–night Laundromat and a used bookstore. I'd plugged in the code Kit had recited at the gate and pulled in to park in a spot right next to a solitary door.

I continued with my question. "Is it safe for you to live here?"

"Yes. It's safe." She dug in her purse for her house keys as she exited the truck and I followed. "I have an alarm system and most people don't know I live here—the celebrity home maps have it all wrong because they list my old place. I've never had any problems, but recently we've stepped up security with cameras that are monitored 24/7." She gestured to cameras mounted all along the back of the building.

Recently? What the hell did that mean? It was absolutely none of my business, but I tugged her close to get a better look at her face. "Is there a problem *now*?"

She hesitated and I willed her to tell me the truth. The

thought of someone trying to cause trouble for Kit made me want to howl as all of my protective instincts woke up. That link between us because I'd saved her life? Yeah, that was kicking in big time.

She pulled away from my grasp and walked towards the building. "My life is always a little complicated, people wanting access that I cannot allow. My people are taking care of it. They tell me there's nothing to worry about." Her tone was clear that, even though she'd answered my question—the subject was closed.

I let it go. My three weeks in her bed didn't entitle me to a full access VIP pass to the rest of Kit's life.

I followed Kit over to the ugly security door and up a set of steep stairs. So far, I was unimpressed with the digs of a country music star but when I reached the top, it opened into a loft space that stopped me in my tracks. As she flipped on lights and threw her keys on a table, my gaze flickered over the open space, taking in the tall windows, the exposed brick, the living and kitchen area, and the area that was clearly her home office—the walls were covered with gold and platinum albums.

"Surprised?"

I turned to see Kit, observing my reaction. "I like it. I'm just surprised you don't have one of those big mansions with security gates and a pool." I shrugged and smiled at her. "You know, 'Super Kit's' house."

"This place is just for me. Plain old regular Kit." She turned away from me and nervously fiddled with something on the table behind her. She'd been all sexy and brave at the Bluebird but now that we were here—in the moment just before we took the leap from strangers to lovers—she was nervous.

I watched her and marveled at how she constantly surprised me with her different sides. Kit was funny, sarcastic, sweet, and strong. But, now she was vulnerable and tender—and I wanted to walk over and hold her until she didn't look so lost. I wanted to help her with the problem with her label and management team. I was hard–wired to do it. Hell, I ran into burning buildings for a living.

I was three steps in her direction, when what I was contemplating hit me like a ton of bricks. This thing between us was *not* about becoming part of her life. This was about three weeks of fun and no strings. I couldn't afford to forget the ground rules.

Turning, I walked over to her display of awards and albums, and let my gaze wander over the signs of her success. Among the display were many photos of Kit with famous musicians, actors, and someone who looked suspiciously like the President of the United States. Fuck me.

Shaking my head, I looked around and noticed a guitar and piano surrounded by stacks of paper that, upon closer observation, were filled with lyrics and musical chords.

"Sorry about the mess." I turned around to find Kit standing behind me. "I'm a complete slob when I'm writing."

She started to pick up the papers and I squatted down to help her organize the piles. I was impressed by the volume of work. She may have been a party girl in the past, but now she was clearly working her ass off. Letting out a low whistle, I said, "You sure do have a lot of songs here. Are these about anyone I know?"

She winked at me and smiled. "I never write and tell."

"Protecting the guilty?"

"Something like that."

Placing the last of the papers in her hands, I laughed, "So, are you going to write one about me?"

"Nope." Her tone was instantly chilly and I physically felt the temperature change in the room.

Shit. I'd touched a sore subject and wasn't sure how to proceed. *That's what happens when you forget the ground rules. Just sex. No talking. Talking always gets you in trouble.* She was still silent so I decided to go with the humor angle. "You wanna think about that a minute before you just shoot me down?"

"Sorry, but I won't be writing a song about you."

Warily, I watched as she got up and took the papers over to a desk. Still looking down at her work, Kit continued, "I only write songs about men I fall in love with or who break my heart." She turned and caught me with her gaze. "We aren't going to do anything crazy like fall in love or get hurt, are we?"

Oh, hell. I'd walked into a minefield and had no clue where the danger was. Removing my tongue from the roof of my mouth, I swallowed hard and searched for the words that wouldn't get me sent home with a major case of blue balls.

"No. We aren't going to do anything crazy."

We stared at each other and I recognized what passed between us—a silent agreement—that we would not cross over the line that was drawn in the sand. I was fine with it since I had no intention to go there again. I knew what held me back—broken promises, disappointment, loss. If half of what was printed in the magazines was true, I knew Kit had her reasons to stay away from the pitfalls of love and relationships, as well.

Now that we understood each other, it was time.

I stood up and walked over to where she stood, leaning against her desk. I watched her closely, taking the cues from her. She remained silent and still for so long that I'd almost decided the affair would end here, but then she reached out and gently brushed her thumb across my lower lip and my stomach dropped a couple of feet. I was hard, aching, and I had never wanted a woman so much in my life.

Stepping forward, I pressed the entire length of my body against hers, groaning with the enjoyment of all her sexy curves. I lifted my hand to cup her face as my desire surged to flashpoint in about thirty seconds. I moved my hand back until my fingers wove into her hair, wrapping several curls in my grip and tugging her head backwards. I bit back my own groan when she gasped, her lips parting on the sound. Starving for her taste, I took her mouth in a bruising kiss. Our tongues tangled together in a slow glide and I thought I controlled the kiss until she pressed her body against my cock and my brain short–circuited.

Releasing her mouth, I stared into her violet–blue eyes, lost to everything but the sensation of being here with her, right now.

"Now see? You *are* Super Kit." I licked my lip, tasting her on my mouth. "Because when you go all soft and hot in my arms, I'm *sure* I can fly."

She half–laughed and half–moaned when I nipped at the soft flesh behind her ear and then licked it softly to sooth the sting.

"Kit?"

"Hmmm?"

"Let's go to bed."

CHAPTER TEN
Kit

"Yes."

It was like the one word flipped a switch for Max and he'd decided that we'd waited long enough. I agreed completely and only let out a little squeal when he lifted me in a fireman's hold over his shoulder and carried me across my loft to the bedroom. He stopped at the edge of my bed and slowly lowered me to the floor, making sure that every inch of my body stroked along his on the way down.

"I didn't get to do that the night we met, so..." His grin was contagious and I found myself smiling back at him.

"You could do it again." I took a step forward and ran both of my hands over his chest. I had this urge to touch him, to feel his warmth and let it burn me up. "But next time, we need to be naked."

"That's how we did it at the fireman's academy."

"Really?"

"Thank God, no." Max laid his hands on the bare skin of my shoulders, stroking down with a light touch along the length of both my arms. I closed my eyes in pleasure. This simple gesture woke up all the nerve endings under my skin, making every inch of me super sensitive, tingly. I moved against him, needing to do something to alleviate the heavy weight of lust in my belly, between my legs.

His hands briefly circled my waist, skating over my hips; the heat from his touch searing me through the fabric of my dress. I looked up at his face and saw him watching his hands progress down my body, stopping at the hem of my dress. He toyed with the fabric, pausing as if he were considering his next move.

"I want to take this dress off you, lay you down on your bed and fuck you until neither of us can move."

"Yes." I loved how direct he was with his wants and needs. It was such a turn–on to be free of the double–talk and bullshit in my life. I nodded—it was all I could manage with the excitement making my skin tight, my mouth dry.

He kept his promise, his long fingers clutching the fabric and lifting it over my head in one, long move. The air in the room was chilly against my bare skin, the only protection I had against the cool air was my bra, thong, high–heeled shoes and Max's body as he invaded my space and pulled me up against the hard length of him.

He kissed me, bypassing the slow build–up and coaxing my mouth open with the sensual swipe of his tongue along my lower lip. The man could kiss, his every move calculated to evoke the image of what he could do with his cock and by the time he lifted his head for a deep gulp of much–needed oxygen, I was wet and squeezing my thighs together against the ache.

Max walked us backwards, stopping when I felt the brush of my comforter against the back of my legs. He leaned back, taking another lingering inventory of my body.

"Fuck, but you're gorgeous," he whispered, reaching a hand towards me but stopping short of actually touching. I bit back a whimper, shocked at how much I craved that press of his fingers against any part of me. I needed him that much.

I didn't have the usual urge to make excuses for my cup size, to cover up the freckles that peppered my breasts or to shield my slightly rounded belly from his view. Something about the way he looked at me told me that he was pleased with what the saw, wanted it under him, around him.

"Sit down." Max did touch me then, one finger placed in the space between my breasts where the crisscross of satin was highlighted with a tiny bow. He pushed me back with a gentle shove and I did as I was told, glad to be off legs that I wasn't sure would hold me up much longer.

Max peeled off his jacket, draping it over the bench at the end of the bed. Next was the shirt—pulled out of his waistband—each button undone with a slowness that made me dig my nails into the coverlet. I wanted to do this task, wanted to expose inch upon inch of his flesh to my eyes and my hands but I didn't move. I wanted to see what he would do next. Needed to let him lead me down this path, to show me just how good this could be.

The snowy white shirt joined the jacket on the bench and he stood in front of me, his skin glowing golden in the dim light of my lamps, the moon glow coming through the window. His shoulders were broad, the muscles on his body honed to a fine point, flat brown nipples in the light whorls of dark hair that covered his chest and led in a narrow trail down into his waistband.

His right bicep was covered in a tattoo—a red heart, bisected with a sword and surrounded by long, angel's wings. It was gorgeous, perfectly highlighting the finely cut muscles of his upper arm and rippling with every flex of movement.

He didn't tease either of us, unfastening his belt and button and unzipping the fly while never looking away from my face. I was watching his progress but I knew he was zeroed in on me, no doubt cataloging my quick breathing, hard nipples, and shaking hands. Max was in control of this and I was happy to go along for the ride and just play passenger for a change.

He toed off his shoes and socks and then lowered his pants, stepping out of them and placing them in a pile with his other clothing. He stood before me for a few seconds in a pair of black boxer briefs, his erection pressing hard against the soft cotton, but soon those were gone, too, and he was naked. I sucked in a breath, the exhale stuttering out with the impact of just how fucking gorgeous he was.

His cock, hard and flushed, stood up against his belly

and while I watched, he wrapped his long fingers around it and stroked it from root to tip. Max walked two steps forward and stood right in front of me, his hand still working his length in a slow deliberate glide. My mouth watered with what I knew was coming next. He'd tell me to suck him off and I couldn't wait to taste him, to feel the weight of him against my tongue.

I was not expecting him to lower himself to his knees, place his hands on my thighs and spread me open. He moved in closer, settling inside the notch of my legs and kissed me sweetly, a brushing of his lips against mine. I wove my fingers in his hair, pulling him in closer and trying to speed this up. I knew he wanted me the way I wanted him—so what was with the slow roll?

"Let me enjoy you," Max murmured, in between kisses. I felt his hands travel around my back meeting in the middle to undo my bra. He pulled away from my mouth and dragged the lingerie with him. "I've been waiting forever to suck your tits. I bet they're as sweet as they look."

He dove back in immediately, covering my neck with a trail of hot kisses that took a detour over my collarbone and ended in the valley between my breasts. His stubble rasped against the tender flesh as he pressed his face against me, his breath warm as he closed over a nipple.

His tongue was just as good on my body as it was on my mouth, and I gasped at the way he lit me up from inside. This was more than pleasure; this was ecstasy—the kind of thing that you only read about and never expect to experience. I moaned, long and loud, as he sucked on me, traveling to the other one to deliver the same mind–blowing attention.

I was so strung out on what he was doing to me that I almost didn't notice his one hand sliding low, stopping at the edge of my thong. He stroked back and forth there, one finger tracing the edge of lace with a deliberate slowness that caused my thighs to clench together. I was *this close* to coming and he hadn't even taken my underwear off.

TEMPTATION

His finger finally dipped inside—low—even lower until he parted my flesh, petting my clit with a slow stroke that set off sparklers behind my closed eyelids. I threw my head back, bracing my weight on my arms. My legs fell open—an invitation he couldn't ignore. He didn't.

Max abandoned my breast and dipped his head lower. Soft kisses against my belly tracked his progress until his hot breath, rapid and hollow, skated over my skin. He pulled down the thong, maneuvering it off while keeping my heels on and then spread my legs wider, opening me and exposing me to whatever he wanted.

"I want you to come on my mouth." He looked up at me, his eyes heavy–lidded with his own passion. I could see his cock, hard and heavy in the frame created by my legs and it made me flash hotter, higher. "Then I'm going to slide inside you and make you come again. You okay with that?"

I could only nod. I didn't have enough blood in my brain to actually respond verbally, so I let my body do the talking. I reached up and grabbed his hair and pushed him down towards my sex.

He groaned, the vibration of it combining with the first swipe of his tongue. I shorted out—there was no other word to describe the electric shock that zinged through my body. My toes curled in my heels, my hands abandoning his hair to grasp huge sections of the coverlet, my legs opening even wider in spite of the overload of sensation. I did not want to back down from this. I wanted it all.

His tongue swirled, lapped, and stroked every inch of me as I watched from above. I could not look away. Could not stop sounds coming from me as he drove me higher and higher. Max slid a finger inside me and found that magic sweet spot that was directly related to the "off" switch in my brain and I was nothing but one big nerve ending. Only feeling, only here in this moment with him.

His mouth continued to work me and his finger eased in and out of me, sliding, pressing until I was there... and then over.

I came apart, shaking and falling back onto the bed as he drew the orgasm out. The huge explosion had died down but with his attention, smaller firecracker orgasms rocked my body and matched the sparklers going off behind my closed lids.

I declared this my own personal holiday—complete with a second round of pyrotechnics as soon as possible.

"I'm going to fuck you, Kit. I can't wait." He was staring down at me, rolling a condom over his erection.

I nodded, loving the weight of him as he lowered his entire body on top of mine. It was delicious perfection, and I was immediately overtaken by the sensation of his hard, blunt length sliding into my body. I was ready for him, slick and soft, and I opened up like he was meant to be there. I arched into him, drawing him deeper until he was fully inside me.

I opened my eyes and he was staring at me, his face hard, eyes intense and he began to move. Long strokes where he almost left my body, the ache of loss sharp in my belly. And then he was there again, his cock filling me and touching every spot that built the fire inside me again.

I lifted my legs and wrapped them around his waist, bringing him closer to me, his stroke deeper and Max closed his eyes. He threw his head back, tendons tight in his throat, low grunts escaping him with every thrust.

"Fuck me, Max," I cried out as I dug my fingers into his back, dragging him even closer to me.

"You're so hot. Wet." He gazed down at me again, the words forced out between his clenched teeth. "I *knew* it would be this fucking good. I want to see you come again. I want you to come all over me, Kit."

The hard planes of his abdomen stroked against my clit with every stroke and I needed little encouragement to get there again. It was white hot, and I shattered like glass around him as he shoved his hard length into my body with a desperate edge. He leaned down and took my mouth, his tongue invading me as his hips slammed against me one last time.

I swallowed his moan as his entire body went rigid, the muscles on his back like iron under the sweaty silk of his skin.

It was amazing; over the top. He'd probably ruined me for sex with anyone else, but it was worth it. Every girl should experience a guy like Max. It should be a constitutional right.

I giggled, letting the absurdity of my thoughts wash over me and Max lifted his head to look down at me. He slid out of my body and lowered himself to the bed, one long, heavy leg pinning mine in place. He laid a hand on my belly, a show of possession that I didn't mind.

"Usually women don't laugh after sex with me. Should I be worried about my performance?" he mumbled against my neck, his breath warm.

"Um... no." I pushed back a little to look at him. "Wait. Are you fishing for a compliment?"

"Kit, every man wants you to stroke his ego after you've stroked his cock. It's crazy, but we're built like that in our DNA." His lips turned up into a sensual smile that promised a reward if I delivered. "So, c'mon. Humor me."

"I need to write a song about it."

"Really?"

"It will be a number one. Fans will riot if I don't write it, scream if I don't sing it. You'll be mobbed by women everywhere you go."

"I could deal with that," he was laughing now, his body shaking with it.

"Well, then let me get started on it right away," I said as I moved to get out of the bed. "I don't want to lose the inspiration."

He yanked me back, rolling on top to pin me to the mattress. His smile was still there but it was more feral than cute and I shivered with the promise I saw there. It was going to be a long night.

"You can write that song later." He leaned down and

kissed me by the ear, whispering, "Right now you need more inspiration."

Yes, I did.

CHAPTER ELEVEN
Max

"Oh my God, that is amazing."

I watched in fascination as Kit devoured the ice cream I spooned into her mouth. She sat cross–legged on her bed, holding the gallon of vanilla ice cream that we'd liberally doused with chocolate sauce and her spoon. And she was naked—boldly, completely, and unashamedly naked.

Ice cream and a naked Kit. I could sell this to Ben & Jerry's and make a fortune.

But that would require me to leave this room.

Not a chance.

She scooted closer and scooped up a spoonful of the ice cream to feed to me. I kept my eyes on her and groaned when her tongue darted out to touch her bottom lip, her teeth biting into the swollen plush cushion of her mouth when I closed my own over the spoon and sucked off the sweet dessert. Her hair was tousled around her shoulders, cheeks flushed in the afterglow of her orgasm, ice cream dribbling down her arm. She was natural, uninhibited, and the sexiest fucking thing I had ever seen. My cock was already hard with the idea of having her again.

Sex had always been good for me. What was there not to like? I love women—their curves, tits, ass—every single thing about them was to be enjoyed to the fullest. It was a mandate. They were God's gift to my unworthy gender and we were supposed to worship their bodies at every opportunity.

But Kit... she was something else entirely. Maybe I'd built her up in my mind after watching her for so many years, but what had happened between us wasn't because of her picture on the cover of *Rolling Stone*. That shit had nothing to do with celebrities and fans—that was all raw chemistry between a man and a woman.

"That tickles." She squirmed as my tongue snaked in between her fingers and slurped up the melting ice cream. "If you don't stop, I'll..."

"You'll do what?" I kept my tongue working on her fingers. She didn't pull away. In fact, she inched closer.

"I'll, umm..." She laughed and shook her head in confusion. "...I don't know what I'll do, but it'll probably require hospitalization."

"You don't scare me. I grew up with three sisters."

Kit managed to pull her hand away from me and settled back in the bed. She dipped the spoon and fed me another mouthful. "Three sisters? Are you the only boy?"

I shook my head. "Nope. I have a younger brother. I'm the second oldest of five."

"Five? That must have been fun, growing up with such a big family."

And then I remembered—she was an only child. That explained the longing in her voice and the idea that having to share a bathroom with three sisters was anything but a living hell.

It was my turn to use the spoon. "Yes it was a madhouse. My parents should be sainted since we all lived to adulthood and weren't sold to gypsies."

"Your parents are teachers?"

"My dad is the school superintendent in Lively—a little place just outside of Nashville where I still live. My mom is a kindergarten teacher, and my sisters, April and Elizabeth, are as well. My brother, Josh, is in law school and the baby, Ashley, is still in college at the University of Tennessee."

"Did you go to college?"

"No. Straight into the NFD after high school, but I'm taking classes towards my degree in psychology." I winked at her. "So, you can lie down on my couch and tell me all of your secrets."

She laughed and shook her head, the movement causing her bare breasts to sway, the nipples tight and pink against the paleness of her skin. I settled back against the headboard to enjoy the view and thanked God again for how utterly at ease she was with her nakedness. She was such an odd mix of the public persona and the private parts—all in all, a pretty amazing combination.

But the question remained—how much of the public Kit was the real Kit?

Now was as good a time as any to find out. "I can't remember. Did you go to college?"

She shook her head. "No. I have my GED, but I haven't had any time for college." She set down the tub of ice cream and absently plucked at the sheet twisted around her legs. The nervous gesture reminded me of how her fingers manipulated the guitar strings and I wondered if she even knew she did it. "A college degree is definitely on the list of things I want to do. I'll go when my career slows down."

"Why didn't you get to finish regular high school?"

"I quit high school at sixteen to work and support myself."

I watched as she retreated even further into herself. She wasn't backing away from me, but there was a barrier there—like she was shielding herself from whatever difficult memories my question had brought to the surface. I didn't need to know her story bad enough to kill this mood or bring her down. I opened my mouth to take it all back, but she stopped me with her response.

"My daddy died when I was fifteen and I started working to help support myself and my mama." Kit swallowed hard. "By sixteen she was..." Kit blinked rapidly, briefly focusing on a point just over my shoulder. She stopped, took a deep breath and continued with a voice that had a rough edge. "She was gone and I was on my own. So, I quit school, got my GED, and started working—waiting tables, cleaning houses, singing a little here and there, until Paul Bryant discovered me at an open mic night at the Bluebird Cafe." She looked at me, her smile strained, but there. "I didn't have a normal life or the typical American dream situation, but it worked out all right."

"Is that what you want?" I clarified when she looked baffled. "Normal. The house in the suburbs, two kids, a minivan."

"Yeah. Not today. Not tomorrow, either. I just want..." Kit paused, clearly revising her answer in her head. "Actually, I guess I just want somebody—my somebody. It's been a long time since I've had anything other than the music."

Oh shit. All kinds of alarm bells were going off in my head. Just like earlier when we'd discussed her writing a song about me, I'd stepped into a minefield. Any time a woman started talking about wanting a permanent relationship, it was 50/50 on how it would end.

"You don't want that," she said, reading my silence or my expression like a piece of sheet music. If I was a dick, I'd use this moment to my advantage. Cash in on her honesty and lie to make sure I got to fuck her again. I was many things, but I wasn't that big of a dick.

"No. I don't."

"Ever?"

"No." We stared at each other, the weight of my confession and her dreams threatening to bury this fling alive. I asked the next thing I wanted to know. "Who taught you to write music and play the guitar?"

At that question, Kit smiled and I felt the tension pooled in my gut ease off. Keeping this casual was proving harder than I'd thought it would be. I liked her. She was interesting and I wanted to know more about her. But I reminded myself about the ground rules: I wasn't here to bring her down. I was here for the good stuff—for both of us. *Keep it loose, Butler.*

"My daddy gave me my first guitar. Jolene—the one

you rescued from the fire. Both he and my grandfather played and I learned by watching them. Song writing... well, that just kinda came to me. Just like performing in front of people—once I did it, I was hooked."

"So, you'd do it even if you didn't have a big contract?"

She laughed, but the light didn't quite reach her eyes. "I might get to find out the answer to that question."

I didn't like the worry that settled on her face and I remembered very clearly how upset she'd been just a few hours ago at the Bluebird. Her label was playing hard–ball. I reached out and tried to pull her close. Kit resisted, her body stiff and tense. "Lots of people would kill to get one chance in the music business. I'm getting two—so, no bitchin' allowed."

"No way. You paid your dues. You should get to call the shots."

"And I blew it. As far as everyone is concerned, I'm back at square one." She sighed. "As much as I'd love to push back and tell them to shove it, I'm not in the strongest position to make demands."

"So what? You just..." I stalled out. I really had no idea what any of this meant. "What does that mean?"

"It means that I write the songs they want me to sing and I wear what they want me to wear and I go to work." Her hands clenched into tight fists, so hard her knuckles were white. The tone in her voice was frustrated, angry, and it was clear to anyone that even though this might be the deal, she wasn't happy about it. "It doesn't matter that I'm not that girl anymore. I'm a product and the goal is to sell as much of me to as many people as possible."

I scooted closer and enveloped her in my arms. When she didn't resist the caress, I brushed a kiss across her temple. "It'll be okay."

She looked up at me with vulnerable eyes and it just about did me in.

Kit snuggled her face into my chest, and I lightly stroked my hand up and down the smooth planes of her back—the silence stretching companionably between us. *She's so small and taking on Liam Connor and his label.*

This was dangerous territory. Kit was quickly becoming more than a fantasy and I was a sucker for people who needed me. The combination was going to get me in trouble unless I remembered why I was here.

I fixed and protected on instinct, a combination of my training and what my mom called my "white knight, Neanderthal DNA" and Kit was pushing all my buttons. Not good, but I knew it and that would keep me straight.

Kit stirred in my arms and I loosened my hold enough to lean forward and reach for the tub of ice cream. Her fingers stroked my back and I jumped a little, the featherweight glide across my skin causing me to shiver with pleasure.

"Sorry. I didn't mean to startle you. I just wanted to..." her voice drifted off as she explored my ink. People often paused when they first saw the tattoo on my back, so I was used to her reaction.

A set of angel's wings covered the broad expanse of my back, the detail on each feather making them come alive as the muscles moved under my skin. One wing was the typical angel's wing—white with deeper shading of the lightest grey. The other was black, tipped with the darkest blood red.

"When did you get this?"

"Just after I joined the NFD."

"I know what they are, but what do they mean?"

"It's my light and dark. A reminder of the best and worst of me."

"Why?" I felt her shrink back from me and I turned and caught her wrist. "I shouldn't pry. I'm sorry."

"No. Don't apologize." I was used to explaining them. Some people got it and others got the hell away from me. I thought I knew what Kit would do but I could be wrong—it had happened before. "I have both sides inside me—the good and the bad—and I don't pretend to know which one is stronger. It depends on the day, on the moment. But I know there have been times when I hurt people... a person... and I can't ever take it back."

"So, this is your punishment?"

"No. A reminder. Both sides are equal and have their place, and I don't pretend to try to be a good man all the time. I am who I am, but I do try not to deliberately hurt anyone."

"It's your code."

I shrugged. It was as good a word as any. It had been called an excuse, a shield. "I call it real."

"Do you have any?" I was entirely focused on her when I'd stripped her down earlier, so focused that I couldn't remember if I'd seen any ink. I was torn between whether I wanted her to have one or not. Her skin was so smooth and perfect; I almost hated to think of her fucking it up with a design. But, on the other hand... ink on a woman in the right place was seventh layer of hell hot.

"On my back."

I had to see it. I scooped her up and flipped her over onto her stomach. She protested with a mild "Hey!" but relaxed when she realized what I was doing.

My fingers traced the design, a heart surrounded by barbed–wire and a honeysuckle vine, and I recognized it as the logo for all her albums, T–shirts, and other merchandising. The heart was designed to look solid, but a little battered and bruised. I guessed, after hearing her earlier story about how tough life had been for her, that the design was more than just a kick–ass logo. It was Kit, once again exposing her heart and soul to the world.

"When did you get it?" I slid my fingers a little lower on her back, glancing over the sweet swell of her ass.

"I got that in Texas about two years ago. Jake..." she stumbled over the name of her famous ex–boyfriend, the crazy asshole who'd dumped her for his ex–wife co–star. "...well, he had a fit. Hated it. But, I designed it myself and I haven't regretted it." She glanced back at me, flipping her hair over her shoulder in a sensual move that shot heat right down to the erection that had waned but had never fully gone away.

"It's beautiful."

I leaned over and kissed the tattoo, letting my lips and tongue linger over her silky skin. Kit stretched out, humming in pleasure as my fingers roamed. That sound was addictive. I could make a career out of touching her just to hear her make that sound over and over again.

"It tastes good, too. In fact..." I glanced over to the gallon of melting ice cream and back up at Kit, "...I wonder if you taste good all over."

Kit's eyes grew wide as I flipped her back over, grabbed the ice cream, and drizzled the gooey dessert all over her breasts and stomach. She sucked in a breath at the cold and tried to scoot away, but I held her in place with my body and lowered my head to enjoy my dessert. I lapped up the ice cream, giving little bites here and there to heighten her pleasure. Circling her breast slowly, I laved her nipple with my tongue, knowing how much she loved it. Her tits were sensitive and I knew that if I reached down and stroked her slit, she'd be wet for me.

Having licked her clean, I lifted my head to gaze down at her. Damn, I thought I'd visualized every possible scenario with Kit as my ultimate fantasy girl, but I was wrong. Like this—stretched out and open to me—her eyes begging me to take her, to do whatever I wanted. Fucking heaven.

I couldn't have imagined this fantasy. My imagination wasn't that good.

"Max, are you just going to keep looking or are you going to do something?"

The question made me laugh and get rock hard at the same time. She was a unique mix of innocence and pure sex and the combination made me want to spend hours, days, even weeks exploring the limits of her sexuality.

Oh, I was going to do something alright.

"I'm going to make you come again with my mouth

and my hands and then I'm going to slide my dick into you and make you come all over me." Her eyes widened, a soft "oh" escaping as she reached for me, her body inviting me to take exactly what I wanted. "So, yeah... I'm gonna do something."

Her eyes followed my movements as I parted her thighs and ran my hands over her soft skin. Shifting down so that my shoulders rested between her legs, I soaked in the sight of the thin line of hair covering her sex, the pink folds already wet with her arousal.

She writhed against me, moaning low in her throat. My dick twitched against my belly, urging me to just grab a condom and mount up. We'd both enjoy it; I could get her off that way but I wanted more. I reached beneath me and grabbed my cock at the base, willing it to settle down so I could do this right.

"Kit, what I want to do to you."

Her eyes were glued to where my hand stroked my erection. "Anything. Just do it."

"Get on your hands and knees. Ass up high."

She complied so sweetly, lowering her head to the bed as she offered herself to me. I moved in behind her, covering her back with my body. My cock nestled perfectly between her cheeks, providing just enough heat and friction to keep me on the edge. Kit pressed back against me and I closed my eyes against the almost–too–good sparks of sensation that rippled up my spine.

I was no newbie, but Kit had the ability to bring me down fast.

I pushed her long, thick hair over her shoulder, pressing kisses along the delicate bones of her spine as I made my way down her back. I paused to linger over her tattoo, tracing the heart with my tongue as she moved under me with her restless need.

"Max, please."

"I know, baby. I'm right there with you." I moved lower, kissing the soft flesh of her ass and lower until I could see the core of her. I lowered myself to my stomach, stretching out on the bed, hissing with the contact as my dick rubbed along the soft sheets. This wasn't going to last long.

I went down on her, my tongue swirling, lips suckling on the tender flesh as she clutched the sheets under her with a growl. I was dying to see her fall apart, to give me her pleasure so I worked her hard and fast—no slow build–up here. It was as if I'd never had her before, as if I hadn't just come an hour ago. Nothing would satisfy until I was inside her.

"Max," she cried out as she came hard, her body half–collapsing onto the bed, the sheets twisting even tighter in her hands.

I lingered as long as I could, drawing out the little shudders that continued to make her moan but I was lost, desperate, almost out of my fucking mind. I reached over to the pile of rubbers on the bed and opened the wrapper, sliding it on one–handed while I looped the other under her body and pressed up on her belly, urging her back on her hands and knees.

I pushed inside her slowly. She was still soft and wet for me and it was easy, the warm, tight clasp of her body almost taking my knees out from under me. I slid out and back in, watching my dick disappear inside her and overcome with the way she offered herself to me so sweetly.

"Fuck, Kit. I wish you could see this." I ran my hands along the length of her back, speeding up my strokes as she began to push back against me. She cried out softly with each thrust and I loved that sound. It was erotic and full of surprise that anything could feel this good.

I leaned over her back, moving my hips faster as my own climax began to spark in my spine, my balls. Her hair had fallen forward, exposing her neck to me and I kissed her there, inhaling her scent. She groaned, her arms shaking where they held her up.

"Max, please."

TEMPTATION

"What, baby?"

"Touch me, I need it," she begged.

"You want me to touch your breasts?" I reached under and palmed her right breast, caressing the hard nipple, loving the way she shuddered under me. "I bet I could make you come this way. Is that what you want?"

One of her arms gave way and she fell forward and I went with her, my body driving deeper into her. The tight clutch of her body almost tipped me over but I wanted her to find her pleasure first. I needed to see it one more time.

Kit began to arch up against me, her movement continuing the deeper thrusts. She was close and I was beyond ready.

I left the sweet weight of her breast and drifted lower, searching for the place where we were joined. Kit was already there, her fingers wet with her lube as mine joined hers in the caress of her clit. Knowing she was touching herself flipped my switch and I was crying out, hips pounding into her as I rode out my orgasm and hers.

We collapsed fully onto the bed, chests heaving, sticky with sweat and ice cream.

"Oh, my God," Kit laughed. "Three weeks of this will probably kill me."

I laughed with her, settling into the curve of her body. Normally I was on my feet, pulling up my jeans and heading for the door but I couldn't move. I didn't want to move.

"We never talked about sleeping over," I hedged, letting my tone carry the question.

Kit rolled over, her head resting on my chest as she tangled her legs with mine.

"If you leave right now, I'll kill you."

I guess that answered that question.

CHAPTER TWELVE
Kit

"I haven't made out in a closet since high school," Max said.

I squirmed in his arms as his soft laugh vibrated over the skin on my neck while he covered me with hot kisses. The storage closest in the back of the rehearsal space was dark, intimate, and just large enough for a party of two.

Rehearsal had been long, but productive. The band was clicking, my voice was strong, and the new material was blending seamlessly into the set list. The tour was selling out, too. I wasn't playing the largest arenas—the label wasn't taking a chance on my singing to empty seats—but the medium–sized venues were full. We were even talking about a couple of nights at Madison Square Garden if the numbers kept rising.

I'd been going over a new song, when I spied Bridget leading someone into the rehearsal space—Max. The sight of his tall, muscled frame encased in blue jeans and a red T–shirt made me mess up my lyrics as I struggled to resist jumping his bones in front of my band and the press covering the rehearsal. His mouth curved into a smile—he was laughing at me even though my screw up was entirely his fault.

I barely remembered the introductions, the television interview with the two of us, or the tour of the rehearsal hall. In all honesty, I hadn't been able to pay attention to anything but the way Max was devouring me with his eyes.

Bridget had cleared her throat and made some comment about getting back to work and for us to "go get that room, already".

So, we did.

The first available room I could find was the storage closet. Which is how I ended up on a table, with my legs wrapped around Max and him nibbling on that spot on my neck that made me nuts.

"Funny, I figured you were an 'under–the–bleachers' guy."

He tightened his arms around me and nipped at my earlobe, making me shiver. "Oh yeah, but that didn't work in the winter." I pressed a warm kiss to his collarbone, inhaling his masculine scent as he continued. "It was harder to get a girl to go into a storage closet with you. I worked on Susie Miller for three months and I never did close the deal. But when spring rolled around... well, she *loved* the bleachers."

I looked up into his smiling face and laughed out loud. "You're a dog."

Max swooped in to reclaim my lips, murmuring "woof" just before he thrust his tongue into my mouth. I wrapped my arms around his neck and my legs around his waist. His body molded into mine perfectly and I shivered at the shot of pure pleasure that raced through me.

I eased off the kiss, stroking the silky strands of hair at the nape of his neck. "Well, I have no experience in closets or under bleachers, but this was the most convenient place for this." Breathless, I leaned in and pressed my forehead against his. "I really needed this."

Talk about an understatement.

Since having sex with Max two nights ago, my mind had constantly drifted back to the way he'd aroused me with his hands, mouth, and body. I'd drifted off to sleep in his arms after the orgasm-inducing gallon of ice cream, but woke up alone in my king-size bed.

My first thought had been, "I miss him" and it scared the shit out of me. I hit the floor and the shower and didn't even think about hitting the snooze button.

"I didn't like waking up alone. I was sleepy, and sticky

from all the ice cream." I narrowed my eyes, as I pulled aside my top to display my shoulder. "You even gave me a hickey!"

Max examined the spot and grinned, no apology anywhere on his face. "I'm sorry about that."

"No, you're not."

"No, I'm not." He leaned over, placing a kiss on my bruise and then moved up my neck to whisper in my ear, "But we both know that if I'd woken you, I would've been late to work."

I bit my lip, stifling a moan as his thumb brushed against my nipple through my shirt.

Max kissed my mouth lightly. "Besides, I left a note and I called you."

Oh, yes, he'd called.

And sent text messages.

The texts were funny, sweet, and so sexy that I'd walked around overheated and distracted—much to the amusement of Bridget and the band and to the annoyance of Ron. But damn, it felt so good to be flirting, making a guy crazy for me, anticipating the next time we could be together. I felt like a normal woman for the first time in a long time. And it felt really good.

Max kept kissing me. Nothing heavy or intense, just a leisurely tracing along my neck, my shoulders, his mouth traveling down to caress the tops of my breasts. It was sexy and romantic and I regretted missing high school if this is what happened during study hall.

"Did you get any work done last night?" he asked. "I wouldn't want to be accused of keeping you from your work."

I laughed. "Oh no, we wouldn't want *that*." Needing to touch him, I traced my lips along his strong jaw. "Lucas and I wrote until one a.m. It was amazing. I had *no idea* what a few orgasms could do for my creativity."

"Well, I guess I could be persuaded to continue giving them to you." His eyes twinkled with good humor.

"Anything I can do to help you pull off the 'must see concert event' of the summer."

I paused, pulling back a fraction to get a look at him. I raised an eyebrow. "I see someone has been reading at the grocery store checkout."

He shrugged, the dimple on his right cheek drawing my attention for a second. The dark stubble on his jaw, the inviting fullness of his lips—they were all too distracting. "It was a long line."

The tips of his ears flushed pink and I realized he was embarrassed. It was so freaking hot, I itched to strip off his clothes and see if he'd turned red all over.

I reached out and stroked his cheek. "Didn't anyone tell you not to believe what you read in those magazines?"

"Why don't you tell me what I *can* believe?" He captured my hand and pressed a kiss to my palm and then held it against his chest. "It said your tour is called 'Beauty and the Beasts' and you're on the road with Mac Daniels and Tyler Grant. Mac drives a Harley and looks like a member of Hell's Angels and Tyler is a pretty–cowboy wannabe."

I laughed. "A pretty–cowboy wannabe?" *Tyler wouldn't like that.*

"It also said you two were lovers once."

I nodded.

Max looked down to our intertwined hands, continuing in a subdued tone, "And the rumor is that you will be," he made a couple of air–quotes, "rekindling the romance on this tour."

Wow. He *really* did read the magazines. I leaned down a little to look him in the eye. "Like I said, you can't believe everything you read in the magazines."

He watched me, his eyes searching mine before he leaned in and kissed me softly. "Good to know. I don't want to be getting in the middle of something."

I brushed my hands over his shoulders, enjoying the play of his muscles underneath his T–shirt. "If I were 'in the middle of something', I wouldn't be here with you."

Shortly after my break–up with Jake and while I was in what I now knew was a manic episode, I'd been lovers with Tyler for a short time. He was the rebound guy—a poor choice on my part—and I'd broken it off. Touring with him wasn't a problem for me, except for the fact that Tyler had never made it a secret that he was open to trying again—to me or the press—and I'd been portrayed as the callous woman who'd broken his heart.

What a load of crap. I'd pegged Tyler early and still stuck to my assessment. He knew that a relationship between us would help his career get to the next level. Country music fans loved a good love story between their stars—June and Johnny, Faith and Tim, George and Tammy—the list was legendary. He was hoping to add our names to the list.

I'd been encouraged by Ron to give it a go when I left rehab, but it was a non–starter for me. Unfortunately for Tyler, he wasn't the one who was distracting me to the extent that I flubbed lyrics I knew like the back of my hand.

I kissed Max and leaned back. "What about you? I'm not getting in the middle of something, am I?"

Max barked out a short laugh. "That would be a 'hell no'."

"That sounded pretty definite."

"A guy has to know his limitations." He shrugged. "We covered this the other night."

I watched him shut down right before my eyes. Max was pretty open, but the subtle shift in his shoulders communicated as loudly as a neon sign that he wasn't going to talk about it anymore. That was fine. We weren't about having a relationship, so he didn't owe me any explanation.

"So, how much time do you think we have in here before you have to get back to work?" he asked.

"Well, I told the band to 'take five' and that's really just a figure of speech, so... Oh!" I arched my neck as Max leaned in and nuzzled the sweet spot behind my ear, his lips soft and his breath warm. I needed to get back, but a few more minutes wouldn't hurt anybody. "So... I guess we have some time... not long though... I'll be missed."

"Then we better make the most of it."

Max cupped my face with his large hands and I lost all thoughts of rehearsal, reporters, and my job as he claimed my mouth. He kissed me over and over again and made me breathless and achy. I knew what he could do to my body and I just wanted to get back here as soon as possible.

I was so lost in the taste and feel of him, that I entirely missed the voices outside the closet door until it was too late. We broke apart, blinking at the sudden onslaught of light that flooded the dimly lit space. Ron stood in the doorway, and he didn't look happy with me. I knew the look because I'd seen it a lot lately.

It brought me crashing back to earth and reality. It was not a soft landing.

Max uttered a quick, "What the hell?" and shifted to shield me from Ron, but I knew the gig was up. Adjusting my clothes, I eased down to the floor and braced myself for the fight I knew was coming.

"Kit! What the hell are you doing in here?" I winced at the outrage and disbelief in every word. "We have a rehearsal hall full of musicians, reporters, and countless other people here on the clock and you're in here making out like some teenager. I know you're going through some sort of mid–twenties life crisis." He waved his hands in the general direction of Max. "But can you at least keep your panties on long enough to do what needs to be done?"

He wasn't wrong.

My face flushed hot with embarrassment as I imagined what this must look like to him. The evidence of my selfish and unprofessional behavior was hard to ignore—my clothes were in disarray, lips swollen. I'd taken one look at Max's sexy bod and blown off my responsibilities. This was not the game plan. Max was the after–hours playtime, not the afternoon delight.

Before I could speak, Max advanced on Ron and when

he spoke it was with serious menace. "You better watch your mouth when you talk to her. I don't know who you think you are but—"

Not easily intimidated, Ron cut him off. "I'm the one who's here to keep her career afloat," he sneered. "What are you doing here? Getting your rocks off with a celebrity so you can brag to your friends? Or sell it to some tabloid?"

Max's hands clenched into fists, his jaw tight as he stepped closer to tower over Ron. "Why don't we take this outside and you can say that again right before I knock..."

Okay, that was enough. I didn't know what the hell was going on between these two but I didn't need this crap right now.

Stepping between the two of them, I pushed them apart. "Are you both out of your mind? You are *not* going to 'take this outside' and beat each other to a bloody pulp." I turned and pointed a finger at Ron. "As you pointed out, we have reporters here today and the last thing we need is to give them a front row seat to a front–page headline that will piss off the label. Am I clear?" I eyeballed them both until they nodded in agreement.

Max grabbed my arm and turned me to look at him. His voice was hard and edged with frustration, "Kit, you can't let him talk to you that way. He deserves to get his ass beaten."

"And you think you're going to be the one to do it?" Ron jeered and Max advanced on him again while growling something about "teaching him a lesson about talking to a woman like that".

I shoved Max back and rounded on him. "Max, zip it. While I appreciate your help, this is none of your business— so, back the hell off."

Ouch. I hadn't said that the right way, but it got my point across.

Max flinched, his face turning to angry stone. "Fine. You want to let him talk to you like you're dirt, you go ahead." He backed up and lifted his hands in a dismissive gesture. "I'm outta here."

Damn. My heart squeezed in my chest as I watched Max stalk off, his back and shoulders rigid with anger. I wanted to go after him, but I had to take care of things here first. As Ron had pointed out, I did have a rehearsal hall full of people waiting on me and I needed to keep my head in the game. Once again, my personal life had to wait.

But it didn't mean Ron was going to get away with acting like a total ass.

I turned to look at Ron and I didn't hold back anything I was feeling. I was going for the Wonder Woman/Xena Warrior Princess vibe but it probably looked more like "woman on the edge". Either way, it did the trick. The smug look slowly melted off his face.

"Ron, if you ever speak to me like that again, *I will fire you.* Tour or no tour, I will drop–kick your ass on to the street so fast it'll be next week before you realize what happened." He opened his mouth to sputter out some excuse and I nipped it in the bud. I clearly needed to establish some boundaries. "My personal life—who I do or do not sleep with—is none of your business as long as I keep it private. Don't *ever* think you can pull that kind of crap with me again. Am I clear?"

He kept his mouth shut and just nodded his agreement. *Smart boy.*

I turned my back on him, walked out of the closet, and made my way back to the rehearsal area to finish my job.

Once that was done, I could find Max and make it right with him.

CHAPTER THIRTEEN
Max

"Kit's manager is a real asshole."

Bridget's eyes widened as her head swiveled in my direction, and I would have laughed if any part of what just went down was even remotely funny. I looked over to where Kit had reentered the rehearsal hall with flushed cheeks and a murderous expression on her face. Ron slumped out behind her and touched her arm to try to get her attention, but Kit shot him a lethal glare and gave him her back.

Good. She was pissed off at that jerk.

And she looked so hot when she was pissed.

I had lost my mind. One minute I was angry enough at Kit to chew nails and then—poof—turned–on to the point where I wished I had a pillow to throw on my lap. God, this woman tied me in knots.

I really needed to get out of here.

I groaned and slid down onto the couch next to Bridget. I stared at the ceiling, breathing deep and trying to get my crazy emotions under control. I'd done what I always did, jumped in and gone immediately to solving the problem by slamming my fist into someone's face. I hadn't done it this time but I'd been damn close.

Bridget tapped me on the arm, her voice anxious. "What the hell happened? I thought you and Kit were off playing 'seven minutes in heaven' in the closet."

I lowered my gaze from the ceiling and noted the concern etched in Bridget's face, despite the sarcastic humor in her question. Jesus.

"We were in the closet doing... stuff... when Ron

walked in and started whaling on Kit to get back to work." I ground my teeth together, my anger still fresh when I recalled the way he'd spoken to her. "Then he insulted her and I lost my cool and threatened him."

"You did what?" Bridget stared at me with her mouth hanging open. "What did he do?"

"He got in my face and we were getting ready to take it outside..."

"You didn't hit him, did you?"

"No. Kit jumped in and told me to butt out of her business." I rose from my seat, intending to leave. I didn't pretend to understand the dynamic between Kit, her manager and the label, but I knew it was fucked up. "And that is what I'm going to do. I can't sit by and watch Kit get treated like shit by that guy. Between Ron and Liam Connor, she seems determined to be a fucking doormat."

I turned when Bridget touched my arm.

I expected her to blast me for criticizing Kit, but her tone was low and calm. "Listen, I need to explain something to you. Kit and Ron—they're in a weird place right now."

"Does that weird place allow him to insult her?" Bridget wasn't going to defend this guy, was she?

"No. It doesn't." Kit's best friend paused and creased her brow in concentration. "They've been fighting a lot lately. He's been riding her pretty hard about jumping through hoops for the label until her new contract is signed. She's focused on making it work, but she's tired. It's caused a lot of strain between them." Bridget gestured around the rehearsal hall. "Remember I told you that the music business isn't really about the music?"

I nodded.

"Kit's contract isn't just about her. It's about all of these people having work. Right now seventy–five people depend upon her in order to make a living and she already feels guilty about the way she screwed up and let them all down. At twenty–one, she's the CEO of a multi–million dollar corporation and it's been like that since she was a teenager." She squeezed my hand as she continued. "Kit's life hasn't been easy. She works to make sure that she can stand on her own and take care of her people. They're her priority—even ahead of her own happiness. So she's not going to just fire Ron when he's being a jerk. This tour is too important. She isn't going to face off with Liam when she isn't sure she can win the fight."

She stood up, giving the "one minute" sign to a young guy holding a clipboard and gesturing for her to come over before turning back to face me. "I know you think she's being a doormat, but she doesn't just have herself to consider." Her mouth formed into a crooked half–smile. "So, cut her a break, okay?"

I took a look around the rehearsal hall. There had to be fifty people working here today and more behind the scenes. How many people did it take to run a tour that lasted months? My gaze settled on Kit. She stood with her band and Tyler Grant, readying their instruments to rehearse a song and all the while Tyler kept hitting on her. A touch here, a squeeze there. A constant public pawing that was starting to piss me off. Kit looked tense, stressed, and so unlike the carefree, sexy woman I'd held in my arms a mere twenty minutes ago.

I looked at Bridget, all the anger gone now. "So, who takes care of Kit?"

"Ha!" She scoffed at my question and patted a hand on my shoulder like I was a little kid. "That's the million dollar question. Kit doesn't let anyone close enough to take care of her. Someone is going to have to make it happen."

She glanced back over her shoulder at the clipboard–guy who was now hopping up and down impatiently for her attention. Returning her gaze to me, she considered me for a long moment before leaning closer, so I was the only one who could hear. "Are you the one?"

I watched her walk away, too stunned at her question to answer. What did she want from me? To be "the one" for Kit? Hell, that wasn't what I signed up for. Even though I cared about Kit, liked her even, a long–term place in her life wasn't going to happen.

Across the room, Kit approached the microphone and launched into a duet with Tyler that I recognized as a hit from a couple of years ago. She turned into a different person once the music started.

She was the woman from the Bluebird again. The creases disappeared from her forehead, she smiled as she interacted with her band, and even Tyler trying to cop a feel didn't faze her. She was in her element, queen of all she surveyed and at peace with the world. With sudden clarity, I understood why Kit wanted these three weeks. Right now, the only place she had to let go and be herself was on the stage.

I remembered my question—who took care of Kit?

For the next three weeks, it would be me. I could do that.

I was strangely at peace with my decision. I could show her a good time and take her away from all the pressures of her job. I'd keep my nose out of her business shit since my involvement only put more stress on her and blurred the lines on what this fling was all about. *Just be the boy–toy. Keep it casual.*

I sat there for another hour, watching Kit rehearse and conduct business with her staff while I figured out a plan to show her a good time. A few quick texts and it was set. Tomorrow was my day off and I planned to make good use of our time together tonight.

She looked exhausted, and when she turned in my direction and I gave her a tentative smile, she cautiously returned. Wrapping up the job, she walked over to where I sat on the couch and joined me on the sofa.

Her hair swirled around her, creating a curtain for her to hide behind. I couldn't see her face but her voice was tired. "I didn't think you'd stay."

"Yeah, well... neither did I." I shrugged my shoulders and huffed out a short laugh. "I figured you'd call security and kick me out." I nudged her with my elbow. "Thanks for not doing that, by the way."

She slid her glance over to me and when she responded her tone was even, but firm. "Max. I appreciate your standing up for me but you... can't." I opened my mouth to justify my actions but she held up a hand and halted any excuse I had. "You're a good guy but I've got to handle this stuff on my own."

Keep it casual.

"No problem. I got out of my swim lane. It won't happen again."

She looked surprised. I guess she was expecting a debate.

"Seriously, I'll be a good boy. I promise." I smiled at her as I crossed my heart.

"I doubt that." Kit groaned and buried her face in her hands. "I'm so sorry for letting that get out of hand. I shouldn't have yelled at you." She lowered her hands and looked at me finally, regret shining in her eyes. "Forgive me?"

"No. No. I stuck my big fat nose where it didn't belong. Besides, Bridget explained to me..."

"What did she tell you?"

"Is there something she shouldn't have?"

"That's not an answer."

Kit looked seriously alarmed, so I jumped in to soothe her fears. Looking around to make sure no one was watching us, I touched her hand. "No deep, dark secrets, I promise. She just explained a few things."

I leaned closer, breathing in her scent. She leaned into me, her head resting on my shoulder and my heart clenched in my chest. Her body was warm, relaxed, and so soft pressed against me. I squeezed her hand and waited for her to look up. When she did, I took one look at her tired eyes and decided on my next move.

Standing up I dragged her with me, heading towards the doorway. "Come on. Let's get out of here."

TEMPTATION

She dug in her heels and tugged until I stopped with a sigh and looked down at her. She smiled sweetly at me, but I wasn't fooled. Especially, when I heard the steel in her voice. "Where are we going?"

"It's a surprise."

She shook her head, wrinkling her nose in protest. "I don't like surprises."

I pushed her out the door. "Somehow I knew you were going to say that."

CHAPTER FOURTEEN
Kit

"So, where are we going?"

Max rolled his eyes at me for the hundredth time and shook his head. "You really don't understand the concept of 'surprise', do you?" He continued with exaggerated patience. "Let me explain this again. If I *tell* you where I'm taking you, then it *isn't* a surprise."

I stuck my tongue out at him and shot death–ray glares at his smug face. "I don't like surprises."

He snorted, but kept his eyes focused on the road. "No kidding."

I stared out the window of his truck, moodily watching the passing scenery. I *really* didn't like surprises. Surprises always ended badly. Even if the planner tried to orchestrate the perfect thing to do, it was always a toss–up as to how the surprisee would take it. I'd watched a reality TV show where a couples' anniversary party started—and ended—as they stumbled through their front door half–naked, with her hand down his pants. Not good.

For me, the memory of a time when I had no control over my life was too fresh for comfort. I'd worked so hard to gain control, to plan when things were going to happen. I wasn't good at *going with the flow*.

The past year had made me really want to hold on tight. When you can't always control your body, it adds a whole new layer of control freak to the mix.

"You don't have to gloat over there. It's not like you don't have your faults." I wanted to bite back my remark the minute it passed my lips. I'd been edgy since my fight with

Ron this morning. That whole scene had been happening more and more lately and I knew that, sooner rather than later, I'd have to do something about Ron.

Max laughed at my attempt to put him on the defensive. He drawled out his response with a nonchalance that made my teeth grind together. "I'm sure I do. In fact, *I* am also a control freak." He cut me a sideways glance. "It takes one to know one."

I squirmed in my seat as he hit too close to the mark. "You guys have to stop watching so much 'Dr. Phil' at the firehouse."

He was shaking his head. "No, no. I'm serious. I get it. You have life smack you around and you try to keep it from happening again by holding on real tight. For the most part it works, but it's exhausting."

Yeah; no kidding. I watched his profile as he drove. "But, sooner or later something breaks free."

"And bites you in the ass."

Max made a turn off the road, his face clouded by the thought of whatever had taken a piece out of his hide. He'd mentioned a bad breakup. *Must have been a bad one. Is there such a thing as a good one?* I reached over and laid my hand on Max's thigh. He glanced down and laced the fingers of his free hand with mine.

He pulled off the main road onto a dirt path that snaked alongside corn and soybean fields. Cattle grazed in the far distance as the day surrendered to the pull of the night. The sky was purple and orange and shot with reddish gold. I lost track of the turns he made as we wound our way through the beautiful hills of Tennessee.

He pulled the truck into a stand of trees bordering a pond and came to a stop alongside at least two dozen other trucks and vehicles. A bonfire flickered from a clearing surrounded by portable folding chairs.

It was a party.

Not one of the industry parties I was used to attending. This one had a couple of kegs, music and a bunch of twenty–somethings enjoying the fact that they were young. This was not what I expected but my heart sped up with excitement.

Max hopped out of the truck and grabbed two chairs from the back before coming over to the passenger side and helping me out.

"You okay with this?" he asked, his arm around my waist as he pulled me close.

"Yeah. Very okay." I leaned into his touch as we navigated the sea of folding chairs, coolers, and couples dancing.

Trucks were pulled up around the perimeter and people sitting on open tailgates waved at Max as we passed by.

"Who are all these people and where are we?" I asked as he claimed our spot by the fire and set up our camp chairs.

"The usual crowd. People I went to school with, firefighters from other stations. They're all cool so you don't need to worry about them being weird about who you are."

"I'm off the clock?"

"Absolutely. No Super Kit here." He dragged me close again and pressed a kiss to my forehead. "Just be a twenty–one–year–old woman with a hot date who can't keep his hands off you."

"I like the sound of that."

"Good." He leaned in to kiss me but we were interrupted by Dean and Shannon appearing out of nowhere. They were good at that—it was *their* superpower.

"Here's a beer, Max. You obviously need to cool down," Dean handed over the bottle with a smile. "And here's a Diet Coke for you, Kit. Max told us it's your favorite."

"It is. Thanks."

"Everybody," Dean shouted out and most of the party–goers turned to listen. "This is Kit and we're all under direct orders from Max not to mention that she's a celebrity and not to ask her for an autograph. No photos and no requests for her to sing at your wedding. I'm looking at you, Tara and Glenn." A pretty girl stuck her tongue out at Dean while the guy who must be Glenn flipped him the bird. "Any violators will have their nuts crushed. Direct quote. Carry on!"

"Dean, you're a jackass." Max shoved his friend, but Dean kept laughing.

"Did you really say all that?" I asked Max.

"Yep."

"Including the nut–crushing thing?"

"Yep." He stuck his hand into the back pocket of my denim skirt and smiled. "I just wanted you to have a good time."

I stared at him. Damn, but he kept surprising me. First Jolene, and now this.

"Good surprise, Max."

"I'm sorry." He cupped his hand to his ear. "Can you repeat that? I'm not sure I caught it."

"Don't push your luck, buddy."

We all sat down, the warmth of the fire just enough to chase away the chill of the summer evening as the sun went down.

"So, how was the Bluebird thing?" Shannon asked.

"It was good," I answered. "More friends than industry people there and that's how I like it." I nudged Max with my elbow. "And our guy did fine. Didn't even break out in hives when they took his pictures."

"The miracle was getting him there at all," Shannon said. "Max is the only person in this town who goes out of his way to avoid anything about the music industry. Ever since Sarah died."

Even if I hadn't been looking at them all, I would have felt the tension descend on the three of them like a downpour. Max tensed and looked ready to beat feet back to his truck while Dean was concerned and Shannon stricken with regret. Whoever Sarah was, she was not a happy conversation starter. I was dying to ask about her but I'd told Max to stay in his box not an hour ago so I needed to give him the same courtesy and respect the boundaries of our fling.

"Well, you handled it like a pro and I'm glad you came," I said, reaching over to grab his hand and weave our fingers together. The tension in his muscles eased when he figured out I wasn't going to push the topic.

"Kit sang this amazing new song. Had the crowd eating out of her hand," Max said with a smile in my direction. "It's going to be her next number one."

"From your mouth to Liam Connor's ears."

"Forget that asshole. He doesn't know a good song when he hears it."

"My favorite is 'Troubled Times'." Shannon shot a glance at Max, daring him to stop her from violating his rules. "If you don't mind, can you tell me about it?"

"I don't mind. I love talking music with people who love it as much as I do." I noticed that several people around us were listening so I pitched my voice a little louder and smiled to include them. "I wrote it when I first got to Nashville. I had two hundred dollars, my guitar, one pair of shoes and three pairs of jeans and T–shirts in a backpack. I was staying at a shelter trying to dodge the cops and social services because I didn't want to be in the system."

Max let go of my hand and placed it on my upper back, his strong fingers warm against my skin as he offered me his support. I accepted it, letting it be what it was.

"I was pretty low and feeling pretty sorry for myself but there was this guy at the shelter who had this dog he couldn't bring inside. One night while he was sleeping, somebody killed his dog. He found him the next morning tied up where he left him." I could still see the image of the old man hunched over the body of the animal, weeping as he held him in his lap. I'd never heard such a lonesome sound in my life. "He was heartbroken and all I could think is that I'd thought I was the only person who had trouble. Somebody else was always going to have it worse than me until it's my turn to be the one on the bottom. I decided then I wasn't going to borrow trouble."

"Live with what you have," Dean added.

"Yep. Sometimes it's good, sometimes bad."

"That must have been hard, growing up on the streets?" Shannon asked.

"I survived." I shrugged it off, refusing to go back there and let it have any of my present. "I was so busy getting by that I didn't realize I'd missed so much until years later. I never got to hang out at a party like this. No football games. I didn't even learn to drive until two years ago."

"Really?" Max was surprised. "I was driving on the farm at twelve."

"I was too young and then I rode the bus or walked when I first came to Nashville. Then when I was old enough to get my license I had people driving me everywhere." I smiled at the leap that my life had made when Paul Brandt found me at the Bluebird.

"So what else didn't you get to do?" Max asked. He waved his arm as if I could have the universe. "Your wish is my command."

I looked around the party, watching the couples sway to the music.

"I never danced at a prom or any school dance."

Max followed my gaze and turned back to look at my face. He put his beer bottle on the ground and stood, lifting me with him. "Come on. We'll fix that right now."

He walked us over to a place near the perimeter of trucks, the firelight not quite reaching as we stepped into the shadows. He wrapped me in his arms and pulled me in close, nuzzling the sweet spot behind my ear that turned my insides to mush.

"Pretend the moon is a disco ball and the trees are crepe paper streamers." He chuckled against my neck. "Dean is spiking the punch and I'm not hearing any part of the power ballad played by the DJ because I'm trying to

ROBIN COVINGTON

figure out if you're going to give it up after the dance is over."

"I'd say your chances are looking good."

"Excellent."

We swayed to the music and I closed my eyes and let him lead. He was warm and strong and I was content to just be held as one song led to two and three. This was up there with one of my best moments ever.

"Thank you, Max. You're sweet to do this for me."

"Are you kidding? You never pass up a chance to hold a beautiful woman close. Dancing is the perfect excuse."

"Sure." I laughed, my cheek resting against his chest.

"Trust me. You do this right and you are 'in like Flynn' later. Women eat this up. I know what I'm talking about."

"So what other opportunity do you never pass up?" I looked up at him and caught my breath. His face was all dark angles and shadows, his eyes hot with desire and mischief. What had been a light and playful sexual tension morphed into something sharper, darker, hotter. His voice was rougher when he spoke.

"You never pass up the chance to do this. Especially with a kickass, passionate woman who knows how to survive."

Max kissed my cheeks, eyelids, and finally my mouth. A simple slide of lips that spiraled into a sensuous thrust and parry of velvet tongues against each other. I wrapped both arms around his neck and hung on for dear life because— have mercy—my knees had liquefied and I doubted they would support me if he let go.

"You also never, never, pass up the chance to take a woman down to the lake in the moonlight and fuck her." He held me close, nuzzling my hair sweetly; his tender actions contradicting the raw passion of his words. I breathed him in until I heard him speak, his voice barely a whisper, "I want to see you, Kit. Under the moon and under me."

Damn.

TEMPTATION

I wasn't going to lie to myself. My heart was *right there*—ready to fall for him if I let down my guard for one minute. Hell, I already liked him. And why wouldn't I? He was passionate, tender, funny, and endearing. Everything I wanted in a guy.

And absolutely unavailable.

We'd set clear ground rules. I'd tried this relationship stuff before and it hadn't lasted. How could it when I spent two–hundred–fifty–plus days a year on the road? Emails, phone calls, and stolen weekends only held it together for so long and then it fell apart. Not suddenly and violently, but wrenchingly, achingly, and in slow motion like on every tabloid TV show. It was a goal to change whatever I needed to in order to have a relationship but that was tabled for a little while.

Right now I had three weeks. Three surprising, sexy, fantasy–fulfilling weeks.

And now, I had a surprise of my own.

Removing myself from Max's embrace, I led him away from the crowd, past the line of trucks and deeper into the gloom of the woods. The lake shone with the moonlight and it was enough to see Max, to find a stand of tall trees that was shielded from the eyes of anyone else from the party.

I pushed him against a tree. As my eyes adjusted to the dimness, I saw him clearly, arms crossed across his broad chest, intently staring at me.

"Your plans are going to have to wait."

He lifted an eyebrow. "Is that right?"

"You might want to hold on to that tree."

I took one step, then another, until I stood right in front of him, our chests touching with each heavy breath. I dropped to my knees at his feet, never breaking eye contact so I saw his expression morph from surprise to "fuck yeah" in a few seconds.

I reached up and unfastened his belt, the top button on his fly and then grabbed the tab on his zipper. He kept his eyes locked on me, the tension in his jaw growing with each click of metal against metal until I reached the end. He'd done me the favor of going commando, so I reached inside and grabbed his cock, stroking it slowly as his knees gave slightly.

I licked across the head, moaning at the salty taste of his pre–cum. His fingers dug into the bark of the tree as he groaned. I'd told him to hang on for the ride.

"What am I going to do to you, Max?" I smiled, as I recalled his words from the night before. "I'm going to do everything."

CHAPTER FIFTEEN
Max

Fuck. She was going to kill me.

I did what I could as she took me in hand and then into her hot, wet mouth—lock my knees and try to stay upright.

There was just enough moonlight for me to see my cock slide in between her pretty little lips. My skin glistened in the night as she sucked me and I fisted my hands with the extreme effort not to grab her hair and take over the slow ride of torture and ecstasy she was taking me on. Moments slid into minutes as I battled with myself to keep my orgasm at bay. It was a workout and sweat dampened my skin then turned cool with the breeze off the lake. I shivered.

She stopped. Oh, Jesus. I almost whimpered at the loss of pleasure.

"Is that good? Anything you want me to change?" Her lips were already swollen and slick with her effort as she stuck out her tongue and licked that spot under the head that made my eyes cross.

It was an effort to keep my eyes open. I didn't want to miss a minute of this. I'd spent a lot of time fantasizing about Kit and I realized that my mind wasn't dirty enough for where she could take me.

She glanced at where I clutched the tree and shook her head.

"Why don't you put those hands to use?" She shook out her dark curls, her expression wicked and mesmerizing. "Grab my hair and show me how you want it. Take control, Max. I can handle it."

Holy hell.

"Are you sure?"

She answered by placing her mouth a hair's breadth from my cockhead, her expression telling me that if I wanted it, I had to take it.

"I hope you mean it."

I wove my fingers in her curls, my palms flat against the back of her head as I took a deep breath and eased myself in her mouth. She was hot, scalding, and sucked me with a tight hold on my dick. She took almost all of me as she tested just how far I could go and still make this good for her.

Kit's eyes shone as they watched me, little sounds of pleasure escaping with each thrust and vibrating around me to add another layer of sensation.

She let go of me, giving me total control of this joining and I set up a rhythm. Not slow. Not fast. Calculated to keep us both on edge, to bring us within sight of the ecstasy but unable to catch it. My body was tight with the effort to make it last, that telltale tingle of warmth in my lower back alerting me to the fact that I was about to lose control.

I was a great collector of blowjobs. I'd begun early with several girls in the hayloft on my family farm and I loved them. Sitting back and taking my pleasure, the God–like control, the carnal bliss at watching a girl work hard to get me off. I loved it. I was a guy and, like any man, I was a pig when my thoughts turned to how down and dirty it could get.

But nothing—not a goddam thing—prepared me for the sight of Kit on her knees, her mouth open for me, her tongue tasting every inch of me.

"Kit, I'm going to come."

She moaned around me and her eyes fluttered closed. I looked down and the picture before me finished me off. Kit's right hand had disappeared under her skirt as she brought herself to a body–jerking orgasm. The knowledge that she got off on this little scene pushed me beyond the edge and I fell into the chasm. My eyes slid shut, my hips thrusting forward as I tried to pull out.

Kit shook her head and gripped my hips to keep me where I was and I shot. I couldn't stop. I couldn't slow down. I could only hang on to her for dear life as she brought me down to where no woman ever had before.

Aw fuck. I was a goner. I was hooked on Kit. She was going to have to beat me off with a stick for the next three weeks now that I knew just how fucking awesome we were together. Damn, it was going to be hard to let her go when our time was up.

Beautiful. Smart. Talented. A sex kitten in and out of bed.

If I was smart, I'd keep her.

I'd never been a smart guy.

"Goddam. Look at you," I whispered, my voice rough and harsh to my ears. "You're gorgeous."

I pulled out of her mouth and yanked her to her feet.

I slid my hand through her hair to cup the back of her neck. She shivered as my lips took a slow slide across her jaw, cheekbones, and barely brushed across her lips. It wasn't enough.

I plunged into her mouth, taking the kiss directly to that crazy point where I was ready to forget where we were, strip her down and take her on the ground. My hands shook, groin tightening when I tasted me on her tongue. I let her go.

She barely contained the protest on her lips as her eyes fluttered open and met my gaze. She swayed a little on her feet. I knew what she was feeling—my world had tilted on its axis, too.

I shoved myself back in my jeans. "My place isn't far from here. This party needs to go there now. I've got a big bed and I want you naked in it all night. My neighbors aren't close enough to hear anything and I feel like making you scream."

She grabbed my arm and tugged. "Let's go."

I smiled and followed her up the path, deciding to leave

my chairs for Dean to bring to me tomorrow. I wasn't going back to the bonfire because if someone tried to start chit chatting, I'd kill them.

I overtook her, clasping her hand in mine as I planned our exit. I was so caught up in Kit and the evening ahead that I didn't notice the cop cars until they turned on the blue lights and hit the siren for a couple of cycles.

I hadn't thought anything could bring me down from my Kit–induced high but this was a buzz–kill.

People scattered, running in opposite directions as they desperately tried to avoid the four police officers. I heard truck doors slamming, engines starting as some lucky bastards made their escape.

We weren't so lucky.

They didn't cuff us but they wasted no time in assisting us into the back of the police car while the several other people they'd caught were leaning up against the second vehicle in a straight line. We sat in silence mainly because I had no fucking clue what to say. I'd had some crazy shit happen on dates but I'd never been arrested for trespassing.

The officers recognized Kit and they were just a few steps away discussing exactly what they were going to do. They'd come here expecting to round up a bunch of rowdy underage drinkers and ended up with a hodge–podge of members of the fire department and a woman whose picture was on the cover of this week's People magazine.

"Kit. I'm sorry."

"It's not your fault." Her voice was low, tense. I wasn't dumb enough to say that it was okay when this clearly was not. "I'll give Ron a call when I get a chance. He'll clear this up."

What she didn't say was obvious—getting us out of the slammer would be easy but keeping it out of the press wouldn't be. It would be impossible to keep it from my boss.

I opened my mouth and then shut it. I really had nothing here.

TEMPTATION

A truck pulled up, its high beams temporarily blinding us all. A collective protest went up from the crowd and luckily the driver killed the lights. A farmer hopped out of the cab and made his way over to the cops. He was in his mid–fifties, wearing a ball cap, T-shirt, jeans and boots and an expression that said he was fucking pissed. The cops immediately went on alert.

"Sir, you need to get back in your truck and leave."

"This is my land—"

"That's fine, sir, but you still need to go."

"I'm sick of all these kids coming here and leaving their trash and messing with my crops," he boomed out, determined to have his say.

This wasn't anything new. For as long as kids have grown up in the country, they've partied in barns, hunting sheds, and open fields, and the property owners have hated it.

"I understand, sir." The larger officer moved over to the man, exposing us to his line of sight. The farmer peered into the vehicle, curious to see who was in the back of the car. He looked away and then returned his gaze to our faces and I knew the minute he recognized Kit. The cops knew it, too; their bodies tensed as he leaned over and shouted, the thin line gone and replaced with a huge grin.

"Is that Kit Landry?" He didn't wait for anyone to answer, taking off his hat as he waved at her. "My name's Brian Wood. I'm a huge fan. My wife is, too. We have every one of your albums."

Kit leaned forward, giving him a small wave and a smile. "Thanks so much. I really appreciate it." She turned towards me and gave me the "go along with it" look. "This is Max."

I waved, following her lead.

"You're that guy who saved her from the fire."

"Yes, sir. Nice to meet you."

Kit took over the conversation again, stepping out of the vehicle and over to Brian. "I'm really sorry about trespassing. We didn't mean to."

"Don't you worry about that; just some harmless kids." He waved off her apology and plowed on as if it was the most normal thing in the world to fan girl all over her while Nashville's men in blue stood by with people they'd arrested based on his complaint.

"She's going to be upset that she missed meeting you. We couldn't get tickets to your concert here. The cheap seats sold out too fast."

Kit reached out and touched his arm, giving him an even bigger smile. "I'd be happy to get y'all tickets and VIP passes to that show as an apology for tonight."

"You can?" He looked at the officers, nudging them with an elbow and chuckling. "That would be so nice. Very nice."

"It's my pleasure." She gestured towards the others still lined up against the other police car. "And we can let everybody go?"

"Oh sure." He could have agreed to let aliens give him an anal probe as focused as he was on digging his phone out of his pocket. He fished it out and held it up with an even bigger grin. "Can I get a picture?"

"Absolutely." Kit took the phone from him and handed it over to the big officer who took it with a smile. I bit back a snicker at how she'd manipulated this entire situation. It was genius. Somebody should have started a slow clap in tribute.

Brian looped a burly arm over her shoulders and pulled her in tight. Kit's eyes got a little bigger with the surprise at being manhandled, but she recovered and smiled for the photograph. In between the time to set up the "just in case" second shot, she turned to me and winked. The expression on her face was pure mischief and it looked good on her. Really good.

I laughed out loud and she joined me. We were both crazy, relieved from dodging the bullet and high on being together. Nothing about this night was what I expected but I was glad I hadn't missed it. And if I believed in that emotion, I might have fallen a little bit in love in the back of that cop car.

CHAPTER SIXTEEN
Kit

I wasn't laughing now.

My hands shook and my vision went blurry as I threw the pictures onto the island in my kitchen and reached for the edge to support myself. My entire body had gone slack, my skin prickly with that feeling that usually preceded throwing up.

The tabloids were full of my little run–in with the law the night before but the coverage was all about how I'd given the property owner the VIP passes and tickets. Brian had wasted no time sending the pictures of us together to a local affiliate and the story he told was the kind of good publicity I could never buy.

But this. What I was looking at was the kind of story that sunk careers and sent you to Branson.

The Daily Scoop had provided the entire package to me and my label as "a courtesy" before they printed them all. I was welcome to provide a comment and they'd be happy to run it. I was going to find this Earle guy at the Daily Scoop and rip his balls off. It wouldn't stop the story from running but it would make me feel better. My ears were still ringing from the irate telephone call from Liam Connor and the sound of him breaking a vase in his office. I didn't know which one he'd shattered but I would find out later at my command appearance in his presence.

Fuck.

I looked down at the photos and papers on my counter and came up short with any way to make this mess any better. This was ugly. This was likely the final nail in the coffin of my career.

The pictures were dark and grainy but what was in them couldn't be denied.

Me.

On my knees.

With Max's cock in my mouth.

And as if the photos weren't bad enough, the accompanying article was ugly. It made me out to be a two-timing slut with Max and Tyler and hinted that I had started drinking again. Just what I needed right now when the label was going to such pains to maintain/fix my image. As Liam had screamed, "America's fucking Sweetheart does not suck off some guy like a twenty-dollar whore." I bit back my reply that she obviously did, but I wisely kept my mouth shut. I wasn't billed as a Pollyanna but this was really over the top and country music sponsors were largely conservative. They overlooked my multicolored hair, the tattoos, and my songs that talked about sex and drinking, but this was going to cost lucrative endorsements for me personally and for my tour.

Bridget and Ron walked over and each took their turn viewing the pictorial train wreck. Their expressions morphed from concern to absolute horror as they saw the photographs. I sat on the nearest barstool, unable to do anything but stare at the shiny silver surface of my fridge.

Bridget sat down beside me and grabbed my hand. "Kit, honey, this is gonna be okay. Your lawyers are going to stop them from printing the article and it will all blow over."

I wasn't convinced, but I appreciated her effort.

"This is bad, Bridget, and we all know it." I leaned forward, resting my cheek on the cool granite countertop. "I wouldn't be surprised if the label used my morals clause to ditch my contract."

"You've been thinking of buying it out."

"There's a whole world of difference between walking away and getting kicked out."

My door buzzer sounded and I glanced at the clock. It

was Max. He'd texted to say he'd be over this morning. I wasn't the only one whose boss was going to be less than thrilled about our sex life getting front page headlines. This new development was going to get him in serious trouble.

"Ron, can you let Max in?"

He cursed, but walked to the door, looking at the video monitor before buzzing him up. When his footsteps got to the door, Ron ripped it open and walked away, but not before giving Max a dirty look. I had no clue what was going on between the two of them, but psychoanalyzing their relationship was the least of my priorities.

"Lover–boy's here."

"Kiss my ass, Ron," Max replied as he walked over to me. He didn't like what he saw because he stopped in his tracks about three steps in front of me. "What happened?"

I gestured towards the pile of career–ending shit on my countertop. "See for yourself." I needed to warn him. "It's bad."

He picked up the sheaf of papers and as he progressed I saw his complexion go from tan to shockingly pale. His hands shook, from anger or what, I don't know, but he was messed up and my heart went out to him.

We weren't just fuck–buddies. We were friends and I hated to see anyone brought down because of me.

"I'm sorry, Max."

His eyes were blazing when he looked at me. Anger... it was pure fury. "For what?"

"You would have never been a target for those vultures if I wasn't in the mix. They are after me and I dragged you into this with me."

"Yeah, I'm sure you had to do a lot of arm–twisting for him to let you give him a blowjob," Ron sneered.

I turned on him. "Ron, shut the hell up. I know what I did. I know you don't approve, but it's done."

"You would have never let this happen if it wasn't for him."

"What the hell are you talking about?"

"You used to be careful." Ron advanced on me, his face screwed up with his own frustration. "You used to know what had to be done and you'd do it. You avoided trouble like him."

"Kit is entitled to live her life—" Max joined the argument, but Ron cut him off.

"Oh, what the fuck do you know about it? You can't even keep your dick in your pants long enough to get through the department Christmas party!" He laughed when Max took a step back, his surprise written all over his face. "What? You didn't think I had you checked out? I knew you were bad news for her after the deep–throat kissing at the commendation ceremony. I told you to stay away. But what the fuck do you care? You got your rocks off and now this affair is over, so get the hell out."

"Don't act like you know what's going on between me and Kit."

"What? Is this a love match now? Are you going to live happily ever after?"

I sucked in a breath at his words as my heart did a leap. I locked eyes with Max as we both faced off over the words that still hung in the air like fog.

Jesus. Why did I wish that Max would answer him? Why did I want him to tell Ron it was different than what he'd said? I was standing on the edge of making a very big mistake when it came to this man and the involvement of my feelings. Every fiber in me screamed for me to tread carefully and I was listening.

"I don't think our status is the issue here. We need to figure out what we're going to do about this story and these pictures. Now," I said.

The silence that followed was complete as we all calmed down. Not even my appliances had the balls to make a sound while we all brainstormed a way to get out of this mess.

Bridget spoke first, her voice low and cool. The eye of the storm, as always. "You have a meeting with Liam

Connor at two. I think you're going to want to meet with your attorneys and security before that one."

"I put a call into the firm and they are looking into a legal injunction to stop the Daily Scoop from printing the pictures," Ron offered, scrolling through his phone. "I have Mandy at the office checking the Internet to make sure they aren't out there already. We need to get Earle Foster to name his source."

I was still staring at Max so I saw his reaction to the reporter's name. He jumped and then rubbed his jaw with a large, calloused hand while walking towards the big bank of windows that faced the street, a nerve twitching in his left temple.

I braced for impact. I'd had enough bad news in my life to know when it was coming.

"He approached me to get a story on you, Kit."

"What?" This was the first I'd heard of any reporter approaching Max. "Why didn't you say anything?"

"I didn't think it was important," he said as he swiveled to face me. "I would never take the money or sell your story and I figured he would go away..." he sighed. "Dean told me to tell you. He told me you'd be hurt if you found out this way." He clenched his fists at his side in frustration. "We were supposed to be about having fun and I didn't want to weigh our time down by bringing up all the crap you were trying to forget. I never thought he would find another source at the party. Never."

"So which one of your buddies sold you out?" Ron asked.

Max sighed and kept his eyes locked on mine. I wanted to reach out and touch him, as if a physical connection would help me sort this out. Did I believe him? My track record with men wasn't great. It would have been no surprise that I'd been fooled—again.

Oh, but I wanted him to be the real deal.

"I have an idea," Max said.

"Give me the name," Ron's finger hovered over the

screen on his phone. "I'll send our security guy over there."

"No," Max said, turning to look at Ron. "If I'm right, then he's my problem and I'll deal with him."

"That's unacceptable," Ron barked.

"Too bad."

"Fine." I put my hands up to stop round two. I was about two seconds away from losing it and I needed to get a plan on the table before I fell apart. "Max will check and let us know what he finds out. But that doesn't answer the question of who dragged the Tyler/Max love–triangle stuff into it."

Max scoffed. "Not me. All I know about Tyler is what you've told me, which is nothing."

I turned to the others. "Okay."

I looked at Ron and he avoided my gaze and I knew... I just *knew*.

I stared at him; my teeth ached from grinding them together. "Are you telling the press I'm dating Tyler? *Cheating* on Tyler?"

"Absolutely not." Ron flushed brightly, his pulse pounding in his throat.

I watched him closely and I could read him like a book. In typical Ron fashion, he was calculating how much I knew and whether he could convince me to do what he wanted. *Son of a bitch.* My vision blurred; my ears rang as I sank to the couch.

"I didn't tell them you were seeing Tyler. But we both know that a strategic use of 'no comment' is very useful."

My eyes crossed in exasperation. "Ron. Are you insane? What are you thinking? They made me look like a nympho in that article. It almost sent Liam into a stroke."

"Kit, get your head out of your ass and back into reality." His tone was even but the edge was scathing. "Music is not enough to keep an artist on the charts anymore. You need to keep your face on the magazine covers and your name on the lips of every talk–show host. Hell, you aren't even on the A–list for Jimmy Fallon anymore. When you were with Tyler, your numbers went through the roof. The fans loved it and you were at the top. A love triangle is just that much better."

I stood, needing to move. "Ron, have you looked at our numbers lately? They're growing and my interview requests are steadily increasing. I'm co–headlining the number–one concert of the summer and it's not because of who I'm sleeping with. My music is enough to keep me at the top of the charts."

He snorted in derision. "I am well aware that your success is not because of who you're sleeping with." He pointed a finger at Max. "This guy? Who is he anyway? Some nobody whose asshole buddy sold all of your bedroom secrets to the tabloids."

Max stepped forward, his voice hard with anger. "The last time you spoke to her like that, I backed off because she asked me to." His hands clenched at his sides in a white–knuckled fist. "But it won't stop me this time. Do you have any idea what you're doing to her? Don't you have any loyalty at all?"

Ron sneered. "Oh, you're one to talk about loyalty to Kit. You're going to fuck her and then move on. Get out of my face and let me do my job."

I stared at the two of them arguing and my brain hurt with the effort it took to process all the crap thrown at me in the last twenty–four hours. I knew what I had to do. Ron wasn't going to be happy and neither was Max. Fuck; I wasn't happy about it, either.

"Ron, call the publicist and issue a denial of any romantic relationship with Tyler." He sputtered to say something and I raised my hand to stop him. "Also, confirm that Max and I were seeing each other but that it's over." I heard Max mutter a low "fuck, no" but ignored him. "I'll call Tyler and warn him. This will hurt his ego and he'll be an ass on tour, but that's how it'll have to be. I'll record that duet with him as an apology."

Ron shifted on his feet, his face red with frustration

and his jaw clenched with the effort to shut up and do as he was told. Finally, he gave a curt nod of agreement.

I looked at Bridget and took a deep breath. "I want a drink..."

"Kit." Bridget's voice was soft, understanding of what I was asking in her eyes.

"So, I need you to clear my calendar today after my meeting with Liam so I can go talk to Cyrus. I'll be okay." Cyrus was my sponsor and he knew everything. He was the one safe place I had when I was like this. When I was at the crossroads of good and bad decisions. I was feeling edgy, like I was craving something I couldn't name. I knew the signs of my illness and I knew when I needed help. A good talk with Cyrus and I'd get past this.

Right now, I needed air and space and to get away from their sad, scared, concerned faces looking at me. I walked out of my kitchen, turned the corner and bolted up the stairs that led to my rooftop terrace.

I emerged at the top of the stairs, sunshine warming my icy limbs and boosting my energy level a little bit. I stood at the railing, watching the people on the street below and wondered how I'd arrived at this place in my life. I was faced with so many decisions, and no path looked familiar or correct.

I needed to deal with Ron. He was somebody I didn't know anymore and I wasn't sure I wanted to. At twenty–one I was bone–tired, overwhelmed, and more scared than when I'd arrived in Nashville with no job, no money, and no home.

"Kit."

It was Max.

"Go away." I just couldn't deal with him right now. I was starting to feel a little out of control and I needed to focus, to work through my exercises that were designed to help me deal with panic attacks, my cravings for alcohol.

"No. I want you to talk to me."

"Not now. I need time to think."

I felt him walk up behind me and, even though I anticipated his touch, it still moved me. I wanted to turn and let him hold me and lose myself in him but playtime was over.

"I swear I didn't talk to the reporter."

"I believe you."

"You do?" He turned me to face him, his face holding too much hope for me to string him along.

"It doesn't matter. I have to focus on fixing this and I can't worry about this thing between us. I just can't."

Hell, it hurt to say it but I was right. My life was too crazy, too fucked up to try to navigate whatever this was. And no matter how much I wanted to take the time to figure it out, I was out of that commodity.

"I can help you deal with this. Don't shut me out."

"I've got people to help me with this."

"People on your payroll. People with their own agendas." He pointed back towards the stairs. "You can't trust Ron. You know that, right?"

I just stared at him. I wasn't going to argue with him about it. The possibility of parting ways with Ron had been on my "to do" list and, with the last conversation, it had moved to the top. Max took my silence as agreement and plowed on.

"Kit. Let me help you."

"No. I can't." He tried to pull me close and I pushed him away, shifting just out of his reach. It was too hard to do this when he was touching me. "Just go away. Call Ron if you need help dealing with the NFD."

"So that's it? What about our three weeks?"

"I'm sure you'll find a suitable replacement in no time."

"What if I don't want to?"

"Don't." I sighed.

"Don't what?" he asked, stepping closer and backing me up against the wall. "Don't let me help you?"

"Don't make this more than it is!" I snapped, pressing both hands against his chest to force him to give me space.

My hands were shaking and I clenched them at my sides, hoping he didn't see the tremor. "We set the parameters of this and nothing included you becoming any part of my life. Because, newsflash Max—this is my life. It's complicated and messy and I don't have time or energy to..."

I lost steam when he stepped forward; cupping my face in his large, warm hands. His eyes were fierce, contradicting the gentleness of his tone.

"Stop," he said. I shook my head, raising my hands to pull his away, but my actions stalled and I ended up wrapping my fingers around his wrists, leaning into his touch. "Just stop and let me help you. You don't have to do this by yourself. Not anymore."

I wanted him. Wanted to let him stay and be my rock. But what I hoped he was offering and what he meant did not match.

"Max. Nothing has changed." I found the strength to pull his hands away and step backwards. "We knew this had a shelf–life when we started. I'm calling it early. You need to go."

"And if I don't want to end it?"

"It doesn't matter. I do."

I'd known it would hit the mark and I had excellent aim. Max looked as wretched as I felt and *I* was the one killing this thing. Whatever we could have been was done.

"Kit."

I lifted my hands to keep him from coming any closer. "Please, Max."

He stared me down, waiting me out to see if I would cave.

"This isn't over right now. I will not accept it. I respect that you need space to deal with your shit but I'm not going anywhere."

All I could do was stare at him. I had nothing except the headache that was now spiraling behind my right eye. I must have looked like I meant business because after a few moments he nodded and turned his back on me. I watched him as he progressed across the terrace, never taking my eyes off him as he descended the stairs and disappeared.

I wanted to call him back so badly it was like a physical ache in my marrow. Every part of me hurt with the effort to stay where I was. I turned and leaned on the terrace wall and reached for my phone.

There was one more person I needed to worry about. I thumbed the screen and placed the call. The phone rang once, twice and then the voice of my mother's nurse came across the line.

"Lilah? It's Kit. No, no I'm okay." I closed my eyes and steadied my voice. If I didn't, Lilah would worry about me and I needed her to focus her emotions elsewhere. "How's she doing today? That's good. Listen; let me know if anything weird happens. No... nothing to worry about... the publicity is heating up and it could get a little crazy... I won't be there tomorrow... okay, call Josef or me if you need anything... I mean it—*anything*. I'll be there as soon as I can... Bye."

I ended the call and brushed away the tears that burned my eyes. I was so tired but I had to hang in there. A few meetings. A potential lawsuit. Liam Connor was going to be a dick and I needed to bring my A–game. We'd figure it out. I'd paid for the best lawyers and security for a reason. Same shit, different day in this business.

I wiped at my cheeks, cursing the stupid tears that were running down them and a fucking reporter named Earle Foster.

CHAPTER SEVENTEEN
Max

I walked into the firehouse looking for one person.

"Max," Dean called out as I walked past him.

I didn't even slow down. Dean's known me long enough to understand what was about to go down. He ran up behind me and our movement drew the attention of the rest of the guys on duty. I was going to have an audience and I didn't give a shit. The more people to back up how this went down, the better.

I found Bobby in the truck bay and I knew the minute he saw me. Fear has a look and he was the poster child for terror.

"How much?" I advanced on him, using my height and bulk to my advantage. He cowered and I was glad. *Be very scared, motherfucker.* "How much did he pay you for the pictures?"

"Man, c'mon." Bobby backed up two steps and I followed him. "This is how it goes. She's a celebrity and she should know better than to blow you at a party where everyone can see."

I hit him. I was aiming for his fucking ugly mouth but he dodged and I landed it on his nose. I felt the crunch and saw the blood. I'd likely broken it and I didn't care one little bit. When I was done with him, his nose would be a minor problem.

"You asshole. You broke my nose!" The pain pissed him off and gave him a backbone because he got up in my face and kept talking. "I'm your *brother.* You're coming after me because I sold some pictures of a drunk, shitty singer

147

who's probably fucked half the town to get her record deal? Dude, you of all people know what women will do to get a contract. They've all been on their backs."

"Bobby—" Dean's voice cut in over my shoulder, his tone full of warning. "You don't want to go there."

"What? We don't talk about Sarah. Everybody knows that she fucked around on him with that producer."

"This isn't about Sarah and I asked you a question... how much?" I was like ice, stone–cold and serious about getting my answer and the SD card.

"Fuck you." Bobby spat blood on the floor and dared me to make my move with a "come on" wave of his fingers.

That was his second mistake. I jumped him and beat him with every ounce of anger in my body. I punched him until he fell down and then I pinned him to the ground for another round. He was tough and he landed some good punches on my face and stomach. I tasted blood but it didn't slow me down—I had purpose. I didn't do this for me. I was doing this for Kit and for the vulnerable look in her eyes when she said she wanted a drink and for the tears she cried when she'd thought I'd gone inside.

And I did this for the way my chest hurt when she'd pushed me out of her life and ended us.

"Butler! Stop this now!" The voice of my captain barely pierced the haze of fury, but his arm latched around my neck as he yanked me off Bobby got my attention. He manhandled me up and shoved me towards Dean with a terse "keep him on a leash" and then he leaned over to jerk Bobby to his feet.

"What the fuck is going on here?" He was looking at Bobby when he asked the question, but he turned to me for the response. "Butler? You're still in deep shit with the director and me over your trespassing. Don't think we didn't hear about it because your new friend got the charges dropped."

"Yes, sir."

"So why did I come in here and find you beating on a

brother firefighter? In *my* fucking house?"

I didn't want to tell him but I had no choice. I wasn't going to add insubordination to my list of infractions. "He took pictures of me and Kit at a party and sold them to a tabloid reporter."

"And what were you doing in these pictures? Anything that would violate department rules?"

"No, sir."

I knew what his next question was going to be and to say that telling him the answer was the last thing I wanted to do was an understatement. Not just for my sake; he was the one who'd caught me fucking the director's niece at the Christmas party, so my sexcapades weren't a big mystery. I didn't want everyone to know about Kit. We'd been secluded, in a private area and Bobby had followed us. There was a good chance that no one else knew about it. And if Kit's lawyers succeeded in getting the article stopped, then I didn't need to expose her actions to all the guys standing around and watching the show.

"So what was in the pictures?" The captain's tone told me he wasn't going to ask again.

I walked closer to him, close enough so only he could hear me. "We're having sex in the pictures. She's giving me a blowjob."

To his credit he didn't even blink, only a muscle twitch by his left eye gave away any reaction.

"I see." He looked at Bobby. "Is this true?"

"Yes, sir."

"And you accepted money?" Bobby nodded and he bit back a foul curse. "How much?"

"One thousand dollars."

I saw red; my jaw clenched so hard that pain shot up my temple. He'd gone cheap when he'd thrown her under the bus. Fucking Bobby.

"Where are these pictures? Did you make copies?" Bobby mumbled "on my phone" and "no" and the captain held his hand out. "Give it to me."

Bobby handed it over and I watched as the captain pulled out the SD card and handed it to me.

"Give this to Ms. Landry. I'll call her manager and let him know that if she wants to sue Mr. Taylor, the department will fully cooperate."

"Yes, sir." I shoved the card in my pocket, knowing it was not the end of this. There was no way I was getting away with whaling on Bobby, no matter the reason. It was NFD policy.

I was right.

"Butler, you're suspended for two days without pay for fighting at the house. I'll write it up and you have five days to grieve the reprimand."

It was a light reprimand, since I could have received a week without pay but it was going in my jacket. As of right now, I could kiss the next round of promotion boards goodbye. Fuck it. I'd do it again.

"Taylor, get cleaned up and report to my office immediately. You're suspended indefinitely, pending a full review. I don't think I need to tell you that your behavior casts a pall on the department and violates every tenet of common decency." The captain's voice was like a whip and I was really glad it wasn't aimed at my ass. "And bottom line, that's a shitty thing to do to a brother. How is he or anyone else here supposed to trust you to have their back at a call?"

The message was loud and clear: Bobby might lose his job.

Look at me not giving a shit.

Everyone filed out of the bay since the show was over, and I turned to head out to my truck and head home. It had been the shittiest day and there was a six–pack and my back porch calling my name.

But I had to do one thing first.

I dug in my pocket for the SD card, holding it out to Dean. He looked confused, but took it from me, no questions asked. This was why we'd been friends our whole lives.

"I'll call Bridget, Kit's P.A., and tell her you're bringing this over."

"Why don't you deliver it?" he called after me as I walked out of the bay and into the sunshine.

"Because she doesn't want to see me anymore."

And there wasn't a damn thing I could do about it—no matter how much I wanted to.

CHAPTER EIGHTEEN
Max

It wasn't any surprise at all to find my mom waiting for me when I got home.

I pulled into my yard and parked my truck alongside her little Prius in the shady spot under the magnolias my great–grandparents planted many years ago. She was sitting on the broad front steps of the farmhouse that had been in my family since before the Civil War. It was mine now, my early inheritance from my Grandpa Butler who held the note that I paid every month. He was living it up and charming the ladies at the Augusta Senior Living Village now.

I climbed out of the truck, grabbed the beer off the passenger seat and walked over to sit next to her. She didn't waste any time making her point.

"Dean said you got suspended for two days."

"Fucking Dean." I didn't even dodge the smack she leveled against the back of my head for my language. Some families put money in a jar for every curse word; we had my mom's half–hearted attempts to give us brain damage. I pried the top off a bottle with my keychain and handed it to her and then opened my own.

"You want to talk about it?"

Did I want to? No.

Was she going to stay here until I did? Yes.

"Are you going to tell me how you ended up in a sex tape with Kit Landry?"

I made a mental note to kill Dean the next time I saw him.

I turned and faced my mother. She was looking at me

with the same look she'd worn when she'd caught me half–naked on the living room couch with Tamara Riggs. She'd calmly sent Tamara home and then proceeded to pierce me with her steady gaze until I confessed everything and willingly listened to the "sex talk". Ten years later, she still knew how to make me talk.

"It wasn't a sex tape." I cleared my throat and took a drink from my bottle. "It was just... you know... pictures."

"Uh, huh." She sounded skeptical and reached over to adjust the collar on my shirt. "You two seemed to have hit it off."

I needed to tread carefully here. She was circling in for the kill. "Well... you know... we've become friends."

"That's great, Max." She smiled and took a sip from her own bottle.

I knew it was coming. There was no way my mom was letting me off the hook on this one. As a rule, I didn't talk with my mom about the women I slept with. My dad, either. I didn't bring them home, so there was nothing to discuss.

Her voice was deceptively soft and sweet. "Would that be what they call 'friends with benefits'?"

"Mom!"

She turned back to me and shrugged her shoulders. "Did I get it wrong? That's what Ashley told me the term is these days."

Why in hell was she talking to my little sister about this?

Pain started throbbing at my temples. I covered my eyes. "No, Mom, you got it right."

"Good." She sounded inordinately pleased with herself and then confused. "So, what does that mean exactly?"

Maybe Ashley hadn't explained *everything* to Mom.

"It means that it's... umm... casual."

"I see." Her voice was slightly disapproving.

I waited and occupied myself by watching the bees buzz around the honeysuckle on the fence. I knew this trick. My mom would sit quietly and patiently wait for her victim to cave in under the weight of the silence and spill the beans.

Oh, hell.

"Mom, we're just hanging out until she goes on her tour. Well, we were. It's no big deal." How could I explain this? And why wasn't I telling her that Kit kicked me to the curb? She'd said it was over but I wasn't ready for her to end our time together. "Kit works too hard and she's got no one to take care of her. We started just to give her a break, to have some fun, that's all."

My mom turned and nailed me with her cool, gray eyes. "Max. What are you doing?"

"I just told you."

She shook her head slowly. "You just told me you care about this girl enough to notice that she needs someone to take care of her." She stopped me when I tried to interrupt. "It doesn't surprise me that you stepped in to try to help, but I *am* surprised you picked her."

"Mom. We're spending some time together. End of story." I needed to make this clear. "This was never going to be anything more than these three weeks. Our worlds wouldn't work together."

"Here we go again," she sighed, and set her beer bottle on the deck with a loud clunk.

"What does *that* mean?"

"Ever since Sarah died, you've divided up your life into these tiny little compartments. Work. This house. Sex." She smiled at the look of surprise on my face. "I'm your mother; I'm not deaf, dumb, or blind."

"Mom."

"Don't '*Mom*' me."

Her voice had that scary "don't mess with me or you're grounded" tone, so I shut up and let her finish.

"Sarah cheated on you and then she died and you never got the chance to come to terms with what happened. No one blames you for having lots of 'friends'." She gently smoothed back my hair from my face. "But you can't expect to live like this forever to protect your heart."

I ducked out from under her touch and away from her piercing gaze. "I don't want to talk about this."

"Big surprise. You've never been a talker—so be a listener." She chuckled lightly and patted my knee. "Some of the best things in life are the ones you don't see coming."

Smiling, my mom stood up and handed me her beer, leaned over to kiss me on the cheek and walked down the steps. She got to her car and paused, shouting across the yard, "Call your dad. He wants to know if you kicked Bobby's ass. He's always hated that guy."

I laughed, lifting my bottle as she drove away. Leave it to my mom to come by, bust my balls, and get me thinking about shit I did not want to think about. Like Sarah, relationships, and Kit Landry.

The last few hours had been a nightmare—worse for her. The thing with Kit had been going along fine and now it was a mess. And while I'd normally be out of here with all the crap happening, I wasn't headed for the door even though she'd opened it up and told me to find my way out.

What the hell was I doing?

I knew what.

Kit was amazing. She was easy to talk to, to laugh with, and she was the hottest little firecracker I'd ever had in bed. I was only signed up for a three-week gig and I was already dreading the day when she would no longer be part of my life.

I wanted my three weeks. After that? I had no clue.

CHAPTER NINETEEN
Kit

You know it's a bad day when the main evidence in a lawsuit is a picture of you giving a guy a blowjob.

I exited the judge's chambers with my full entourage behind me—Ron, Bridget, my attorney, and my bodyguard. In spite of what the public thought, my life was more late night drive–thrus than red carpets but I was glad for the perks today as we headed out the back of the Federal Courthouse and avoided any press in the front.

I settled into the backseat of the black Suburban, kicking off my heels as I sank down into the leather seat. I leaned back and closed my eyes, wishing I could take the day off but I only had time for a quick nap, rehearsal, and then a late flight to New York City for several promo appearances.

"Well, I'm glad the judge ruled in our favor," Bridget said.

"Judge Fairfax is known to be fair and sympathetic to violation of privacy cases," my attorney, Patrick Sweeney, commented while he checked the messages on his cell phone. "The Daily Scoop has to destroy the photographs and they cannot print *that* story, but they *can* still run one about your love triangle with Max and Tyler."

"I'm not involved with Tyler," I grumbled, not even opening my eyes. I don't know why I bothered to protest; that story had taken hold and was running on every major media source. Ron was getting his wish, as my record sales and radio play were picking up. He never passed up the chance to give me an "I told you so" look.

"If they base the story on 'unnamed sources' then they

can do it," Patrick explained. "I've got a paralegal at the firm who will be monitoring their stories on you. If they screw up, I'll be all over them."

I looked over at him, reaching out to give his hand a squeeze. "Thank you so much. I don't know what I would have done if they'd printed those pictures."

"Well, let's try not having public sex again and we won't have to find out," Ron muttered from the front seat of the car.

I ignored him. I'd been doing a lot of that since yesterday in my apartment when I'd discovered he was stirring up the Tyler crap in the press. Patrick shot me a look and I knew he was thinking that I needed to do something about my manager. I was glad I had him working on that, as well.

"I'll call the NFD later and tell them the ruling. As you can imagine, they were concerned about the photo getting out as well since it also involved one of their firefighters. They will use your statement and today's case in the disciplinary hearing against Bobby Taylor."

"What about Max?" I asked, looking out the window as downtown Nashville slid by. I had another two weeks here before hitting the road and I couldn't wait. On tour, I could just focus on the shows, the music, and my career. It was my norm, my comfort zone, and I was so ready to get back there. But I couldn't even fool myself that I wouldn't miss Max. I would; very much.

"He was suspended for the fighting, not the photo, so there isn't much I can do for him unless you want to send a note and try to get it lifted from his record."

"He did beat the crap out of Bobby for you," Bridget said. "I think it's the least you can do for a guy who is such a hero."

"I can't believe he got the SD card for me." Dean had shown up and handed it over and filled in the blanks on what had happened at the firehouse. Max had done it again—saved my ass from the fire but I still couldn't call him.

If I did, then we would keep going for the next two weeks and I'd be in danger of getting in over my head. I was already into him and fourteen more days wouldn't slow that down. The other night at the Bluebird I'd sung a new song, the one about not wanting to risk getting too close because I knew I would fall. At the time, I didn't have anyone in mind but now I did. The song seemed almost like wish fulfillment.

I could fall in love with him.

I was half–way there already.

I wasn't sure if he would ever feel the same way.

Max wasn't a player. He was a straight–up guy who didn't want any type of commitment and I got that. I didn't really understand the why but I knew it involved a woman in his past. I knew that fighting against a memory was the hardest thing to do and I didn't want to lose that battle a second time.

But I owed him thanks for what he did for me and it was a debt I could not fail to pay, no matter what it might cost me.

CHAPTER TWENTY
Max

I was acting like a crazed middle–school girl.

While the rest of A–shift was downstairs in the TV room, I flopped down on my bunk in the firehouse and hit the speed dial on my phone. Again.

Kit was in New York making the rounds of the talk shows, but I persisted in trying to talk to her about what happened.

The love triangle story had broken and the number of reporters stalking me was ridiculous. I wondered if they really thought my response to their questions was ever going to be anything but "no comment".

I wasn't ashamed of being with Kit, but I was embarrassed for her and what the article and photos made her out to be. Most people congratulated *me* on scoring big, while some of the public treated her like a fallen woman. Luckily, her real fans stuck by her and the sales for her concerts had skyrocketed. I guess the saying was right—the only bad publicity is no publicity.

My only real problem was the reaction of the NFD—they weren't thrilled, but after a very long apology session with the director and a statement from Kit, I was off suspension, had received my back pay and the incident was wiped from my record.

But Kit wasn't so forgiving.

Since the day in her loft, she'd frozen me out of her life. She refused to take my calls or answer my emails and texts. I was one restraining order away from stalker status but I couldn't stop myself. I'd tried to give her the space she'd asked for but after four days, I was officially going out of my mind. I had to talk to her.

Kit was one of the strongest women I knew and I cringed at the thought that I was part of the stress that had brought her to her knees. Not telling her about the reporter was stupid. But letting her find out about it the way she did was worse than stupid.

I let the phone ring and I jumped with surprise when I heard a real, live voice come over the line. Kit's voice. Not a recorded message.

"Max."

It was the same, sexy voice I heard in my dreams. Not the sparkly, pre–packaged version she used in interviews, this was the totally genuine voice that latched on to something deep inside me and wouldn't let go. I refused to think about how close that something was to my heart.

I hesitated, waiting for her to tell me off and demand I lose her phone number.

"Max? Are you there?"

"I'm sorry."

"What are you sorry about?" I heard her breath catch over the line, giving away her emotion. I wasn't the only one struggling with what this had become. "You got the SD card for me. Thank you."

"I'd do it again. I'm no Boy Scout or even anybody you'd take home to your parents, but I'm not an asshole and I'm not cruel."

"I believe you."

"But?"

"I'm not in a place to handle what's going down between us. This has gotten complicated." Kit sighed heavily, her voice edgy. "I want to trust you, but my head's telling me I don't really know you."

I cut her off. "You *do* know me." I leaned into the phone, as if I could get physically closer to her by focusing on her voice. "You know me. Just like *I know you*."

The moments passed like an eternity until she spoke

and I could breathe again. "I don't know how to cut you off right now."

"Then don't. I'm holding you to my three weeks."

"And then?"

"One day at a time." I lived in the moment all the time. Why treat this any differently?

The silence on the line stretched out but I could be patient. I knew when I was going to get my way and Kit was already considering it. She hadn't shot me down, so I was still in the game.

"One day at a time," she said.

I closed my eyes. The relief I felt at her words almost made me dizzy.

Not wanting to overstep the boundaries of our "friends with benefits" arrangement, my next question was cautious. "I heard you after I left."

"What do you mean? Heard what?"

"I don't know who Lilah is, but if you're in trouble—"

She cut me off right away, the fear in her voice when I expected anger, freaking me out.

"Max... I can't talk to you about that."

"Kit, please."

Her voice was firm. "Max. I can't. Not right now."

"Alright. Alright. Don't worry about it." I hadn't missed that she'd said "right now"—did that mean she might someday? Did I want her to? This whole situation was fucked up, totally out of my comfort zone but I couldn't find the energy to back away. I also hated to rock the boat with my next comment, but it needed to be said. "You can trust me. I hope you know that."

Surprisingly, she shifted the subject entirely. "Who couldn't you trust, Max? Who is Sarah?"

I sat up and swung my legs over the side of my bunk, my entire body rigid with tension. Now it was my turn to let the silence stretch out between us as I considered my options. I could refuse to answer her questions or I could offer her the trust I kept asking of her. "So, we're going to have this conversation?"

"Is there a reason why we shouldn't?" Kit countered softly.

"Oh, I can think of about a million." I chuckled, my throat dry. "Including the one that says this is crossing the line of the terms of our agreement."

"You said we know each other. This will help us get to know each other better."

"Uh huh." Fuck it. I could do this. Kit and I had already crossed the line; what was going on between us was so blurry, I'm not even sure I could find the chalk line.

"Sarah was a girl I loved. She broke my heart and then she died."

"Oh, Max. I'm so sorry."

I swallowed hard, fighting every instinct to shut down this conversation because thinking about it made it feel like yesterday instead of six years ago.

"We lived together and I found out she was cheating on me with her boss, a record producer. He was older, had more money, and she fell for every slick line he fed her. I was in the fire academy, making no money, and all I could offer her was little pay and a future of wondering if this was the time I never returned from my shift."

"How did you find out?"

"I saw a text from him and everything suddenly made sense—all the traveling together, the nights she was working late at the office." I swallowed hard because this is where the story got rough. There were some things you never got over and this was mine. "We got in a fight at a party and she took off in her car. She'd been drinking, so I followed her and when I caught up with her, she'd flipped it on a curve. It was too late."

"Oh, my God, Max."

"When Dean found us, I was working on her even though I knew." I coughed, my throat tight. No matter what Sarah had done, no matter how much she'd hurt me, she didn't deserve to take her last breath on the side of the road.

"That's my story."

"You still love her." It sounded more like a statement than a question to my ears but I heard what she was asking.

"No. But I did." I was in for a penny; might as well give the pound of flesh, too. "I really did and then I was really hurt. I never want to feel that way again. I just don't think the high is worth the low."

As the words passed my lips, I realized that I wasn't so sure anymore. Just two weeks ago I would have guaranteed my answer, but with this woman in my life my limitations felt more like shackles instead of safety nets.

"Enough about me. If I keep this up then I'll have to turn in my man–card."

She laughed and just the sound loosened the tightness that I'd been carrying around since she'd kicked me out of her apartment.

"So, Kit. What's your story?"

"Don't you read People magazine?"

Her laugh was awkward and I recognized it for what it was—a lame attempt to avoid the spotlight. She wasn't getting off that easily.

"Didn't you tell me not to believe anything I read in a magazine?" When she hesitated, I leaned into the phone and whispered, "Baby."

"Yeah?"

"Just tell me."

"I loved Jake Cooper and he loved me. I know he did no matter how it turned out. For a year, we were able to keep it together. I cut back on my touring and he turned down a movie but eventually our careers demanded more of our time. He wanted me to scale back my ambition, but I couldn't make the leap. I was afraid."

"Afraid? Of what?"

"Career suicide. Lost opportunity. Missed chances to make money and secure the future for me and the ones who depended on me. It was only a few years ago that I was a homeless teen living on the streets. Jake grew up in the suburbs in a gated community and he had no way to understand where I was coming from."

I knew what came next. Unless you were living under a rock, the whole world knew.

"Things were bad between us and then he went to Japan to work on a movie and I stayed in the U.S. His ex–wife was his co–star and they started sleeping together again."

"What an asshole."

"Yep. But, that wasn't the reason I left him."

"I think it was reason enough."

She hummed in agreement. "I ended it because I wasn't the woman who was going to make him happy. The things he wanted us to do to be together—it wasn't wrong. That's what normal people do and I figured that if I couldn't or wouldn't do it for him then I needed to let him go." Kit attempted a non–committal tone as if the decision hadn't been a difficult one to make, but the pain in her voice gave it away. "We loved each other—I loved him—but it wasn't enough."

I remembered the headlines that followed Kit the year after the break–up. There were the missed concerts, the delay of her album because she was a no–show at the recording studio, and the reports of drinking and rehab.

Kit guessed my train of thought. "Everything printed about me was true. The drinking. The men. I missed work because I was drunk or hung over or in some random guy's room. I haven't had a drink in a year. Haven't wanted one until recently." Her voice was weary. "I've been hitting extra meetings, talking to my sponsor as I work through it all."

Okay. So we were both fucked up when it came to relationships and that was never destined to end well. I should get out now while the getting was good but I knew I wouldn't.

I'd thought I was a fan before I met her but "Kit the Singer" was only a fraction of what the awesome "Kit the Woman" was. Jake Cooper had been a clueless douchebag and I was running for the second place title because I intended to walk away when this was all over. Or would I stay? I had a lot of thinking to do in the next two weeks.

Voices came over the line and I could hear Kit murmuring to someone in the background. When she came back on the line, her voice had switched into business mode. "I have to go."

"Hey, don't worry about it. You go do what you have to do and I'll see you when you get back to Nashville. Okay?" My fingers itched to touch her and I would have given anything to kiss her at that moment, but that was going to have to wait.

She agreed and ended the call and I flopped back on my bunk and stared at the bed above me. The crisscross of wire that supported the mattress on the upper bunk perfectly matched my emotions.

My head was telling me not to get involved any deeper with Kit but I knew it was too late. I *was* involved. I wasn't calling it a love match, but friendship was definitely in the mix and that made all the lines a little blurry.

And for the first time since Sarah, I didn't mind.

But it did scare the shit out of me.

CHAPTER TWENTY–ONE
Kit

"Is that a new song?"

Surprised by his question, I strummed my guitar and looked over to where Max was lying on the picnic blanket. We hadn't talked much since our telephone call. I'd left New York for a short press junket in the Northwest and bad weather in Nashville had pulled Max into a double–shift at the station that ended early this morning. I'd expected him to grab some sleep and then call me later, but he'd called before eight and asked if I wanted to go fishing and have a picnic.

I'd thrown together a cooler full of food and drinks, and grabbed my guitar just in time to meet him downstairs in his truck. We'd driven in silence to private Butler land far out of Nashville.

So far we'd eaten, with Max inhaling the fried chicken, but his fishing pole was still in the truck. He'd collapsed on the blanket and I watched him.

Max didn't look good. Haggard and exhausted, he had dark shadows under his eyes and his usual, easy conversation was nonexistent.

I knew what was wrong and I let him have his peace. The TV news and the newspaper were full of what Max had dealt with on his long shift. With tourist season in full swing, the bad weather had caused several major accidents with several fatalities. One accident resulted in the deaths of three people, one being a child, and Max's station had responded to the call.

So, I didn't press him to talk. I had no idea what to say

that would soothe his hurt. He needed time to process everything that had happened and I was content to sit by and work on the song I couldn't get out of my head.

I still owed him an answer to his question. "Yep. A new one. But, the words aren't coming to me." I struggled to articulate what I was feeling since I couldn't get it on paper. "It's not a love song, it's not a sad song, it's..."

"It's bittersweet."

I closed my eyes and looked up into the sky as I continued to strum. The sun shone a warm red behind my eyelids. He was right. It was bittersweet and needed the perfect lyric. But that would be for another day. I needed to concentrate to the get words down and I couldn't do that, knowing what Max was dealing with.

I opened my eyes and looked at Max. His eyes were closed, his chest rising and falling in a rhythm that usually led to a nap. Damn, but he was beautiful. With the sun glinting off his ebony hair and his tan skin gleaming, he looked like a dark angel. I laughed at that word choice—he'd always been my angel.

"I like this place." I soaked in the crystal clear lake, the grassy lawn leading down to the pier and the beautiful, old shade trees. It was secluded, quiet, and perfect for getting away from what troubled you. "Is this a favorite?"

"One of them. I come here to relax. To get away." His voice was gravelly and he cleared his throat before continuing. "Thanks for coming. I've never brought a woman here before."

My stomach did a triple somersault. What did that mean about how he felt about me? Something between us had shifted, changed. It was still too early to tell but I felt like we were on the edge of moving into new territory for us; something that would take longer than three weeks to figure out.

I'd missed him in New York and he'd preoccupied my thoughts more often than I liked. The week between the awful day in my loft and when I'd finally taken his call had been terrible. It was crazy how much I missed him and how much that fact didn't bother me. But, what I wanted in my personal life was the total opposite of what Max wanted in a relationship. Realistically, this was all it could ever be and I had to accept it.

I placed my guitar in its case next to the blanket and stretched out next to Max. He reached out with one arm and dragged me closer, our knees touching, eyes locked on each other. I reached out and stroked his face. He closed his eyes, leaning into my touch.

"Do you want to talk about it?" I asked.

He kept his eyes closed. "No."

I kept up the stroking, running my fingers through the soft strands of his hair, a whisper–light trace across the stubble on his jaw, down his muscled bicep. He wasn't asleep.

"Are you ever scared?"

He opened his eyes, dark lashes and the darkish circles on his skin making the amber stand out.

"Fuck, yeah; every time."

"Then why do you do it?"

He shifted up on one elbow, looking down at me, the sun behind him making his tanned skin deepen to a bronzed gold. He didn't give me his usual Max smile. His eyes were somber, the lines around his mouth and eyes tight with tension.

"Are you ever scared? To do what you do?" he asked.

"It's not the same."

"Answer the question." He toyed with the top button on my sundress, slipping it through the hole.

"Yes. I get scared."

"So why do you do it?" Another button slipped through the hole, the rough callouses of his fingers awakening the nerve endings under my skin

"Because no one else can do what I do. Nobody else can sing my songs."

"So ask me again." He leaned forward, kissing the skin

he was exposing, a lick of his tongue, a nip of his teeth.

I arched into his touch, squirming underneath him as my belly grew warm and my nipples hard. I could barely think about the question with him all over me.

"So why do you do it?" I asked as he put his finger in his mouth and then lowered the wet digit to circle my nipple, blowing on it gently.

"I do it because nobody else can. It's my song, in a way."

He lifted up and stared down at me, desire mixing with something else in his eyes. Sadness. Regret. Grief. I bit back the tears in my eyes. He didn't need that from me.

I cupped his jaw, stroking over his lower lip. "Was it bad today?"

He closed his eyes, his jaw tight. "Yes."

"Can you talk about it?"

"I—" He swallowed hard, fingers gripping the blanket. I wanted to take the question back. He'd come here to forget and I'd invited his nightmare. "There was a kid. We couldn't get them out."

I gasped, understanding the horror immediately. The TV screen had been filled with the car fire.

"What do you need?" I would give him anything but I didn't know where to start. He needed to give me an idea and I would let my heart show me the rest of the way.

"I need you." He lay on his back, on the blanket, his eyes fixed on me. "I was back at the house, putting away the gear, getting cleaned up and all I could think about was you. Do you know why?"

I shook my head.

"Because when I look at you, everything else fades. It just disappears and I can breathe again." He reached up, his fingers toying with a curl, wrapping it around his finger. "I need you to make it all disappear. You're the only thing I want to see."

I leaned over, lowering my lips to his mouth. I pressed my lips to his, the sweetest glide filled with every ounce of my feeling. I pulled back, watching him until his eyes opened in a lazy, sensual motion.

"Just look at me."

Max stared at me as I sat up completely, shrugging off the sundress and letting the sunshine warm my skin all over. I let my fingers dance across my skin, my breasts, in between my thighs. I was teasing myself, enticing Max with the movement. Drawing him into my spell.

"Just look at me," I repeated as I slipped off my bra, one strap at a time, letting the weight of the cups pull it down. The breeze off the lake was cool against my fevered flesh, tightening my nipples into hard peaks. I needed his touch, the wet slick of his tongue on my body, but this was about Max.

Max's eyes were hot and needy as he watched my progress, his hand rubbing against the erection filling the front of his shorts. I snaked a hand around my back and undid the clasp, throwing my bra to the side. I hooked two fingers into my underwear and slid them off my body until I kneeled in front of Max in nothing but my skin.

I was wide open. Pouring everything I had, everything I felt, into this moment with him. He looked me over, his gaze scorching me as he drank me in.

"Just look at me."

I leaned forward from my kneeling position and undid the button on his shorts, pushing them down and off his body. He was hard, large and hot as I closed my hand around him, squeezing and stroking until he writhed under my touch. He never broke eye contact with me and I was wet just from the sounds he made. Rough. Needy. Raw.

"Fuck. More." He groaned, writhing under each stroke of his cock. His fingers clenched the blanket at his sides, twisting the fabric. He was gorgeous, skin smooth and damp with sweat. "Please, Kit. More. I need you."

I ached to touch myself, to ease the deep need building between my thighs, but I held off. This was about Max. This was all for Max.

I straddled his waist, reaching for the condom I'd stowed in the basket. I placed it on him quickly, positioning my slick center over him.

"Just look at me."

I slid down his length, gasping with the fullness of him. He was so hard, so thick. I stroked my hands over his chest, enjoying his masculinity.

He reached up and cupped my face, caressing my cheeks with his thumbs. "You're so beautiful."

I blinked back the tears. I was not safe with this man. I wanted to protect him, to soothe him, to laugh with him, to be with him. He'd worked his way inside my heart and I'd done nothing to stop him. It was as if my heart knew what my head would not admit.

He was it for me. He could be—was—my everything.

I traced the contours of his face, his cheekbones, his eyelids, his lips, and then back up to lightly caress the dark shadows underneath his eyes. "You look so tired. You should be at home sleeping."

His sooty black eyelashes fluttered open, the desire swirling in his eyes causing my breath to catch in my throat. Max reached up, grabbed my hand, and pressed a kiss onto the palm.

"I need you, Kit." His gaze caught my own in a stare of unapologetic need and desire. "You're all I need."

"Max."

"Always need you."

He pulled me down and kissed me, his tongue thrusting inside my mouth with a brutal, possessive hunger. I claimed him back, elated to know that I was not alone in this feeling. I needed him to know that he wasn't alone, either.

I released his mouth and sat up, beginning that slow rise and fall that would bring him release, maybe bring him comfort. I was so wet, my body clasped him on each stroke and I felt the loss of him when he pulled out and the hunger building each time he thrust back in.

I want you.

I need you.
I love you.

I used my body to tell him all the things that I would not say. All the things I knew he did not want to hear. But I shouted them in my head as we rode the wave together. When I came it was sudden, wrenching a long, deep moan from me that I shouted into the open air. Max groaned, his fingers digging painfully into my hips as he shoved me down as he thrust upwards, going deep inside me. I felt him come, swelling inside as he found the oblivion he needed.

I collapsed against him, our bodies slick against each other and warm with the sunshine and our exertion. Max held me and I held him, our bodies shivering with the aftershock. We held each other until the sweat cooled on our bodies and our heartbeats slowed down in tandem. We held each other as we both fell asleep—Max finding his peace and me finding my home.

CHAPTER TWENTY–TWO
Max

"So, what are you trying to do? Feel good or forget?"

I looked up from the bourbon in my hand and into the face of my best friend. He leaned heavily on the bar and shook his head at me like he already knew the answer to his question. "Dean, don't start. I'm not in the mood."

Dean signaled to the bartender to bring him a beer. When he turned back to me, his voice was brimming with sarcasm. "Yeah, I needed you to tell me that. *Thank God*, I came over to get that newsflash."

I took a drink from my glass. "What do you want?"

"I want to know what has you heading straight for the hard stuff." He nodded towards the glass in my hand.

I knocked back another swig of the whiskey before looking at him. "I'm fine."

"Go sell that shit somewhere else. Are you still thinking about the shift? You took off pretty fast after the debrief."

I sighed and slammed my glass down on the bar, spilling some of it on the counter. *Dean's just worried about you. No need to bite his head off.* I tried again with less asshole in my tone. "No. I'm okay about the shift. I just..." I struggled with how to describe what was eating me up. "I'm just..."

Giving up, I grabbed my second drink and glanced over his shoulder across the room. My gaze automatically found Kit, beautiful and animated, as she posed for pictures and signed autographs for some of the crowd at Stoney's, a local bar and grill owned by a retired firefighter, Mike Stoneman. Always gracious, Kit happily complied with her fans' requests. As usual, she was making every person feel as if they were the only person in the room.

Dean interrupted my thoughts. "So, where did you go? I tried your phone for hours."

I took another drink, grimaced at the bitter taste, and savored the burn. A couple more of these and I wouldn't give a shit about the shift or anything else. "I went to the lake." I anticipated his next question and muttered, "With Kit."

Dean's arm paused in mid–air as he lifted his beer to his mouth. His eyes shifted to me as his mouth dropped open in shock. "You never take women to the lake."

"I know."

"Not even Sarah."

"*I know.*"

Dean placed his beer on the bar and rubbed his hand over his face. "Is that a good thing?"

"I don't know." And I didn't. I stared at the mirror over the bar, watching Kit's reflection as I remembered the events of the morning. "I don't know. I got off the shift and she's the first person I thought to call." I glanced at Dean with a shrug. "I needed to see her."

Dean stared at me like I'd just spoken in pig latin. "Well, that's good. Right?"

"I don't know." Damn, I sounded like a broken record. "I just needed to be with her."

I'd known in my gut that she was exactly what I needed. And she was perfect. She'd known when I'd needed to sit and brood and when I'd needed to laugh. Then, she'd offered herself to me, so sweetly and openly, and I was unable to do anything but bury myself inside her body and make love to her with a ferocity that shocked me.

Make love to her.

Not just sex.

Oh hell. I'm in trouble. I squeezed my eyes shut at the memory of the way I felt the minute I'd entered her soft, warm body. I'd worried I was going to be too rough, that I would hurt her. And I was right. I *was* going to hurt her.

"I'm falling for her," I said.

"Oh."

"Yeah. Oh." I opened my eyes to see Dean gearing up to launch into a "this is great" speech and I cut him off. "It won't work. I can't do it."

"Bullshit. That's just Sarah talking."

My frustration bubbled to the surface and I growled. "No. That's the truth. I'll fuck this up eventually. I don't know how to do this."

Dean's face flushed with anger. "Bullshit. You'll figure it out like the rest of us assholes."

I refused to debate this with him. I knew me. I knew my limitations and I would fuck this up and when I did, Kit would dump my ass and I would be in the hurt locker. It would be ten times worse than Sarah and I just couldn't do it.

I already needed her too much.

Dean nudged my shoulder as Kit headed over to us with her cheeks flushed and eyes bright. Her cheerfulness faltered when she glanced in my direction. God only knows what she saw in my face because I felt like I was raw and ripped open.

"You want a drink?" Dean asked.

"Just a Diet Coke, please."

Kit glanced towards me, her eyes lingering for a moment on my bourbon. I did not make eye contact with either of them, instead watching the activity in the mirror over the bar.

Dean ordered her drink and pointed towards the crowd in the bar. "I can't believe you got Stoney to smile. I didn't think he actually *had* teeth."

Dean nudged me again, and I tried to join in on the conversation, but I couldn't stop thinking about what I knew I had to do. Minutes crawled by and I seethed until I couldn't stand it any longer.

I put my glass down and touched Kit's arm to interrupt her conversation with Dean. "We need to go."

My voice was more gruff than I'd intended and she pulled away from my touch with a confused and hurt expression on her face. I sucked in a breath and gave myself a do–over. "Don't you have an early photo shoot tomorrow? We should go."

Nodding, she shot me a questioning look before turning to Dean and making her excuses to leave. On autopilot, I took her arm and headed out of the bar and across the parking lot towards my truck.

Kit stopped and turned and faced off with me. I couldn't look at her.

"Max. Are you okay?"

Just do it Max. End it. I looked at the neon sign on the bar and avoided her eyes as I hedged. "I'm just tired. I need to go."

The bustle of traffic and the distant sound of a siren filled the silence.

"Do you want to go to my place?"

I shook my head, my eyes still glued on the garish neon. "No. I don't think so. I just need to go home."

"Okay... you just want to call me tomorrow?"

I turned to face her and she faltered. What she saw in my face caused her features to cloud over with a wariness I hated to see. I hated that I was the one to put it there.

I fought the urge to hit something as I ended the best two weeks of my life. "No. I don't think I should call you anymore. This needs to end now."

She stepped back and raised an arm up over her stomach, as if reacting to a physical blow.

Determined to get it over with, I plowed ahead. "You were right. We both knew this was going to be a short–term thing. I just think we should end it now. It would be better."

Her eyes searched my face as her mouth struggled to form words. She cleared her throat, her voice raw. "Did I do something wrong?"

"No. It's not you. It's me."

Fuck, that was a terrible thing to say. I was an asshole.

She might have been hurt two seconds before but now she was pissed. "I can't believe you used that line on me. You're dumping me with one of the worst excuses ever." Kit walked up and poked me in the chest. "If you want to end this, then just tell me why it's over. Don't hide behind some lame–ass line you think is going to spare my tender feelings."

Unable to maintain eye contact, I looked over to a group of people exiting the bar and struggled to say something that would soften the blow. But I didn't trust myself to speak and not take it all back. I turned and Kit was no longer standing beside me. She was walking towards the sidewalk and talking to someone on her cell.

What the hell?

"Yeah I need a cab at Stoney's... that's the one... I'll be waiting." She clicked the phone shut and continued walking on the sidewalk towards the front of the bar.

I sprinted to catch up to her. "I'll drive you home."

"We're done, Max. I called a cab and it'll be here soon. Just leave me alone."

I stood there on the sidewalk as she waited for her cab.

You can't just let it end this way. Time to be a grown–up and be honest about why this was such a colossal mistake.

Desperate, I blurted out the truth. "I can't do this. I like you."

Kit's face registered surprise for the briefest moment and then she was pissed again. "You *like* me? You sound like a middle–school boy."

She was right. I tried to figure out a way to explain why I had to get out before it was too late to salvage my heart.

"The other night, Shannon got to pick the movie at the station and she chose the chick flick where that British guy hooked up with the movie star. You know the one I'm talking about?"

Kit nodded. "I know the one but what does that have to do with us?"

"I'm getting to it." I took a step closer. "At the end, she

comes to him and lays it all out there. Tells him she loves him, the whole nine yards, but he turns her down. He explains that he's just a regular guy and when she dumps him he'll have to deal with seeing her face on TV, in magazines—everywhere—and he wouldn't be able to handle it."

"And?"

"That guy? He's me. I wanted to be with my fantasy–girl and then walk away with no regrets just like I always do, but I didn't expect to care about you. I didn't expect to need you." I tentatively reached out, capturing her hand. "And I do need you. So fucking much. This is more than a fling to me and I have to get out while I can. Because *when* it ends, *when* I fuck it up, I'll be the one having to live in this town with your face and music everywhere."

I stroked my thumb gently over her palm, memorizing the way her tiny hand fit inside my own, the softness of her skin. She was the most beautiful thing I'd ever seen. Funny, open, giving and way out of my league. I had to get out now before I couldn't walk away.

She looked at me and I hated the sadness etched onto her face.

"In that scene, she also reminded him that all this stuff was just nonsense—not real—she was just a regular girl," she said.

She stepped forward and placed her hand on my chest and I leaned into the warmth of her touch.

"I'm just me, Max. All the famous stuff, it isn't me. I thought you knew that."

"If you'd stayed the fantasy, I could handle it. But you didn't. That's why I need to walk away now."

It was the truth, but I wished like hell I could take it back. Kit looked at me for a long time, like she was trying to see if there was any argument to make and I knew the second she knew it was useless. She nodded slightly and it was done.

I stepped closer, pulling her into my arms and holding

her close as I memorized her soft curves. I buried my face in her hair and inhaled her unique scent. Even though it couldn't last, I didn't regret being with her. She pulled back and gazed at me.

"It was this morning, wasn't it?"

I just stared at her, unsure about how to answer her question.

"That was real—what happened between us. It was real," she said.

"Yes, it was."

"You don't want real."

"I—" Oh fuck. "I don't need real."

"That's bullshit. Everybody needs real." Kit reached up and touched my cheek and I leaned into it. I couldn't help myself. "We just tell ourselves we don't want it because we're scared."

That hit too close. Too close. "I don't need it."

"Sure you don't." She dropped her hand and I missed her warmth. "We could be good together. You're going to regret this, you know?"

"I already do." And that was the most honest fucking thing I'd ever said in my life. "I just can't go where this is headed. What you want is not what I want. That hasn't changed."

As her cab pulled up, she shook off my touch and I braced for the final goodbye. It was for the best. I had a chance to land on my feet if I got out now.

Everything was in slow motion as the cabbie rolled down the window and asked if Kit was his fare. She said something to the guy but I couldn't hear it over the roaring in my ears. When she turned back to me, she had a fake smile pasted on her face and her eyes were bright with moisture. Standing on her tiptoes, she softly kissed me, and then climbed into the cab.

I watched the cab turn the corner towards Kit's loft and drive away.

And then she was gone.

I knew it was the right thing.
It was the grown–up thing.
Being a grown up sucked.

CHAPTER TWENTY–THREE
Kit

"Kit!"

"Tyler!"

"Look over here!"

I pasted a smile on my face and struck a pose for the cameras on the red carpet constructed by the label in their large, opulently appointed lobby. The event, a party to celebrate the kick–off of my tour, was loud, crowded, and seemed to go on for hours. My feet hurt in the ludicrously high heels my stylist had picked out for me, and my jaw ached from the constant smiling for the photographers.

And my heart hurt.

The dull ache had started three days earlier in the parking lot outside of Stoney's Bar, when Max kicked me to the curb. *No, that was harsh. He didn't kick me to the curb—he broke up with me. And he didn't even do that because we weren't together.*

"Kit, darlin'."

A couple of times I'd almost called him, but my finger stalled over the "call" button and I'd closed the phone without dialing. His position was clear and I needed to respect it and move on. I couldn't have him. I'd known it from the beginning. Now I needed to get on with my tour and life; without Max.

"Kit, darlin'. Are you ok?"

Tyler's voice jerked me back to the present, back to the glare of the lights and the click of the photographers' cameras. Dazed and disoriented, I leaned into Tyler's side as he steadied me. Tyler gazed at me with affection and desire and I pressed closer, selfishly seeking comfort where I could find it. Tyler smiled in reaction and his gaze shifted down to my mouth while his grip on my waist tightened. Alarm bells rang faintly in my head as he leaned closer, brushing his lips against mine in a soft kiss.

I sighed, all the tension in my body easing away as I returned Tyler's kiss. He was familiar, safe, and it was so easy to just lean in to him and forget all of my angst about the tour, Ron, and Max.

Max.

Oh no. This is wrong.

Ignoring the flashes going off like the Fourth of July, I pushed away from Tyler and stumbled back in the direction of my dressing area. Reporters were yelling at me but I waved them off and ran as fast as I could in those ridiculous shoes. I needed a few minutes to remember who the fuck I was and who I wasn't. I wasn't a woman who kissed one man while I thought of someone else.

Tyler was close on my heels, so I sped up, made eye contact with my security, and nodded my head in Tyler's direction. My mountain of muscle quirked an eyebrow at me and nodded just before he closed in and blocked the door that I quickly opened and closed behind me.

Once inside, I let loose a strangled scream, ripped the ridiculous shoes off and hurled them across the room. The sudden peace and quiet in the room sucked out the last ounce of my adrenaline and I took the few steps to my dressing table and sank down on a chair before my legs gave out. Stricken, I stared at my reflection. I was proud of my ability to slip into my alter ego and handle any situation life threw at me. I *never* lost it in front of the press. Never let the mask slip.

"Super Kit" was invincible.

I sighed, grabbed a makeup brush and started touching up my face. I was disgusted at myself—I'd used Tyler. I was a jerk and, in a colossally dumb move, did it in front of a ton of photographers. My hand stilled in applying the makeup as

I gave myself the ass–chewing I needed. "Get your head in the game. You have too much riding on this tour to get sidetracked by emotional bullshit."

A knock on the door halted my lecture–for–one. "Not now, Tyler. Give me a minute!"

"It's not Tyler." Bridget's voice was muffled through the door. "Can I come in?"

I went over to the door, opening it just enough to let Bridget and my attorney, Patrick, into the room. Surprised, I reached out and gave him a big hug.

"Patrick, what are you doing here? Don't you have a new baby at home?"

His eyes twinkled at the mention of his newborn son. "I'm on my way there right now, but I wanted to drop off the papers you had me draw up." He handed an envelope to me, his smile dimming with the change of subject. "Are you sure you want to give Ron such a generous severance package?"

I sat down on the couch and drew the papers out of the envelope. "He was the key to my success and I can't forget that fact. Even if—" I faltered as I looked over the papers and then up at my two friends. I was confused.

"What's this?" I pointed at the top three papers.

Bridget and Patrick exchanged a look and suddenly I knew what was going on here. "Ron has been the one feeding information to the press about your activities with Max, your supposed relationship with Tyler. He's also made questionable deals for you where he got kick–backs. Big bribes. Lucrative bribes. My team found evidence that goes back almost to the beginning of your professional relationship." He gestured to the pile. "He has not done his duty to you and I think you should fire him for cause and refuse to give him a severance package."

"Can I do that?"

"According to his contract, he forfeits his severance if he violates the terms and conditions of his contract."

"And you can prove that he did?"

Patrick nodded. "*And* that he was planning to continue with your next album. I have an inside person at the label who states that Ron had meetings with Liam Connor and promised he would kill the new songs, your new sound. He was going to get a bigger cut directly from Liam on your new contract, as well."

"Really?" I sat back on the sofa and part of me wasn't surprised at all. Things between us had been rocky at best—hostile on a good day lately—but I couldn't believe he would actively stab me in the back. But I had to be realistic about where I was in my career at this moment. "I can't fire him now. I'm about to go on tour."

"Kit, I called Paul Brandt," Bridget joined in. "He said he's on the next plane and he'll stay until we find a replacement for Ron."

Paul would be able to hit the ground running. And he would come to me if I needed him—and I needed him now. I didn't want to drag him into this but I didn't see any choice.

I stared down at the papers lying on the table, wondering what else could go wrong. I needed to focus and make a decision now.

"Do it. Fire Ron with no severance."

"He'll probably sue."

"Great. Just what I need—another scandal." But I was past worrying about that. I needed to act and deal with the fallout, whatever that might be. "Do it anyway and get Paul here. We don't have much time."

I'd made my decision and the rapid knock on my door and "five minutes Ms. Landry" indicated that my duties at the party wouldn't wait for this latest development. Rising up from the couch, I mentally prepared to deal with the crowd waiting outside my door. A squeeze from Bridget, and a "hang in there" from Patrick was all I had time for before I opened the door and entered the party full of press, label management, and Tyler. Kissing him now seemed so minor in comparison to everything else that was falling apart in my life.

Josef, my head of security, stuck close to me as we moved through the crowd, heading towards the area set up for the speeches and the press Q & A. I shook off the drama of the last few moments, put on my "Super Kit" persona, smiled, and waved hello to those who called out good wishes. Someone came up behind me, too close, and I figured it was Tyler. I turned to ask him to walk over to the podium with me.

It wasn't Tyler.

I stepped back from the microphone shoved way too far into my personal space. "I'm sorry, but the press conference will start in a few minutes. Okay?"

The reporter, one I didn't know, pressed forward. "Why'd you lie, Kit?"

Confused, I looked over my shoulder, making sure Josef was watching the exchange. I gave a nod in the reporter's direction and began to walk away. He kept after me, still shoving that damn microphone in my face. The scene was starting to draw attention and conversation muted as we passed by.

Josef stepped in behind me, his deep voice asking the reporter to back off. I didn't turn around. I knew better. If I turned around it was like feeding a feral cat. You do it once and they never fucking go away. Years of dealing with aggressive paparazzi had taught me to keep the smile on, the chin up, and keep on walking. However, the next question shouted at me was enough to make me break all my rules.

"Kit, why'd you lie about your mother?"

Ice settled in my veins as the words sunk in. I turned, my lips stiff. "What?"

The room, now so quiet you could hear a pin drop, heard every word he said in reply. "I asked why you lied about your mother being dead when you've had her locked away in a private sanitarium for the past five years?"

The floor heaved. I could actually feel the blood draining from my body. Ron. Max. My stupid kiss with

Tyler. The stress of the tour. All of it came crashing down on me as my vision turned red and my hands shook with anger.

I came out swinging like Sugar Ray Leonard or Mike Tyson. I caught him by surprise and the first punch caught him in the face. Pain shot through my hand but I didn't care. He groaned, dropped the microphone, and went down on one knee as he clutched his bleeding nose.

I went for him again, grabbing his shirt as I yelled at him. "What do you know about my mother?"

The reporter sneered as Josef grabbed him from behind and hauled him to his feet. He kept talking. "I'm talking about the fact that she's a pathetic mess, a trashed out junkie, and a whore." He spit blood onto the floor near my feet right before my security team dragged him away. "I was going to give you a chance to give me an exclusive, but you had to go and act like a crazy bitch. Now, you can deal with it."

I went for him again but Josef's two strong arms around my waist restrained me. I fought him but it was futile. I'd hired Josef for his brains and his bulk and he was using both right now.

"I'm fine. Fine. Let me go," I said.

He did as I asked and I pushed my way through a crowd that, in the wake of my fury, parted like the Red Sea.

This was bad.

I needed to check on my mom, and then I needed to figure out the plan for damage control because the label was going to flip out. This could be disastrous for my career, but I'd be damned if I was going down without a fight.

***

Max

"Good morning, Mary Sunshine."

I blinked at the light pouring through the windows of the firehouse kitchen and tried to figure out who the fuck was talking to me. I stumbled the last few steps, rubbing my eyes and stretching my arms. Dean was seated at the bar, so

I nodded to him and went straight to the coffeemaker, poured a cup, and gulped down the first hot swallow. It burned, but the jolt of heat was exactly what I'd needed. I leaned against the counter and noticed Dean staring at me.

"What?" I was annoyed, and I made no attempt to disguise that fact.

"Nothing. I'm just surprised to see you here this morning."

"I *am* on shift with you."

Dean took a sip before he continued with poorly–disguised sarcasm. "You had a hot date last night. I figured you'd be sleeping over at Alison's place."

Oh shit. "Look, Dean, if you have something to say..."

"All I'm saying is that you usually spend the night with Alison when you guys hook up. I figured last night was no different."

Dean paused and took another leisurely sip of coffee while I waited for the other shoe to drop. When it came, his disapproval made me wince.

"I guess I was wrong about you after all. You rebounded pretty damn quick. I mean, you broke it off with Kit three days ago and then you show up last night with Alison." Dean fixed me with a level stare that made me squirm. "I was wrong about you not being mercenary enough to handle this whole affair thing. You're a pro."

"I didn't sleep with Alison."

"Look man, it's none of my business. You can sleep with whoever you..."

I cut him off. "You're right. It's none of your fucking business, but since you decided to stick your nose in anyway, shut up and listen to me." The silence between us crackled and I took the time to steady my temper. "I didn't sleep with Alison. Nothing happened. When it came down to it, I couldn't."

Dean sighed and rubbed his hands over his face. When he looked at me he had that sad and concerned look that he did so well. I preferred pissed.

"What happened?"

I didn't even know where to start. I wasn't even sure what happened last night, only that it ended with Alison pissed and my sleeping alone at the firehouse. Damned if I knew what to say. The women usually waited until after I fucked them to get mad at me.

Dean solved my dilemma by asking what he wanted to know. "Did you go to Alison's after you left Stoney's?"

"Yeah. She wanted me to stay over and I thought I was into it. But, I just couldn't. Nothing felt right with her, and I ended up making a really lame excuse and left. I didn't want to drive all the way out to my house, so I came here."

I sat down on the barstool next to Dean. Alison had been really hurt when I bailed on her and that was the last thing I'd wanted to do. But I did it anyway. "I knew the minute I kissed her that it was a no–go." I decided to say what had been rolling though my head on a constant loop for three days. "I can't stop thinking about Kit."

Talk about an understatement.

I'd thought about her every second since she'd left in the cab. I'd reached for the phone to call her so many times that I'd locked it in the glove compartment of my truck to take away the temptation. I dreamed about her and woke up so hard I wanted to crawl out of my skin. I thought about her when I was on calls—something not only dangerous to myself but also to my fellow firefighters.

When Sarah died, work was the only respite from the constant gnawing in my gut. The vision of her lying half in and half out of the car and the last terrible words we spoke to each other showed up in my dreams. But this time, even work wasn't helping. And as I'd predicted, I couldn't even listen to the goddamn radio without her songs coming on and in this city, good luck trying to find a non–country station. I was fucked because there was no getting away from it.

"Call her. Admit you screwed up," Dean said.

"I can't."

"Then figure out how to get over her."

"I can't."

And I don't want to.

Suddenly, it was clear. No matter how this had started, I needed her in my life. She was everything I wanted and by some fluke of the universe, she wanted me. The morning at the lake, the way she'd known what I needed, known how to soothe the hurt from my shift, had scared the crap out of me. I might run into burning buildings but she was the brave one that day. She'd made herself vulnerable and open to this thing growing between us. I'd seen it in her eyes, heard it in the way she'd said my name, and saw it in her hurt expression when I'd stood in a dirty parking lot and threw it away.

I jumped when Shannon poked her head around the corner. "Max! You've got to turn on the TV. Kit's in trouble. She got in a fight or something."

Not waiting for her to finish, I grabbed the remote for the kitchen TV. I punched a button and the local country music channel blazed to life with a picture of Kit kissing Tyler. I jerked back. *No fucking way.*

Shannon touched my arm and murmured, "Ignore that. It's nothing."

When Kit pulled away from Tyler, with a horrified look on her face, I let out the breath I'd been holding. In the next second, I lost all ability to speak as Kit launched herself at a reporter and clocked him with a right jab to his jaw. The man fell to his knees, but instead of backing off, he snarled something at Kit which caused her to hit the guy repeatedly until Josef pulled her off and took her away from public view.

What the hell?

"She's got a nice right hook," Dean said. I ignored him.

The TV program reverted to two reporters speaking animatedly, while a mug shot of a woman—a woman who looked like an older, tired version of Kit—was displayed on the screen. I turned up the volume, and focused on the screen and the perky, female anchor.

"*...breaking news regarding country music star, Kit Landry. Last night at a label press party, Kit was approached by a reporter who disclosed that her mother has been institutionalized for the past five years. This news comes as a shock to the star's fans as it was commonly reported that her mother passed away several years before she came to Nashville. The usually cool and collected singer was removed by security after she physically attacked the reporter.*"

A male anchor picked up the story while a photo of Kit flashed onto the screen. "*That's right, Tammy. The story, which appeared in this morning's edition of the Daily Scoop, states that Elizabeth Landry was repeatedly arrested for drug possession, drug dealing, and prostitution while Kit was growing up. According to the article, she finally suffered an overdose which left her mentally disabled one year after Kit's father died in an accident. It also reports that Kit took over her care and moved her to a private sanitarium just after her first record deal was signed. The real question is why Kit lied about her mother for all this time.*"

Tammy nodded vigorously as she responded, "*Well, Jim, the singer is holding a press conference at her label headquarters in about an hour and her team says she'll answer everyone's questions. Her publicist also announced that her manager, Ron Trent, has been fired and her previous manager, Paul Brandt, is coming out of retirement to take over until a permanent replacement can be found. All of this is right on the heels of Kit's return after a stint in rehab after a year of erratic emotional behavior leading many to ask if the singer suffers from the same illness as her mother. Stay tuned. We'll carry the entire press conference live in an hour.*"

I turned off the TV and rubbed my hand over my face. My mind reeled with all the information. Kit had been carrying around some serious secrets the past few years. Secrets she couldn't share with me since I'd given her no reason to think I'd stick around. That was going to change.

I pushed through the crowd of people coming into the kitchen and headed towards the door and my truck. Just as I turned the doorknob, a hand closed around my arm, pulling me back. It was Dean.

"You going where I think you're going?"

"Yeah. I'm going to see Kit. I don't know how I'm going to get to her, but I've got to try." And then I remembered—I was on duty today. "Shit. You'll tell the captain and get someone to cover for me?"

"You know I will." Dean reached around, opened the door, and pushed me out the door. "Go get her, man. And don't take no for an answer. She needs you and you need her."

I nodded and, in spite of the angst twisting in my gut, I sprinted across the parking lot, jumped in my truck, and pulled out. I wasn't entirely sure Kit would see me. Reaching for my phone, I pulled up Bridget's number and hit the "send" button. If Kit had her phone off or wouldn't take the call, Bridget was my best bet.

She picked up on the third ring and did nothing to hide her surprise. "Max?"

I pulled out onto the road and headed towards downtown Nashville. "Yeah, Bridget; it's me."

She didn't hesitate to let me know where I stood. "Look Max, this isn't a good time right now. I need to get back to Kit and you're *the last* person I want to talk to right now."

I cut her off before she got wound up and hung up on me. "I'll cut to the chase then. I'm coming to the press conference and I need you to get me in. I need to see Kit."

Bridget laughed into the phone and I could picture her shaking her head in disbelief.

"Max, you broke it off with her because you couldn't handle whatever was happening between the two of you. Now the shit has really hit the fan. Why would I let you within ten feet of her?"

"You're right. I was a chicken–shit and bailed on her. I'm not gonna argue—"

"Thanks for your honesty. I'm hanging up now."

In a panic, I blurted out the first thing that came to my mind. "No, don't hang up! I'm the one. That's why you have to let me in. I'm the one!"

"The one *what?*"

The words rushed out of me so easily, I knew it was the truth. "Remember, when I asked you who took care of Kit and you told me nobody took care of her? Then you asked me if I was the one who would do it and I couldn't answer you?" When she didn't say anything I plowed on. "Well, *I'm the one.* I'm the one to take care of her. And you've got to get me in there so I can prove it to her. Please. Help me."

The silence stretched across the line for what seemed like hours. *Come on, Bridget; you know I'm right. Just help me out.* I turned on to the block that held the office of her music label and faltered at all of the news personnel and fans milling around the street. I found a spot and pulled the truck over, my hands remaining in a death grip on the steering wheel.

Bridget sighed. "Come around the back and I'll get you in." Just before she ended the call, her voice took on a warning tone. "But Max, if you hurt her again, I'll kill you."

I jumped out of the truck and sprinted across the street towards the woman who made me break all of my own rules. My heart pounded with adrenaline, the rush similar to what I experienced when I entered a burning building. There was no fire here but I knew my life was at stake—and God help me—this was scarier.

CHAPTER TWENTY–FOUR
Kit

It was times like this that I really missed my daddy.

I looked around the waiting room set up adjacent to the place where I would hold a press conference in less than an hour. It bustled with people from my staff and the record label—all focused on fixing the train wreck formerly known as my career. Liam Connor shot nasty looks at me from across the room and I had to dig deep into the grown–up part of me to resist flipping him the bird. *Calm down. All you have to do is bare your soul to a roomful of strangers. Piece of cake.*

I hadn't slept in twenty–four hours. I was running on fumes, ibuprofen, and a Red Bull Bridget had shoved into my hands about two hours ago. Breakfast of champions. Even though this was stressful, I was more than a little relieved that my secret was out and I didn't have to carry it around anymore. Ron had done me a favor when he'd spilled the beans about my mother, but I still hated his guts. I still didn't understand why he hadn't told everything about me but I wasn't going to wait for that other shoe to drop.

I'd talked to Lilah an hour ago and my mother was in her room with extra meds to keep her from getting upset. While security kept the reporters out of the Shady Grove Assisted Living Facility, the additional noise and bustle agitated my mom and the other patients.

I'd taken care of one responsibility—on to the next couple hundred obligations.

I looked around and couldn't find one person I wasn't responsible for in this room. Even Bridget was both a friend and an employee, and I was terrified of letting them down.

I'd already jeopardized everything by trusting Ron.

"It wasn't your fault."

I jumped as a big hand settled on my shoulder. Turning around, I looked up into the clear, blue eyes of Paul Brandt—the man who had been my father figure, my boss, the biggest pain in my ass, and my biggest supporter. God, I loved him. I was humbled that he, with no questions asked, had left Texas to help me.

He tapped me on the nose in that way he did to cheer me up. "It wasn't your fault. You trusted him and he betrayed you. Nobody blames you and you shouldn't blame yourself."

I broke eye contact, the shame leaving a bitter taste in my mouth. "Paul, I should have known."

He cursed under his breath before grabbing my elbow and leading me away from prying ears. His eyes laser–locked on my face until I was forced to look him in the eye.

"Kitten, you listen to me and take it as the gospel truth. This was not *your* fault. You had a viper in your camp and didn't even know it. You've always taken responsibility for everyone around you, but you can't control the bad choices that other people make." He towered over me, and leaned in close and gentled his tone. "I love you and you're the bravest kid I know. You took care of your grandparents, your dad and, then, you took care of your mother whenever she strolled back into town to get clean." Pain flashed in his eyes as he recounted the sad details of my life as if I didn't already know them. "You've spent your life taking care of other people and let your own needs fall by the wayside."

I was irrationally defensive and angry at his words. "Paul, I worked hard to make things better for the ones I love. I'm not going to apologize for doing what was right."

"Honey, it ain't right if it makes you take responsibility for something that you didn't see coming. Kitten, I've watched you give and give and not take anything for yourself." Paul counted his points off on his fingers. "You don't go on vacation. You haven't tried any of the new projects that have been offered to you because they don't fit your current image. Hell, you gave up Jake because you thought that he deserved to be happy more than you do."

I opened my mouth to argue with him, but he was right. I'd been afraid to want things for myself when, one day, they'd be gone. I lived on the fringes of my own life. But I didn't know if I had the strength to do it differently in the future. Max had been the biggest risk I'd taken in a long time and look how that had turned out.

Hugging Paul tightly, I mumbled against his chest. "Have you been watching Oprah again?"

"Dr. Phil." When I raised an eyebrow at him he protested, "What? The man's a genius."

Laughing, I released him and turned towards the mirror mounted on the wall behind me to fix my makeup which was probably messed up from all the emotional crap going down today. "I promise I'll think about what you said." I pulled out my makeup. I could still feel him watching me and knew my answer didn't satisfy him.

"Think about it? Kitten, you need to get a life. A life that includes a man who loves you and is looking out for you." He paused. "Bridget said there was someone who she thought might be that guy."

I froze mid–swipe. "Bridget talks too much."

Paul laughed. "Maybe so. But you don't tell me squat, so I'm glad she does." He sidled up next to me and leaned back against the table, his arms crossed casually in front of his chest. He wasn't fooling me.

"So, he wasn't the guy?"

I dug into my bag looking for my mascara and maybe avoiding looking at him. "Didn't Bridget fill you in?"

"I'd rather hear it from you."

I gave up and put down the tube of makeup. "He wasn't interested in a relationship. Not a bad decision, considering my rock–n–roll lifestyle. He ran for the hills. Smart man."

"Yeah, but you didn't want him to be so smart. Did

ya?"

I ignored the question. I'd dodged the same questions from Bridget for two days after Max had broken things off. Max wanted out and getting back together with him wasn't up to me. For once, none of my celebrity perks could get me what I wanted, because celebrity was exactly what he *didn't* want.

Paul rubbed the back of his neck and chuckled softly as I resumed applying my makeup.

"So, this guy... was he a blonde or brunette?"

"Brunette. Why do you want to know?"

"Just curious." He shrugged and stroked a hand along his jaw. "Bridget said he was a firefighter, so he must have been a big guy. About 6'3"? Broad shoulders and biceps as big as my thigh?"

I dropped the lipstick tube in my hand and leveled a look at Paul. "How could you know that?"

With a slow grin he jutted his chin in a direction over my shoulder. "Because I think he just walked through the door."

Spinning around, my eyes scanned the crowd until I zoned in on the tall figure walking towards me with Bridget.

Max.

His face was blank, but his eyes were the same—golden topaz and filled with simmering heat that caused my heart to go all squishy. Sweet Lord, I'd missed him.

Too much.

I backed up against the table and crossed my arms in front of my chest as he came to a stop right in front of me. My body instinctively leaned towards him and I clenched my hands into fists to keep from touching him. *He's just here because of his hero complex.*

Looking at his handsome face, my emotions bounced from anger, to hurt, to hope, and to relief at just seeing him one more time. And that made me mad all over again.

I swallowed hard and turned loose the first words that came to mind. "What the hell are you doing here?"

CHAPTER TWENTY–FIVE
Max

I had expected her to hit me.

I drank in everything about Kit. I was close enough to smell her perfume and feel the heat of her body. She was rigid with hostility, so I resisted the urge to drag her into my arms and bury my face in her glossy curls. I let my eyes linger on her face, her beautiful face, her graceful neck, and the creamy swell of her breasts in the V–neck of the dress she wore. Finally, my gaze drifted back up to her eyes and when one eyebrow quirked up in a silent inquiry, I remembered that she was still waiting for me to answer her question.

"I came to see if you're all right. You've had a rough couple of days and I thought you could use a friend."

Tears pooled in her eyes for the briefest second just before she blinked them away. Once she'd harnessed her control, Kit met my eyes with the friendly but distant expression I recognized from countless interviews.

"Super Kit" was in the house.

Only her voice, a little shaky, gave away any inner turmoil.

"Thanks, but I have lots of friends as you can see." She waved a hand around the room at the clusters of people surrounding her. "I'm good. No need for you to worry."

She wasn't going to make this easy on me and I didn't blame her. I took a half step closer, gathering enough of my balls to reach out and run a finger along her arm. She inhaled sharply at the contact but didn't move away. The big guy standing next to her moved a little closer—not a direct threat, just making sure I knew he was there.

"I'm glad you're good." I sounded lame and stupid and I cursed my sudden attack of nerves. Our future depended on this moment and I was scared shitless—not of saying too much, but of not saying enough of the right thing.

I decided to go for broke. "I screwed up. I never should've ended things with you, and now that I've got my head out of my ass I'd like another chance."

No taking it back now. This was agony. While I stood there, her expression changed from surprise, to confusion, and then my least favorite—stubborn resistance.

Shaking her head, Kit backed away from my touch as if she were trying to become a part of the table behind her.

"Look, I don't know what the shelf–life is on feeling obligated to a person once you've saved their life, but we're even. You don't have to worry about me. I pay a lot of people to do that."

When I inched closer, she bit her lip and groaned in frustration. "Max, you need to go. I heard what you said loud and clear. This was just a fling and it's over."

Anger at her words, her denial, made me impatient as I stepped even closer, bracketing her body with my larger frame and blocking out everything else. This needed to be about us and only us for at least the next few minutes.

"This was always more than a fling between us and you know it. What we had—" I corrected myself. "What we *have* is something real and I'm done running."

Kit's gasp mingled with those of Bridget and the large man, but my eyes never left her face. I didn't care what the others did as long as they didn't get between me and this woman.

Kit was scared, her breathing shallow and frantic and she swallowed convulsively. I could see her mind churning out excuses but she leaned towards my body in an unspoken expression of need, her body betraying her deepest desire. She wanted me, too.

The moment was broken when a man approached and

signaled to Kit with the "five–minute" sign.

I was out of time.

I brought the conversation back to where it belonged—on the fact that I wasn't going anywhere.

"Kit." She turned her attention back to me and I leaned in close so she couldn't look anywhere else. "I'm not asking for you to make a choice right now, but I *am* going to stay here and help you through this and then I'm going to prove to you that we belong together."

I grabbed her hand and waited as the long moments stretched between us. If I had to get down on my knees and beg, I was prepared to do it.

"You can stay." Kit's voice was quiet and shaky as she withdrew her hand. "Let's see if you feel the same way after the press conference." She nodded at me and turned to follow Bridget out of the room.

I smiled like a goofball and didn't even try to pretend it wasn't for her. I was done hiding how I felt about this woman.

She slipped back into "Super Kit" mode right before my eyes. Shoulders back and focused control on all of her facial expressions. Now that I knew the real Kit, this persona was understandable, but very unsatisfying. I wanted the girl who laughed at my stupid jokes, seduced me at a bonfire, and soothed me on a picnic blanket.

A big hand landed on my shoulder.

"Paul Brandt. I was Kit's manager and I'm filling in since she kicked the weasel to the curb."

I laughed at Paul's reference to Ron. I couldn't have agreed more.

"Max Butler. Kit's..." I struggled with the right words to describe my relationship with Kit.

"I heard what you said, son. I think I have a pretty good idea of what you are to Kit." He looked me up and down with an assessing glance and then motioned for me to follow him. "That took balls. I wasn't inclined to like you, but that impressed me."

I shrugged off the compliment. "I run into burning buildings for a living."

"Uh huh, and I bet that's easier than what you just did."

Walking briskly in the same direction Kit had taken, Paul pushed through a door and suddenly I could hear the rumble of the crowd gathered at the press conference. I spied Kit talking to Liam Connor just behind the side curtains on the stage. He was waving his arms around, clearly agitated. Kit, on the other hand, was focused and ready for the battle.

Paul was watching the scene as well. "That's our girl. Tough as nails when she has to be. The label pinheads are mad at her. They want her to read a prepared statement, but she insists on going off–script and speaking from the heart." His laugh rumbled deep in his chest. "It's the right call. She connects with her fans like nobody's business."

I nodded but I couldn't tear my eyes away from Kit. "Yes, she does. She doesn't give them every part of herself, but what she does let them see is genuine."

But, nobody knew what a big secret she had carried around. I shifted uncomfortably with the knowledge that she hadn't shared it with me.

Paul seemed to read my thoughts. "She didn't trust anybody with the secret of her mama, son. I was with her two years before she let me know about it. She's so used to being the boss that she doesn't know how to lean on other people."

I wearily rubbed the back of my neck. "I get that, I really do. But, I don't understand how she does it."

Paul huffed. "Kit had to grow up fast with very little stability in her life. Believe it or not, this craziness is where she's the most comfortable because she created it and controls it. It's become her safe zone and she is terrified to do anything that'll rock the boat." He leaned over, lowering his voice as people gathered around them. "You seem real determined to stick around so here's a little advice: she thinks being happy—having something for herself—is selfish because it distracts her from her responsibilities. If you want her, you're gonna have to convince her that she can have it all."

I was interrupted from responding as Liam walked to the podium and kicked off the press conference. Every eye in the room was on Kit and I was no exception. I examined her—looking for signs of stress, nervousness, fear—as I willed her to know that I was there.

As if she sensed my focus, Kit turned her head just enough to meet my gaze and my heart stuttered to a stop in my chest. I lifted a hand to wave at her and she did the same to me. A small gesture between us but it was enough for her to know that I was here. If I had my way, we'd have lots of time to talk, to say all the things that needed to be said.
Maybe she didn't think she deserved it all but I wasn't going to stop until I'd changed her mind.

CHAPTER TWENTY–SIX
Kit

Max was here.

Twenty minutes ago, I couldn't imagine anything making this ordeal bearable, but now Max was here and I felt peaceful, almost calm. The fact that my entire outlook was changed by his merely walking through the door should've scared the hell out of me but the moment my fist connected with the nose of that reporter, something inside me had broken free. Other than the absolute conviction that I would not let this moment destroy my career, the rest of my life was up for grabs.

I was shocked, and thrilled, at the way Max maneuvered his way in here and insisted on staying. I had considered fighting him for a moment, but who was I fooling? It was exactly what I'd been hoping, aching for. I just hoped that when he heard what else I was going to reveal at this press conference, that he would want to stay.

Liam finally stopped yapping and signaled to me that it was show time. I scanned the crowd, noting many familiar faces, most of them wearing expressions of concern and encouragement.

I took a deep breath and began. "Thank ya'll for coming here today. I'm sorry for all of the trouble this has caused and hopefully I can make it right. My mother, Elizabeth Landry, is not dead as I have previously let everyone believe. She is alive and has been in a private nursing home since I signed with my label. Her current condition is the result of a drug overdose six years ago during which she suffered severe brain damage. She functions at the level of a three– or four–year–old child and has seizures when placed in stressful situations."

I gripped the podium, not even looking at my notes. I knew what I wanted to say. "I would like to tell you that I lied about her being dead solely because it was in her best interest, but that would be untrue. Yes, I wanted her to be safe and in a healthy place, but I lied because I was embarrassed." Tears gathered in my eyes so I dipped my head and wiped them away before pressing forward. "My mother is bipolar. Her mental illness was undiagnosed and untreated for a very long time and even after we knew, she refused to stay on her medication. To make the situation worse she became an alcoholic, an addict, and she sold her body for drugs. She'd leave for a while and then show up strung–out and broke. The pattern was always the same: she would clean up, make promises to stay straight, and then go back on the street. It was bad enough when my father was alive but when he passed, her care fell on my shoulders. As you can imagine, it was a heavy burden for a fifteen–year–old girl."

It was so quiet in the room I could hear the air rushing in the vents. For someone who was used to crowds of singing fans, this was a little unnerving.

"My life was consumed with dodging the foster care people and surviving as best I could. Early on, a reporter assumed she was dead and I let the lie continue. I was embarrassed. I was tired of having to explain that my mother was a junkie. It was more convenient to let everyone believe she was dead."

I paused and looked around, meeting every eye squarely. I was done with the shame. This was way off script and Liam Connor was going to have a fit. He'd have to get over it. I wasn't going to have any more secrets hanging over my head.

"If you know anything about bipolar disorder then you know it is hereditary and after my episode a year ago, I started treatment with a psychiatrist and was diagnosed as suffering from hypomania. It is a form of bipolar disorder that causes those of us with the illness to have manic or depressive episodes. When I had an episode after my break–up with Jake, I started drinking heavily, forgetting my obligations—you all reported on it so I will spare us all the gory details." I paused to take a breath when the crowd laughed quietly. "I do not require medication and I am treating my illness with diet and exercise with the help of my physician. Of course, I am under constant medical care to treat my mental illness and my alcoholism. I am truly sorr..."

I heard a loud scuffle behind me and I turned around. The voices got louder; the activity just off the stage became chaotic and people jostled to see the cause of the disruption. The press started mumbling, most of them rising from their seats to get a better look. I had no idea what was going on until the source of the noise was rushing towards me.

"You bitch!" Ron, disheveled and drunk off his ass, lurched onto the stage and headed straight for me. "You stupid bitch! You can't fire me!"

Stunned by his appearance and his venom, I stumbled backwards and tried to dodge his fists. Ron grabbed my arm and ripped the sleeve of my jacket before I could get away from him. Stumbling, I fell down and my head hit the table. I was conscious but so disoriented that it was impossible to differentiate between the stars in my eyes and the flashes from the cameras.

Ron followed me down, yelling at me with breath rank with alcohol and I curled up in a ball to avoid his blows. I was getting desperate when Ron's weight was suddenly lifted off me. Struggling to catch my breath, I grabbed a chair and stood up just in time to see Max hit Ron squarely in the stomach.

Ron staggered back two steps, shook it off and lunged towards Max—spewing filth and hate about me. Flailing wildly, his fist connected with the side of Max's mouth, drawing blood. Max wiped at the blood, glanced at his hand, and with a smirk hauled his fist back and nailed Ron right upside the head. Ron went down like a tree and, just like that, the circus was over.

My ears were ringing from hitting the table. I was swept up by Max as Josef and the hotel security staff descended upon the fallen form of Ron. Max murmured in my ear, "I've got you" and the chaos of the press shouting and cameras flashing faded into the background as he carried me off the stage and towards the back of the building.

I hung onto Max, as Paul and Bridget led us through back offices and down the stairs to the back entrance of the building.

"Are you okay? Can you stand?" Max peered down into my face, his hand reaching up to smooth back my crazy hair.

I nodded, holding on tightly as he lowered me to the ground; his arm looped around my waist, holding me firmly at his side.

Liam Connor appeared at my side, his face flushed but his suit impeccable. Apparently he'd avoided the drama.

"Kit, you weren't supposed to talk about *your* mental illness," he said.

"Nice security detail dickhead," Max said, putting his body in between us. "I'm getting her out of here."

"We need to talk," Liam insisted but Max cut him off with a shove to the chest.

"Not now."

"Don't put your hands on me," Liam growled.

"Fucking leave her alone."

Paul stepped up and inserted himself between them, his voice the only calm in the middle of all this crazy. "We aren't going to do this now. You hear me?"

I watched as the two men faced off, Paul's bulk beating Liam by about forty pounds and three inches.

"Fine. I want her in my office tomorrow." Liam gave up more easily than I thought he would but he couldn't resist giving Max a dark look as he turned to go. He was not happy and I wasn't looking forward to our chat.

Bridget fished her keys out of her pocket and handed

them to Max. "You take my car and get her out of here. She can't go home, and the usual places will be mobbed. You have somewhere in mind?"

"Yeah," Max grabbed the keys. "I'll take her home with me. It'll take them a while to figure it out and she'll be safe there."

"Kitten, you okay with this plan? You feel safe going with Mr. Butler, here?" Paul asked.

I don't want to be anywhere else. I tightened my grip on Max. "Yes."

Paul nodded and swatted Max on the shoulder. "All right then. You get going and we'll take care of this mess."

Max loosened his hold and looked down at me, his gaze concerned and tense and filled with something else I was afraid to name. He hauled me up in his arms and planted a swift, hard kiss on my mouth. "You ready?"

"Yes." I looked up at him, biting my lower lip before making my request. "Can I get you to take me somewhere else first?"

CHAPTER TWENTY-SEVEN
Max

The sign at the entrance read "Shady Grove Assisted Living Facilty" wasn't what I expected at all. In my head, I envisioned something out of One Flew Over the Cuckoo's Nest complete with Jack Nicholson yelling at us as we walked the hall to her mother's room with scary medical equipment lining the hallways.

This place was more like a resort. Security gates at the beginning of the compound opened when I asked Kit for the code—the only thing she'd spoken since we'd left except for answering "no" when I asked if she needed Shannon to come by and look her over. I was uncomfortable with the silence, my gut tight and muscles taut with everything that had already gone down today and what I knew was coming.

I had no idea what to expect. No idea what kind of shape Mrs. Landry would be in. And I was scared. This was important, these moments would determine if I got the chance to be with Kit or whether we were over. This was a test and I'd never had the chance to study.

I followed the way Kit pointed with a shaking hand and that pretty much wrecked my soul. My White Knight syndrome was in overdrive when it came to this woman and I was amped up enough to fight whatever dragon showed its face. I would slay anyone and anything to wipe that tremor from her muscle memory.

We passed a large building with a sign that told me it was the social hall surrounded with tennis courts and a pool. This was not a nursing home—I remembered from the search for Grandpa Butler that this place consisted of separate villas purchased by the resident where they could have live–in help to assist them with day–to–day living. I also remembered that it was as expensive as fuck.

"This is it. Number 22," Kit said and pointed me towards the two–car garage. Whoever was inside knew we were coming because one of the doors went up and I pulled in.

"Wait." Kit laid a hand on my harm when I reached for the door handle. "Wait until the door is completely down."

"Is that how you avoided being seen?" I asked.

She nodded. "Nobody saw me coming or going. It was crazy enough to work."

"What about visitors?"

"My mom doesn't get any visitors other than her doctor." She looked over at me in the gloom, her fingers tensing under my own. "You'll see."

The door to the house opened and a woman in her mid–fifties with dark blonde hair and glasses stepped into the opening, motioning us inside. I jumped out and hurried over to Kit, helping her out of the car and noticing her try and hide the wince when she moved. She wouldn't let me call Shannon but I'd check her over later.

"Katie," the woman called out when she pulled Kit into a total body hug. Kit wrapped her own arms around her neck and they stood there for a few moments. From the shaking of her shoulders, I could tell Kit was crying and I could do nothing but stand by in impotent rage and hope I got the chance to beat the living shit out of Ron. It would be worth the loss of my career to see that guy bloody.

"Hey. Hey." The older woman pulled out of the embrace, looking down at Kit with eyes and cheeks damp. "Why don't you introduce me to this guy? You've never brought a bodyguard before. Is it that bad?"

Kit chuckled and shook her head, wiping her fingers under her eyes before turning to me. "Max this is Lilah Pierce, my mom's nurse. This is Max. He's..."

"I'm her boyfriend," I answered, focusing on Lilah so I

missed the reaction on Kit's face. I didn't need to see it, I'm sure it matched the answering hammering of my heart in my chest. I couldn't believe how easily the word had slipped out and I didn't know why I said it. Boyfriend status was something that was granted, not taken, and we had not talked about it. But I took the slide of Kit's hand into my own as silent agreement to this step in whatever direction we were headed.

"She's having a good day. We had lunch a little while ago and she'll have a nap in about an hour." Lilah cut a glance to me. "I think she'll be okay with a new face today. You might want to read to her."

I followed both down a hallway into an open kitchen and sitting area to a covered, bricked patio. The area was partially shaded from the sun and protected from anyone's view by a high privacy fence. There was a seating area and on one of the two sofas sat Elizabeth Landry, Kit's mother.

She looked older than she was, hair mostly gray and pulled back in a ponytail. Thin with slumped posture, her skin was rough and looked like she'd spent way too many hours in the sun without sunscreen. When she looked up and saw Kit, the smile was warm and a little shy.

Kit let go of my hand and walked over to her mom and sat down but she didn't reach out to hug her right away. She sat still, hands on her lap while she spoke softly to the woman who had given birth to her twenty—one years ago.

"Elizabeth doesn't always like to be touched," Lilah explained beside me. "It might take a few moments for her to warm up to Katie being here."

"Is it because of the stroke?"

"Yes. Her reaction to touch, noise, food, all varies according to the day. I could give a long medical explanation but the bottom line is that her brain was fried by the abuse it took and now it just doesn't work right. We aren't sure how she will react and sometimes it can be violent so we normally don't initiate it." Lilah motioned for me to sit down at the table with her, both of us pulling up chairs. We watched Kit and her mom, the older woman now resting a hand on her daughter's knee listening as Kit read the child's book in her hand.

"Why do you call her Katie?" I asked the first thing that came to mind, needing to understand this whole situation better.

"That's what her mother calls her. Her given name is Katherine," Lilah said. "Kit is her stage name."

I wondered what else I didn't know about the woman I'd fallen for. Judging from her announcement at the press conference it was quite a lot.

I sat there watching them for half an hour, Kit reading a book my three-year-old niece knew by heart while her mom giggled and laughed and chanted back her favorite parts. Kit would end the book and Elizabeth would beg for her to read it "one more time" which Kit would do right away.

It was sweet and heartbreaking. Here Kit was, once again taking care of one more person in her life. Once again the question popped into my mind: Who took care of Kit?

It would be me. I was the one who could do it.

Lilah rose from her chair and walked over to them. "It's time for you to lie down, Elizabeth."

They both looked up at her, the disappointment of having their time ended as clear as the blue Tennessee summer sky. They both stood to say their goodbyes.

"Bye Mama. I'll see you next week."

"You read to me again?" Elizabeth asked, her concern genuine and earnest. "You read to me?"

"Yes, Mama. I'll read to you."

They both stood there and even from where I sat, I could see Kit's entire body leaning forward, willing her mother to embrace her. Pleading with her to allow a touch. I held my breath, sending up my own prayers that Kit would get the touch she so clearly craved.

It wasn't happening today. Elizabeth turned to Lilah and smiled, shuffling off into the house with her nurse close behind her. Kit watched them go, her arms wrapped around her body as if to chase away a chill.

I walked up behind her and laid a hand on her shoulder. She spun around and launched herself at me, the sobs wracking her body. I stood firm and strong, a wall built for her to rail against, to push against as she fought to exorcise these demons.

I rubbed her back, kissing her hair and the skin over her temple as she calmed down.

"I'm sorry for falling apart like that," she mumbled against my chest. "I'm sorry."

"After the day you've had you deserve to let it all out. I'm here. Do what you need to."

"I won't..." She stuttered over her words. Clearing her throat and beginning again. "The way she is... I won't be like that. It's not her illness, it was the stroke from the overdose. I'm sick but... but that isn't..."

Jesus. She was worried about that?

"Kit, I couldn't care less if that was how you would end up. I want you. We'd figure it out together."

She didn't answer and I could feel the tension in her body as she thought about it, analyzed whether it was realistic for the long term. I could withstand the scrutiny. I could prove I wasn't going anywhere if I had to.

We stood still for a while as I held her, neither of us speaking. There wasn't much to be said. This situation sucked all the way around and there wasn't a damn thing I could do about it—except give her an escape.

It was time to take Kit home with me.

CHAPTER TWENTY–EIGHT
Max

"Kit, it's all clear."

I glanced over to where she was crouched on the floorboard of the car. Eight years on the job at NFD had come in handy. I knew the city like the back of my hand and the crisscross of little known backstreets and shortcuts had enabled me to get her away from the press. A glance into the rearview mirror confirmed that no one was behind us as we entered the Lively city limits.

Kit maneuvered into the seat and groaned as she stretched her limbs. She rubbed her head and winced in pain.

I'll kill that guy if he hurt her.

"Are you sure you're okay? Do you want a doctor?"

Kit winced again as her fingers touched a tender spot. "No. I'm fine."

"My cousin, Robert, is a doctor and he lives nearby. I can call him."

"No, I'm okay. Just a little sore." As I turned off the road and on to a private lane marked "Butler Farm", Kit leaned forward to peer out the front window. "Is this *your* farm?"

"Partially. I bought the land with my cousins Robert and Amy two years ago from my Grandpa Butler." I pointed towards a lane that led to a modern house. "Robert built that for himself and Amy's husband farms her part." I turned the car down a long, tree–lined driveway that led into a clearing where a large white farmhouse stood surrounded by roses. I pulled to a stop at the steps that led to the wide, wrap-around porch before turning to Kit with a grin. "I bought the house and 10 acres. Stay where you are and I'll help you out."

I jumped out of the car and rushed around to meet her. She ignored my order and emerged, disheveled, but steady on her feet, with her shoes in her hands and her torn jacket thrown over her arm. Kit stopped abruptly and looked at the house and the yard with wide eyes.

"Max. It's beautiful! I expect the Waltons to come out any minute!"

I chuckled as I led her up the steps to the front door. "I wish. I could use John Boy's help with the heavy lifting." At her perplexed expression I guided her through the door, explaining, "I'm renovating."

I watched her face as she entered and viewed the interior of my house for the first time. I kept the architectural details intact, but removed some walls and put in large banks of windows to let in the sunlight. From the front door, were the original maple floors as they led through the open family room and kitchen anchored by a large stone fireplace.

I led her into the kitchen before I asked, "Do you like it?"

Her smile gave away her answer. "This is gorgeous. It's amazing."

I didn't try to hide my pride as I showed off my home. "I do what I can as I get the money and I bribe the guys at the firehouse with beer and burgers to help me out. I'm done with renovating the back rooms. I enclosed the back porch with glass to make it a three–season room but I still need to work on the living room, study, and dining room." I motioned towards a large staircase. "It has five bedrooms upstairs—four now—I took a small one and made it into a master bath and walk–in closet."

I was babbling. I shut up and brought her hand up to my chest. "I should've brought you here sooner."

I understood why I hadn't. Bringing Kit here meant I

couldn't ignore my feelings for her. Now, with Kit standing in my home, I could see a future with her in this house. In my life.

I saw all of the emotions swirling in Kit's eyes—fear, vulnerability, desire and an emotion I hoped I wasn't misreading. *Stay with me. Make this place a home.* The house was silent except for the sound of the grandfather clock ticking in the hall and our heavy breathing. I reached out and grasped her waist, pulling her close. She melted against me as I cupped her face and leaned in to sample the sweetness of her mouth.

I don't know how I ever thought I could give this up.

I brushed my lips softly against hers, barely a promise of a kiss before I pulled back. My hesitation was met by a whimper from Kit as her hands laced through my hair and pulled me back to her mouth. My first real taste of her was electric. The slide of velvet tongues flamed my passion and I angled my mouth over hers possessively—the pressure on my cut lip making me wince.

Kit pulled back, her lips wet from my assault but her eyes full of concern. "You're hurt." Her thumb brushed over my injury gently and that touch made me feel like a million dollars. "You're bleeding. Let me clean that up."

I tightened my hold on her as she tried to pull away. "I'm fine."

She cupped my face between her palms, her voice low. "Let me take care of you."

I nodded and led her to the family room. Sitting her down on the couch, I retrieved the first aid kit from the kitchen and returned to sit down beside her. I soaked Kit in as she busied herself with pulling out the necessary items with her small, slender fingers. She refused to meet my gaze, her face a mask of concentration as she swabbed and cleaned my lip with careful motions. Content just to have her near, I took the time to gaze at the face I'd missed so much. Even tired from the events of the past few days, she was still the most gorgeous girl I'd ever seen.

"I think you'll live." Her eyes traveled over my face and down my body looking for signs of another injury. She "tskd" when she spied my knuckles, scraped raw and a little bloody from hitting Ron. She smiled as she cleaned the abrasions. "It must have felt good to finally hit the weasel."

I laughed. "Yeah, it did. He was asking for it." My tone sobered as I continued. "I'm sorry I wasn't able to stop him before he hurt you. I'm sorry I let you down. That *I* hurt you."

Kit dipped her head, hiding her face from my inspection while she silently busied herself with applying the ointment. Her motions stilled as she sighed and brought my hand up to rest against her wet cheek.

I cupped her chin and tipped her face up until I could see the tears. "Kit. Baby, don't cry. You're killing me."

Her violet eyes were darkened with confusion and pain and I held onto her hand, anxious to keep the physical connection.

"Max. This is so... I... I just need to know what you want."

What did I want? That was easy.

Her.

"What do I want? I want to stop missing you. I want to stop looking for bits of paper with lyrics on them showing up in my pockets. I want to stop thinking of that stupid frog when I hear a Merle Haggard song. I want to hear your songs on the radio and know they're about me." I leaned in closer, my hands gripped her shoulders, lips only a breath away from hers, and our eyes locked. "I want you in my bed. In this house. In my life. Underneath me. Around me. I want my name on your lips as you come apart all over me."

My hands clenched with need as I pressed a brief kiss against her mouth before saying the thing I never thought I would ever say again.

"I want you to tell me that you love me because I love you and I honestly don't know how to live without you."

CHAPTER TWENTY–NINE
Kit

He loved me.

Max loved me and wanted me. I was breathless and I took a deep breath to calm my erratically beating heart as I inched closer and pressed my mouth against his.

"I love you, Max."

He slid his arms around me and pulled me close, groaning in his chest as he swept inside my mouth with his tongue. *More. All of you.* I wove my fingers into his hair anchoring him in place for my greedy mouth. It had been too long. We scrambled against each other—desperate to feel skin against skin, soft curves against hard angles.

I was hungry for him, reaching under his shirt, rucking it up to lift it from his body. I needed to see him, to feel him. I trembled and Max hissed into my hair at the first touch of my palms against the sleek, heated skin of his abdomen and around to the muscled expanse of his back.

"Baby, you always make me feel so good." Max breathed the words against my cheek before he savagely reclaimed my mouth. "Let me make you feel good. You know how much I love to see you come."

His words made me shudder as his calloused hands covered my breasts, rubbing my nipples until they hardened underneath the silk of my dress. With one hand, he tunneled under my hair and unfastened the halter top, letting it fall down to expose me to the burn of his gaze and the rough caress of his hands.

"Make me come. Please." I wanted nothing more than to lose myself in him, in how he could make me feel. Max could make all of the crap of the last twenty–four hours go away and I needed the oblivion. I needed him.

I moaned and arched upwards as he took a nipple in his mouth, sucking and nibbling on it until it was hard and sensitized to the point of pleasure/pain.

It was almost too much. I was slick between my legs, clenching them together in search of what he offered, what I knew he could deliver. I tugged him up my body but he refused to let me control this lovemaking.

"Kit. I need to fuck you. I need to know you're mine."

"I'm yours."

"Yes. You are."

His look was feral, his movements rough as he lifted me up, unzipping my dress and pushing it down and off my body. I shivered as he stripped off my thong, and blazed a trail down my body with his lips and teeth—nipping and laving my skin, stopping only to push me back on to the couch and expose my nakedness to his gaze.

I was possessed. Taken. Like every touch and every look branded me as his.

For as long as I remembered, I'd wanted to belong to someone and now I did.

He watched me as he pushed between my thighs and tongued my wet core, making love to me with his mouth. His pace was unrelenting as he pushed me higher and higher, as if he needed to seal our words with this physical act. My body went boneless as he pushed inside me with two fingers, pumping sleekly and deeply. Without warning, my body bowed off the couch and I pushed up against his mouth as my climax washed over me like a wave of fire.

He was burning me alive, branding me and I'd never craved anything more.

"Fuck, you taste good. Like honey."

Max rose up, unfastened his jeans and shoved them down his legs, his cock hard and stiff against his stomach, a delicious drop of pre–cum on its tip. Before I could tell him how much I wanted him, Max leaned over me, capturing my mouth in a kiss that tasted of my arousal as his cock brushed against my slick, sensitive sex. Mindlessly filled with the need to have him inside me, I struggled up against him, urging his body to fill me, stretch me.

Breaking off the kiss, he ran his tongue up my jaw and let it circle the outer shell of my ear before dipping down to nip at my earlobe. He pulled back and I protested, silencing my complaint when I saw that he was pausing only to put on a condom.

I gasped as he entered me with one thrust, kissing me roughly and holding my hips in a bruising grip. I didn't want him to be gentle and he wasn't. I needed this connection to erase the last few days of being apart.

He pounded into me, hard and deep, and I met him thrust for thrust, our cries mingling along with the sweat on our straining bodies. Max grasped my thighs and lifted me higher against his body, angling me in a way that allowed him to rub against my clit with every push and pull. I tightened my grip on his biceps, his eyes locking with me just as my climax hit and pulled him over the edge with me.

He collapsed on top of me, panting harshly while his lips tenderly skimmed my forehead, cheeks, lips, and finally settled against my neck. His weight was a comfort, a solid reminder that I wasn't alone. I was loved.

He shifted to the side and pulled a blanket over us as we settled into the couch. Max caressed my face with gentle hands, urging my lips up to accept his gentle kiss. He broke it off and whispered against my cheek. "I love you."

"I love you, too." I snuggled into his embrace, rubbing my face against his neck and inhaling the unique scent of Max, sweat, and our lovemaking that lingered on his skin. In spite of this perfect moment, doubts were crowding into my mind and I clung to him, wishing we could stay in this moment forever. How would we really make this work?

Max sensed my struggle and pulled back to look into my face. "What's going on?"

"Are you sure?" I traced his jawline, loving the scratchy

feel of his beard against my fingertips. I shivered as I remembered how it had felt against the skin of my thighs and breasts. "Our life will never be normal. Even if I cut back, this will never be a regular kind of life together."

Max shifted and leaned up on one elbow. "I know that. But, I can't live without you. I tried and it didn't work." He kissed the tip of my nose and smiled. "Besides, I'm beginning to think that normal is overrated. We'll figure it out. We'll make our own normal."

"That sounds so good. I want that." Brushing aside my doubts, I snuggled into his embrace as he shifted back on the couch. I was happy. Max loved me and it *would* be different this time.

Like he said, we would find our own normal—together.

CHAPTER THIRTY
Max

I woke slowly from the most amazing dream.

It was always the same; Kit in my bed, dark curls spilling over my sheets, as I worshipped every inch of her deliciously fuckable body.

This morning was even better, because the pictures in my head were in Technicolor and my sheets even smelled like her. Groaning, I rolled over, pulling my pillow against my face, inhaling the delicious scent of Kit—a combination of summer, honeysuckle, and pure sex.

Lying there, the smell of fresh coffee and the sound of her sweet singing wafted over me and made me smile.

It wasn't a dream.

I shifted under the sheets as memories of last night drifted across my mind. I was hard, aching as I stroked up and down slowly, drawing out the pleasure. When I woke up with Kit on the couch I'd picked her up and carried her up the stairs to my bedroom, placing her gently on my bed.

In the twilight, Kit had climbed on top of me—driving me crazy with her soft hands. Her mouth had been hungry, sweet, and I'd let her lead the way. All of her doubts from earlier seemed to disappear as she took control of my body. Drawn in by the spell she cast over me, I made no effort to hide just how desperately I wanted her. She teased me with her lips and hands, and it had taken all my strength to resist taking over as she grasped my cock in her small hand and led me into her body.

That time was slow and sweet. No words were spoken. She'd fallen apart in my arms and I'd held her close as my climax surged through my body, leaving me sated and spent. Unwilling to break our connection, I'd stayed inside her as we drifted back to sleep.

We needed to talk. To figure out how this was going to work between us. She had doubts and so did I but I wanted to figure them out together. For the first time in forever, the thought of committing to someone didn't scare me. I wanted it and I was going to have it.

I got up, determined to go down to the kitchen and drag Kit back to bed. Breakfast could wait. I dragged on a pair of jeans, and left them unbuttoned, padded barefoot down the stairs, and skidded to a stop when I got a good look at the scene in my kitchen.

I leaned against the doorway and watched her make my house into a home.

Kit was standing at the stovetop, my shirt reaching to the middle of her thighs and her hair tousled from the night in my bed. She sang softly to herself as she bustled around, preparing pancakes and eggs.

"You look good in my shirt."

Kit looked over her shoulder, eyes wide with surprise but warm with love. I pushed away from the wall and walked over to her, wrapping my arms around her waist and pressing my front against her back. She melted against me and sighed as I pressed a soft kiss to her neck.

"Good morning."

She sighed again as my mouth traveled up to the sensitive spot behind her ear. Her voice was breathless and I smiled at her reaction to me. "Good morning to you." Kit gestured at the stove. "I was making you breakfast."

I nibbled back down her neck as I snaked a hand under the edge of my shirt to caress her silky thigh. "I was hoping to have breakfast in bed."

She moaned as my fingers brushed against her wet folds and higher to caress the smooth skin of her belly. She wriggled against me, rubbing her ass against my erection. Holy shit that felt good.

"I made you pancakes...Oh!"

I was done playing unless I was doing it in my bed. I lifted her over my shoulder, snagged the bottle of syrup off the counter and turned to head back to the bedroom. Kit squirmed in my hold and squealed as I smacked her ass. "Hold still. You're gonna love it, baby. I'm gonna lick every inch of—"

The sight of someone standing in my foyer brought me to an abrupt halt.

"Mom!"

Holy shit. My dad was also standing at the front door, a grin twitching at the edges of his mouth.

Kit was absolutely still, but I could feel her groan of embarrassment buried against my shoulder. I slowly lowered her to the ground, and once her feet hit the wood floor, she turned and faced my parents, fussing with her hair and tugging the oversized shirt further down her legs.

It was kind of cute. We'd laugh about this someday but from the feel of her elbow jamming into my side, I didn't think it would be anytime soon.

My dad cleared his throat, breaking the embarrassed silence as he strode towards the kitchen. "Coffee smells good. Think I'll get a cup."

"How did they get in?" Kit whispered.

"They have a key."

Kit took off up the stairs with a mumbled "going to put some clothes on" and I followed my dad into the kitchen. The passing of cups, milk, and sugar busied our hands as we studiously avoided the fact my parents had clearly interrupted an intimate moment.

Taking a sip of the hot brew, I asked, "What are you guys doing here so early?"

Kit made her reappearance, wearing a pair of my sweatpants, and I handed her a cup, pulling her close beside me.

"We tried to call but no one answered." My mother reached out and grasped Kit's hand in compassion. "We saw what happened to you, dear. It was terrible." She turned to me, her eyes filled with pride. "And we saw what you did to protect her."

"Proud of you, son." My dad patted my shoulder and then shifted to lean against the counter. "When we couldn't get you on the phone, we figured you two were squirreled away here. There's a bunch of reporters camped out at the top of the lane. Robert blocked the road, so they can't get down here unless they crawl through the woods." He flashed an apologetic glance towards Kit. "We probably gave away your location, though. I think the ones who were camped out at our house followed us here. I'm sorry."

Kit smiled back. "Don't apologize, Mr. Butler. Welcome to my world." She sighed, and put her coffee down on the counter. "I should apologize for disrupting your life."

"It's John. And you didn't do anything you need to apologize for. This will all blow over and we'll be back to normal before you know it."

"Damn! That coffee smells good! Is there more?"

I turned to see Dean, followed closely by Bridget, saunter into my kitchen and head straight for the coffeepot.

"The door was open so we just came on in." Smiling at the Butlers, he introduced Bridget before he continued, "The station, Kit's loft, are all a mob scene. Bridget called me once my shift was over and she followed me in your truck."

"The label needs you back pronto. The buzz has all been in your favor, but with the tour kicking off in three days, they are howling to get you back in town for promo work. Paul's working out the details but we need you. Sorry," Bridget said.

I watched Kit closely; her expression was tense. I gathered her close to my side and pressed a kiss to her hair as she asked, "What about Ron?"

Weird looks passed between the four visitors and my stomach clenched in response. "What's going on guys?"

Dean was the one to answer. "Ron's still in custody. Both you and Kit need to go and give statements so they can press charges. That's the good part." He rubbed the back of his neck and hesitated. "The bad part is that he's saying you assaulted, threatened, and harassed him, Max. He's hired a lawyer who keeps talking to the press and stirring it all up."

I shrugged. "So what? He can't prove it."

Dean continued. "The department has placed you on administrative suspension without pay until this gets cleared up. The director's pissed and wants to talk to you today. You *know* how he hates bad press."

"I protected her. What the fuck did they expect me to do? Let that asshole hurt her?"

"It's not just the fight." Dean held a hand up to stop me from interrupting. "You left the shift to go to Kit. I tried to cover, but they know. You were AWOL."

Shocked, I released Kit and walked over to the large fireplace that dominated the family room. Leaning on the mantle, I breathed in deeply, controlling my temper and collecting my thoughts. This was manageable. I would talk to the chief and the police and get back to work.

"What?" Kit asked from behind me. "You left work to come to me?"

I turned and faced the bank of upset and concerned faces in front of me. "Of course I did. You needed me. I'd do it again if I had to."

"Could you lose your job?" Her expression told me that she already knew the answer and it was not going to go over well.

"Yes."

"And you would do it again?"

"Yes."

"What about your promotion?"

I scoffed. "Not going to happen now."

Kit stared at me, her expression unreadable. I didn't know her well enough to understand every nuance and right now I cursed that fact. She closed her eyes briefly, cutting herself off from me completely. I made a move towards her and her eyes flew open and she bolted, heading out of the kitchen. She was clearly upset.

Following her, I caught up with her in my room just in time to see her pulling on her clothes. "Kit, baby? What are you doing?"

"I'm going. I've got to fix this mess."

"Okay. Just hang on a second and I'll get dressed and go with you."

She stopped, her eyes only briefly meeting mine before darting away. She clutched her shoes to her chest and scurried past me and into the hallway. "No. I'm going alone."

I grabbed her arm and spun her around to face me just before she reached the stairs. "Kit. I'm going with you. Remember last night? We do this together from now on."

Tears pooled in her eyes as she shook her head, her voice a broken whisper. "No. This won't work."

Shock rolled through me and loosened my grip on her, allowing her to slip down the stairs. I barely registered the others as they piled out of the kitchen just in time to witness my life falling apart.

My voice was loud and harsh as I shouted at her retreating back. "What do you mean, *this won't work*? We've barely gotten started and you're giving up?" I raced down the stairs two at a time and caught her at the bottom. "What about the fact that we love each other?"

"Max, we both know that isn't enough. Our lives are too different and mine has already ruined yours. Your parents have reporters camped on their lawn and you're practically a prisoner in your own house. Not to mention the fact that you might lose your job!" She wiped at her wet cheeks with the back of her hand. "My life is in chaos and I go on tour in a few days and I'll be gone for months. Trust me. We've been living in a bubble—a wonderful bubble where the press left us alone and we didn't have to deal with reality. But trust me, those days are over and the reality of my life will tear us apart." Her breath hiccupped in her chest. "I don't want you to end up hating me because I can't be what you need."

"What are you talking about?" I saw the fear, heard it in her voice. I was scared, too, but I was more afraid of losing her and never taking the chance. I reached out, pulling her close to me. "Kit, don't do this. My job will be fine. Your job will be fine. We'll work out the rest. Together." I leaned in close to press my forehead against hers as I pleaded, "I love you so much. Just hang on to me baby. We'll be all right, I promise."

She rested against me and a little of the tension loosened in my chest. Her hand wove through my hair as she pulled me into a kiss that was full of tenderness and something else I couldn't name. With a whimper, Kit released my mouth and stepped far enough away that I could see the expression on her face. Suddenly, I knew what else had been in that kiss.

It was goodbye.

I was pissed. Anger shot through me. "So, you're gonna do this? You're afraid and you're going to run? What is this? Fucking payback for what I did?" I gestured wildly at the front door. "All this craziness? That's nothing. But you're too afraid to take the chance and even though I suck at any kind of relationship, I know I can't do it by myself." Running my hands through my hair, my voice caught as pain squeezed my heart. Jesus, this was worse than Sarah. Knowing Kit was out there and I couldn't have her might kill me. "You and me, together? It would be hard, but I know we'd be worth it. It could shatter into a million fucking pieces and it would still be worth it."

I stared at her, daring her to take the leap with me. If this had any chance of working, we both had to be committed one hundred percent.

"Max." Her voice was barely above a whisper but it was like she was shouting at me. That one word told me

TEMPTATION

everything I needed to know. She was already gone.

I turned away from her, heading up the stairs to wash her smell off my body and burn the sheets.

CHAPTER THIRTY–ONE
Max

My eyes were gritty from too little sleep.

Three weeks had passed since Kit walked out of my house and my life. The last time I'd seen her was the day after she'd shot us all to hell. I'd arrived at the police station to give my statement just as she was leaving and our eyes had met for the briefest moment before I turned away. I couldn't stand the sight of her when I couldn't have her. She looked beautiful as always, but in that second, I saw the pain and hurt that shadowed her eyes but, for once, my hero complex didn't take over. She'd made her decision and she could live with it.

Just like I would.

My suspension from work only lasted two days. In the end, Kit had called the director—explaining how I had protected her from Ron—and I'd been reinstated immediately. I was grateful. The job was the only thing that kept me from losing my mind. At work, I could pretend to ignore the pitying looks from my family and friends.

Just like the one Dean was giving me right now.

I shifted on my seat inside the fire truck as it raced down the street to the third call of the night.

"Dean, cut it out."

Dean didn't even pretend to misunderstand. "You look like shit. When's the last time you slept?"

I adjusted my helmet to block my face. "Last night."

"Uh huh." Dean continued to examine me. "I didn't ask 'when was the last time you tossed and turned and paced the night away'."

I stared down at my boots, saying nothing. I wasn't going to spill my guts and dwell on something I couldn't change.

"Max."

"Don't." I met his eyes across the truck and gritted my teeth. "She's gone. Let's just do the job."

The back doors opened and I jumped down to the ground, surveying the scene. I got my orders and made my way into the three–story apartment building, checking rooms, carrying victims out to safety—focusing on the job. Time passed quickly, and soon I was on the second floor, conducting one last sweep before calling the "all clear."

Inside, the fire was dying down but it was still loud. I heard an ominous crack but couldn't tell where it was coming from. A tingling awareness spread across the back of my neck. It was time to get out.

Instinct propelled me towards the exit just as the ceiling heaved above me. Two steps from my goal, debris rained down on my head and shoulders. I reached for my communication device but it was too late.

A large object landed across my back and I slammed to the floor under its weight. I couldn't breathe. I scrabbled to move away the heavy debris. I tried not to panic but it was hard, with what felt like an elephant sitting on my back. It was getting hotter, the noise louder, as the fire sparked back to life overhead.

I clawed at the rubble and dislodged my helmet and it rolled to the side. Succumbing to the pain, I saw the picture of Kit tucked into the inside band just before everything went black.

CHAPTER THIRTY–TWO
Kit

The applause was deafening.

I waved to the audience and left the stage of the Grand Ole Opry, heading towards my dressing room to prepare for the interview segment and then my final performance of the night. I was bone–tired. Getting here had required a red–eye flight from Florida, so I pushed open the door and headed straight for the fridge and my new best friend—Mr. Red Bull. Bridget was on the telephone, so I kicked off my shoes and plopped down on the couch.

The first set was behind me and I breathed a sigh of relief. I longed to get out of Nashville, back on the road, and away from all the memories of Max. On the road, I still hurt, but it was easier to focus on the music and the fans without seeing him on every corner. I welcomed the grind of the road. Most nights I fell into my bunk in a dreamless stupor but I still dreaded the morning when my brain clicked into gear and the pain came rushing back.

I'd blown it this time. My fear had forced me to make a rash, stupid decision that hurt Max deeply. The crazy part was that I didn't even know why I'd done it anymore. My doctor said it was a panic attack brought on by all the crap that had happened and that my sense of desolation and fear was a normal part of it.

All I knew was that I'd been overcome with the overwhelming feeling that staying with Max would hurt him.

His face outside the police station had been cold, hard, and devoid of any emotion towards me, except indifference. He probably hated me and I didn't blame him. I hated the cowardice I'd let control me, but it was too late to change it. My chance with Max was over and I had no one to blame but myself.

I popped one eye open when Bridget signed off her call, ready to ask about the details of our flight, when a phone rang—the "Stand By Your Man" ringtone signaling that it was mine.

Bridget scooped it up off the dressing table and flipped it open with a cheerful greeting. Her smile slipped as she listened briefly, murmured for the person to hang on, and held the phone out to me. Her voice was grim.

"It's Dean. It's about Max."

My hand stilled in mid–air. It was bad news. I knew it. Maybe the worst news. With icy fingers, I took the phone from Bridget and brought it up to my ear.

"This is Kit."

"I thought you might want to know." Dean's usually jovial voice was tense and anxious. "Max is hurt. We're on shift and he was in a building when it collapsed."

I found it hard to speak around the band that was constricting around my heart. "Is... is he okay?"

Dean paused as people shouted around him. I could hear him cup the phone closer to his mouth. "I don't know the extent of his injuries. We got him out of the building and he's on the bus headed to NashGen. He was unconscious. Hold on a second." Dean answered a series of rapid questions and came back to the phone. "Look, I gotta go. I'll see you at the hospital."

I sat there, unable to move, as the dial tone sounded in my ear. Only two thoughts swirled in my mind: one, I had to get to Max, and two, that if I got the chance, I would make him love me again.

I jumped off the couch, my focus on getting to Max.

Bridget was right behind me, scooping up purses and keys.

"I'm going with you."

I hit the backstage hallway and broke into a run. People

moved out of my way while casting puzzled looks in my direction. Paul came jogging up and stopped my momentum with a hand on my shoulder.

"Kit, where are you going? We have a show in," he looked at his watch, "ten minutes."

I leaned on his arm, scared shitless and close to losing the battle to keep it together. "Max is hurt. He could be—" I bit my lip, unable to voice my greatest fear. "I have to go to him."

"You know, if you walk out of the Opry, the label will tank your new contract." His voice was firm; matter–of–fact. No judgment there.

"I don't care." *I would give up my whole career for Max to be alright.* I'd figure out the career part once I knew he was okay.

Nodding, Paul kissed my forehead quickly and pushed me towards the door. "Good girl. I'll fix it here. Go!"

Bridget and I bolted out of the artists' entrance of the Opry and headed straight for her car. I was silent as we careened through traffic, praying for Max to be alright. Could you be okay if a building fell on you? Would they let me see him? The fifteen–minute ride was torture and I barely let the car come to a stop outside the ER before I jumped out and bolted for the entrance.

The waiting area smelled like antiseptic and burnt coffee and was filled with firefighting personnel, EMTs, and policemen. Ignoring the pointing fingers of those who recognized me, I scanned the crowd for Dean. Giving up, I approached a nurse to ask about Max, when I heard my name shouted above the noise. Turning, Dean waved me over.

He grasped my arm and led me to a room filled with firemen. "He's still unconscious and they moved him upstairs."

"Can I see him?"

Dean pushed me through the door. "We'll see. I'll take you up."

TEMPTATION

We emerged from the elevator on the third floor and immediately stepped into a waiting room full of people. Several nodded to Dean, and I ignored the whispers that erupted in my wake. It seemed like an eternity until I turned a corner and entered a hospital room where John and Olivia Butler sat, next to a hospital bed.

I blinked, my eyes adjusting to the low light in the room and the hushed hospital sounds of machines whirring and soft–soled shoes squeaking on tile floors.

My heart fell to my feet. I forgot how to breathe.

Max sat on the edge of the bed, shirtless with a pair of scrub pants. His face and body were covered with scrapes and cuts. It was the bandage on his head, tinted red with blood just over his left temple that made me weak.

I wanted to run to him and make sure he was all right but his hostile demeanor stopped me. His amber eyes grew dark when he saw me, suspicion and hurt tightening his jaw.

"What are you doing here?" he asked, not an ounce of welcome in his tone. I'd made a mistake. I was too late.

"Dean called me," I stumbled over my tongue, suddenly realizing how far out on the ledge I was with no safety net. "I wanted to see that you were okay."

"I look better than I feel," he answered, his tone flat and emotionless.

"Oh."

"You've done your duty. You can go."

"Max!" His mother scolded him from her perch by the bed. I blushed with embarrassment. I had no right to be here.

I moved to leave but a hand on my arm stopped me.

"Are you a friend of my grandson?"

I turned. A much older man, who possessed Max's strong jaw and large build, was watching me closely. Startled, I looked around. Their faces were worried, frantic. I had no right to be here.

"I'm sorry." I offered an apology towards Olivia Butler. "I should go. I'm intruding."

I turned to go, but gentle pressure on my arm stopped my leaving. Max's grandpa held me back, his face kind and full of understanding.

"Young lady, the important thing to remember is that you came." His curious gaze examined me and I remembered that I still wore my costume from the Opry. "I can presume from your lovely outfit that you were at quite a fancy shindig and left in quite a hurry."

"I was at the Opry. I have a show tonight."

"I see." His eyes were gentle as he squeezed my hand in encouragement. "You don't walk out of the Opry for just anyone. My grandson must be very important to you."

"Grandpa," Max said in warning from across the room.

I blinked back the tears gathering in my eyes, my voice barely above a whisper. "Very important." I swallowed back the fear and told the absolute truth, making eye contact with Max as I spoke. "He means everything to me. I love him." I started to back out of the room. "But I was scared and I have no right to be here. Not now. I'm sorry."

I really did turn to go this time. I wasn't welcome. Too late to salvage what we'd had. I'd get on my tour bus and back on the road. Sooner or later, I'd forget him. In the meantime, I'd get a shitload of good song material.

I was two steps out of the door when I heard his voice. "Wait."

I froze, not really sure if I'd heard him or imagined it like I had in so many dreams the last few weeks.

"Kit. I can't get off this bed without falling down. Get back in here." His mom whispered something that sounded like "you're being rude" and he added, "Please."

I eased back into the room, staring at him from the spot just inside the door. Max just stared at me and I had no idea whether he wanted me to stay in place or go to him. The air in the room crackled with everything between us, the uncertainty and longing I saw in his gaze.

"Can you give us a minute?" Max asked his parents and Grandpa and they all hustled to beat feet out the door.

A soft chuckle escaped the lips of Grandpa Butler as he walked past me. He stopped and whispered his two cents. "Trust me, darlin'; I've seen him mope around these last few weeks. That hurt will be forgotten once Max hears you tell him you love him. Tell the boy what he's been dyin' to hear."

"Grandpa," Max barked and the older man scurried through the door with a big wink.

I liked him. Very much.

Max and I stared at each other, the seconds measuring like hours in my twisted gut. I had no idea where to start.

"You left the Opry," Max stated but every word was drenched in a question.

"Yes."

"That's not going to make Liam happy."

"No, it won't," I agreed. "But I wasn't thinking about making him happy when I left."

"What were you thinking?"

"I was thinking that you might be gone and I'd never get to ask you."

"Ask me what?" His gaze was hot and leveled at my own. I couldn't look away. I wanted him to see just how real this all was. To believe me.

"Ask you to take me back. To say I'm sorry for giving into my panic and fear and hurting you." He didn't respond but he didn't look away, so I walked towards him, my voice cracking with all the emotion just trying to break out of me. "I wanted to ask you to love me again like in that movie star film. To tell you that I'm just a girl who screwed up and wants your love even if I don't deserve it. For today. For forever."

I was standing in front of him now. So close my body brushed up against his knees. He smelled like smoke and antiseptic and Max and I just wanted to latch onto him and inhale.

"What about your job?" he asked, his voice so low I had to lean in to catch it. The movement brought me within kissing distance of him and I fought the urge to lay one on him and seal all my words that way.

"I don't know. I might not have a label. I may start my own. I don't know." I shook my head. "I know I'm stronger with you. I'm better with you."

"And if your career is over?"

"Then, it's over. I'll figure something out. I can play anywhere. I've got options."

"Uh oh. 'Super Kit' is in the house."

I shook my head. "I don't need her when I've got you."

"Stupid jackasses. They don't know what they've got."

I laughed. "Is that right?"

"Yes." He reached out and grabbed my hands, lifting them up and around his neck as he opened his legs. I slid in there, tightening my hold on him and hanging on for dear life. I know my heart was pounding like a drumbeat in one of my songs but I didn't care. Max didn't either. "I am not a stupid jackass. I know what I've got."

"And what is that?"

"I've got you."

"Yes, you've got me."

He tugged me down and our lips met in a soft sweet kiss. His voice was low but I heard every precious word.

"Don't leave me again," he pleaded. "You'll always be enough for me. The only one for me. I love *you*, Kit."

I wrapped my arms around him and held on tightly, as our mouths gently caressed each other.

I broke off the kiss as the room spontaneously erupted in applause, hoots, and catcalls. I looked over my shoulder to see the doorway filled with his family and friends offering smiles, teary eyes, and congratulations.

"Now about the whole 'Super Kit' thing." His gravelly voice brought my attention back to his handsome face. "I kind of like the idea of you in a cape—and nothing else."

"On one condition."

He cocked an eyebrow at me. "Anything."

I leaned in closer, my lips only a breath away from his.

TEMPTATION

"You need to change the locks on your front door."
    "Deal."

EPILOGUE

Three months later

The sign read, "Lively, Tennessee. The place folks love to call home."

I squirmed in my seat in the back of the chauffer-driven car, excited by the marker that told me that I was five miles from the place I had wanted to be all summer—home. I had a number-one single, "Angel", on the charts and a new album due out in the Fall. I was on top of the world.

I'd decided not to renew my contract with Liam Connor and was exploring starting my own label while entertaining offers from a couple of big name recording companies. I had time to decide and was in no hurry. My life was full and my own.

The tour had been unbelievably successful with every show sold out and extra dates added and filled to capacity, as well. I'd loved every minute on stage with the fans, and the band was closer than ever. With Ron gone from the scene, the fun and camaraderie had returned in full force.

It felt like it was when I first started—before I let business become more important than the music. Before I'd let image be more important than the truth.

It had been an amazing summer.

But, each passing day I'd counted down the time to when I could return to Tennessee and to the man who held my heart. Max. I had missed him terribly. I'd flown home frequently and he'd come to see me when he got time away from the station. He'd even spent his week–long vacation on the road with me, witnessing the craziness of my life on the road first–hand. To my relief and delight, Max fit in like he was born for the road. The band loved him, the crew loved him, and the fans loved him.

Especially the female fans.

I giggled as I remembered the first time he'd attended a "meet and greet" and been bombarded with requests for photos from my female fans. At first he'd been surprised and then embarrassed as the ladies had shoved pieces of paper with their phone numbers into his hands. Once the fans had posted those pics on the Internet, it started a pattern that would continue the rest of the tour—requests for Max, photos with Max, and a pile of homemade gifts for Max.

While Max was a good sport about suddenly being thrust into the spotlight, I was careful to keep the intimate details of our relationship between the two of us and I shielded him from exposure as much as I possibly could. But, even when he wasn't with me, he was photographed by the press, as he lived and worked in Nashville. I'd worried silently that it bothered him more than he let on. When I apologized for the press intruding on a private lunch with his parents, he kissed me softly and told me to never apologize again; it was a small price to pay to be with me.

I'd shown him many times that night just how much his support meant to me.

So, when, three weeks after the night at the hospital he'd asked me to move into the farmhouse with him, I'd agreed with one stipulation—that he'd let me install the security gates currently blocking the car at the top of the driveway.

I used my remote control to open them and gathered my things together as the car drove the last mile to the house I now called home. My heart pounded like the drum solo on "Angel" at my first glimpse of the large, white house surrounded by the old–growth oaks and dogwoods planted by Max's grandparents. I blinked back tears as I thought of the love that had been made and would be made in this house.

This is home.

I'd wanted this for so long that I had the urge to pinch myself and get three independent confirmations that this wasn't a dream. If it was, then I was never going to wake up—ever.

The car pulled to a stop at the base of the wrap–around porch, and I hopped out without waiting for the driver to open the door. I'd told Max not to meet me at the airport and I was now anxious to have the reunion I didn't want witnessed by cameras and curious fans.

I scanned the yard as I thanked the driver and signed the invoice for the bill. I heard hammering coming from just beyond the rose garden and I headed around the house to find Max. The garden was in full–bloom, the flowers coaxed to life by Grandpa Butler, and the scent was strong and sweet where it mingled with the smell of fresh cut grass.

My breathing literally skipped when my eyes landed on the best thing I'd seen in two weeks—Max in khaki cargo shorts and a tight, white T–shirt that caressed his muscles.

Will I ever see him and not want him?

He was hammering a shutter next to one of the windows on the front of my new rehearsal space and recording studio, located in the sweet little cottage that had been Grandmother Butler's private retreat. Tears came to my eyes as I remembered the day that Max had walked me down the back path to this little house and handed me the keys, explaining that he wanted to renovate it into a space where I could work from home. He'd brushed away my tears as he teased, "As long as I can visit and try my damnedest to distract you from your work."

And then he'd pulled me into the cottage and demonstrated just how distracting he could be.

Heat pooled in my belly at the memory, and I must have made a sound because Max looked up, his amber eyes widened in surprise and then crinkling up at the edges when he smiled. One minute I was riveted to the spot and the next I was crushed against his chest with his mouth devouring mine in a desperate tangle of lips and tongues. God, he was an addiction for me and I didn't plan on ever kicking this one.

Max lifted me off my feet and I wrapped my legs around his waist as he turned and walked the few steps necessary to press my back against the side of the cottage. I briefly worried about his injury but he'd assured me that he had a doctor's note that said he was fully recovered and I needed to stop worrying about him. The note really said that—an inside joke between Max and his doctor and a way to stop my constant "fussing over him"—his words, not mine.

With my weight supported by the wall, his hands were free to roam my body, teasing under the edge of my T–shirt until his hands moved over my stomach and my ribs to cover my breasts, plucking my nipples through the lace of my bra. I sighed and rolled my head back as Max took advantage of my invitation and pressed hot, wet kisses along the exposed skin of my neck.

Max lifted his head and looked down at me, his eyes blazing with desire, heat, and love. He was so unbelievably gorgeous that he still took my breath away. His mouth widened in his trademark "just for me" sexy smile and his voice was rough with emotion. "Hey."

I smiled back. I'm sure I looked like a goof but I didn't care. This was my man and I loved him more than I ever thought I'd be able to love anyone. "Hey."

His hand reached up to caress my cheek, my eyes closed as I leaned into his warmth. He was my rock, my touchstone, and I could feel my soul filling back up just being in his orbit.

"You're early. I meant to meet you up at the house and give you a proper welcome."

"I think this is pretty perfect." I pulled myself from his embrace and tugged him towards the house. "C'mon, I know how we can make this welcome even better."

To my surprise, Max pulled me back with a shake of his head and a mischievous grin on his face.

"No way. I want you to see your new studio before we go up to the house." He pulled me behind him as he climbed the front steps, turning to face me when we reached the top. "Everything is installed and ready to go. It just needs your personal touch."

Max opened the door, motioning for me to walk inside. I could smell the scents of drywall, paint, and carpet, and as my excitement bubbled to the top I slipped past him and took the first real look at my new recording studio. My eyes scanned the front room which served as the writing/lounge area and was outfitted with two comfy sofas covered in red corduroy, tables in honeyed maple, and an upright piano in the corner. A custom–made entertainment center held a flat screen and Max's gaming systems. Light streamed in through the large windows, making the warm yellow paint gleam like burnished gold. It was warm, inviting—and mine.

I walked towards the back rooms which housed a kitchenette, bathroom with a shower, and my studio. It wasn't as large as the ones in Nashville, but I could record demos here, write songs, and rehearse with the band instead of heading into town. Skipping back into the front room, I saw Max standing there with his hands opened in a gesture of inquiry.

"So, what do you think?"

I crossed the room and jumped into his arms, pressing kisses all over his face as he staggered under the onslaught. "I love it!" I peppered more kisses on his lips as he laughed out loud. "Thank you! Thank you! I love you!"

"This is the right way to say thank you." He curled his hand around the back of my neck and pulled me in for a slow, wet kiss that quickly turned the mood from festive to seductive as he claimed my mouth in a blatant show of possession. I whimpered and Max broke the kiss, gazing down at me with a heavy-lidded stare that told me we would be headed to a bed very soon. Fine by me. It had been too long. "You're very welcome," he nodded towards the long wall behind him, "but you haven't seen the best part yet."

TEMPTATION

I followed the direction of his gesture and had to blink. The wall was covered by a hand made guitar rack mounted on the wall. It was also made of maple, stained a golden color and carved with the most delicate design of honeysuckle and barbed–wire. Just like on my tattoo and album logos. It was beautiful and made with so much love that it shone.

"Oh, Max." I covered my mouth with a shaking hand. Never in my life had someone done something like this for me. I pulled away from his embrace and walked slowly towards the rack. My hands shook even more as I ran my fingers over the wood. It was smooth as glass, cool to the touch, and the design was intricate but beautifully simple.

Max came up behind me, his voice soft in my ear. "Grandpa Butler helped me with the carving and the staining. It holds five guitars," his hand motioned to the middle section of the rack, "with a place of honor for Jolene."

I leaned forward to observe the carving below Jolene's slot more closely. The wood frame was formed into a curved point that held a more detailed carving of the full logo of the heart, vines, and wire. Something extra was carved into the heart and I leaned in closer to read what turned out to be three initials. K.L.B.

Oh. My. God.

My breath stuttered in my chest and my legs wobbled as I slowly turned around, scarcely believing the scene before me—Max on one knee with a velvet ring box in his hand and looking at me with so much love that I wasn't sure that this tiny cabin could hold it all. It wouldn't have surprised me if the windows blew out, the door flying open under the pressure of the emotion. Suddenly afraid that my legs would give out, I grabbed the back of the sofa. This was not the time to face–plant on the floor.

"Kit." He swallowed hard, his voice gravely and rough with his nervousness. "I wish I had your gift with words. I know this is fast and we're young but I've never been so sure of anything in my life." Max reached up with his empty hand and caressed my cheek, brushing away my tears. "I love our crazy life and I love watching you do all of these amazing things with your career. I want to be the one you come home to, the one you need when it gets too tough— the one you write mushy love songs about."

I choked back tears as I half–laughed, half–sobbed at his words. The tears were flowing like someone had opened the faucet and I knew that my makeup was a mess but I didn't care. All I knew was that the most amazing man in the world was asking me to spend forever with him. To make the home I'd dreamed about.

Max opened the box, removed the ring, and slid it onto my finger. The metal quickly warmed to my body temperature and it fit perfectly—like it had always belonged there.

"Marry me, Kit Landry. I love you. I swear that every fucking day of your life you will never doubt that you are the most important person in the world to me."

I didn't even bother to wipe away the tears as I fell to my knees and tackled him. We both fell backward onto the carpet but I could see him clearly when I straddled his body. His grin was wicked, too cocky for a guy who hadn't gotten my answer yet but I think he knew what was coming. "Yes, I'll marry you! I love you."

"Come here. It's been too long."

Max pulled me down to him, capturing my lips in a kiss that quickly turned from tender to needy in the span of a few seconds. It had been too long. These days, any time spent apart from him felt like it was too long.

Max tugged at the hem of my shirt, pulling away from our lip–lock only for the time necessary to lift it off my body. In less than five seconds he had my bra off, his strong calloused hands rubbing against my sensitive skin, teasing my nipples into hard points while my whole body flooded with white–hot arousal.

It never took long for him to get me there and I was on

the edge, fueled by too many nights with only my hands to ease the ache. I leaned over him offering my nipple, audibly stuttering when his hot mouth closed over me. He worked me up with his mouth and tongue—the gentle pulls, the licks and kisses that got me wet and needy. Desperate for him.

"Fuck, yeah, baby," Max growled against my skin as my orgasm hit me like a bolt of lightning.

My mind went blank as my body filled with the pleasure that rolled over me in waves. In spite of it, I was still so hungry for Max that my hands shifted over his body—unable to settle in one spot for very long. With a ragged breath I opened my eyes and looked down at him, begging, "Max, please. I need you."

He lifted his head to gaze into my eyes, a muscle clenched in his jaw with his own effort to remain in control.

"Off. Off," I said impatiently while my fingers got busy unbuttoning and unzipping his shorts. He lifted his hips up and I shoved down the material far enough to give me unobstructed access to him. He was going commando and I immediately grasped his cock in my hand, stroking the long hard length, soaking in every movement of his body, every groan that escaped past his clenched teeth.

I loved every minute with Max but this moment—when I had him completely undone by his need—was a head–rush for me. But it never lasted long.

When Max took over, I was the one adrift, only anchored to this world by him and the way he made me feel like the whole universe centered on the two of us.

He groaned, running his hands over my skirt and making quick work of getting it off me, along with my thong. Finally I was naked and he had full access to where I wanted him most. He lifted his hips so the tip of his erection prodded the entrance of my hot, slippery core. Closing his eyes tightly, he pushed inside me with one thrust. He was big and hard and it had been a long few weeks but even through the ache it felt so damn good that I never wanted it to stop.

His eyes opened and I don't know what killed me most—the fiery passion or the tenderness. His fingers dug into my hips and I could feel his legs shaking with the effort to prolong this moment for a little while longer. "Kit. I love you so much. No one else for me. Ever."

I leaned down, brushing a soft kiss against his lips. "Show me. Prove it."

With a low moan, he rocked his body against mine— sliding in and out of my body—as his mouth claimed every one of my gasps, every single sigh.

I arched my body, riding him to meet his every thrust, pulling him deeper and clinging to him as he pulled out of me.

Max broke the kiss, panting with desire as he lifted his head and licked my nipple, sending sparks of pleasure to my clit. He drew the hard peak into his mouth and suckled deeply before releasing it to do the same thing to its twin. My head swam with the sensations created by him filling me, stretching me as my second climax built low in my belly.

"Come for me, Kit." Max's voice was rough, his breathing hard and labored, stuttering with each deep thrust. "I need to feel you again. Want it. Will always need you."

His words sent me over the edge. Flying. Tumbling. I cried out as my body seized him, drawing him deeper and forcing him to join me in the freefall.

For several long minutes, we laid together on the floor, listening to the sounds out in the garden as they filtered through the open door. The scents of summer roses and sunshine mixed with those of our lovemaking as we drifted along in our private paradise. He nuzzled my cheek, that spot on my neck I loved so much. He shifted us, placing me on my back while he leaned up on his elbow to watch me. I lifted my left hand and played with the ring on my forever finger.

It was classically styled with a large stone in a platinum setting and it was perfect. Not gaudy or showy, just right.

"Max, I love it. It's so beautiful."

"I'm glad you like it." He grinned a slow, lazy smile. "I'm glad you said yes."

"What would you have done if I'd said no?"

"Like *that* would ever happen." He dodged my pinch and laughed. "I would have kept asking you. Wearing you down with sex until you had no other choice but to say yes."

"Manipulative bastard," I grumbled.

"And you're going to be Mrs. Manipulative Bastard."

I grinned up at him, liking how that sounded just fine. I dropped a quick kiss on his lips. "Thank you."

Max cupped his hand behind my neck and drew me close for a lingering kiss before resting his forehead against mine. Smiling softly to himself, he shook his head. "For what?"

Aw man, how could he not know? I reached up with both hands and made sure he heard every word. "Thank you for believing in us when I didn't."

His eyes sparkled with mischief and his smile was big enough to light up the world. I loved knowing that all that joy was because of me, of us. "Baby, don't you get it?" He wound a curl around his finger and gave it a gentle tug. "Loving you is the easiest thing I've ever done. I love being the little man at home."

I laughed at that. Life with Max would never be dull. I kissed him and then leaned back, my mind churning a million miles a minute. *The little man at home...*

"Uh, oh."

Max's voice brought me back to the present.

Busted.

His voice was laced with humor as he touched his finger to my nose. "I *know* that look. You just thought of a song didn't you?" I nodded and he pushed me up, stripped off his T—shirt and pulled it over my head.

He pointed towards the cabinet next to the piano. "That's stocked with your favorite pens and paper."

I looked over towards the cabinet but hesitated. "Are

you sure? I just got home..."

Max laughed and leaned back on the sofa, his hands behind his head. He made a delectable picture—all muscles, silky dark hair on his chest, and miles of tanned sexy skin. "I'm going to lie here and recover, so you've got fifteen minutes to write down what's in your head."

I shivered at his sexy tone. "And then?"

"And then, I'm going to take you up to the house and get to work on distracting you from your job." He paused and flashed a wolfish grin. "At least for the next sixty years or so."

All thoughts of work suddenly left my mind as I pictured just how many ways Max could distract me from my work. *Oh, yum.* I backed towards the door of the cottage, pausing at the doorway.

"How long did you say you needed to recover?"

Max lifted an eyebrow and leaned up on one arm. "What did you have in mind?"

I reached down and grabbed the hem of the T–shirt. "I was wondering if you wanted to work on 'Operation Distract Kit.' You know... get started on that sixty years or so." I lifted the T–shirt up and off my body and shivered at the feral gleam that shadowed his features. "If you're recovered enough, that is."

Max growled low in his chest and leaned towards me. "Why don't you come over here and let me show you just how recovered I am?"

I laughed and turned towards the door, stepping out on the porch. "Why don't you catch me?"

Racing across the lawn towards the house where I would live and love with Max, I threw back my head and laughed.

I needed to write a song about this.

Tomorrow.

Dear Reader—

Thanks so much for reading my book. I really hope you enjoyed Max and Kit's story. If you did, please tell your friends and drop me a line at robin@robincovington romance.com. I'd love to hear from you. And for the latest info on my books, sign up for my newsletter.

And if you are so inclined, please leave a review on Amazon, Barnes & Noble, iBooks, or Goodreads.

I love to explore the theme of fooling around and falling in love in my books and I adore a hero who falls hard. When I'm not writing sexy, sizzling romance, I collect tasty man candy pics, indulge in a little comic book geek love, and obsess over Dean Winchester. Don't send chocolate... send eye–candy!

There are so many great books out there and I'm grateful that you spent your money and time to read my book.

Xx,
Robin

****

Social Media Links:

Website: www.robincovingtonromance.com
Facebook Profile: http://on.fb.me/YSW9n3
Facebook Page: http://on.fb.me/1fCyWuQ
Twitter: @RobinCovington
Pinterest: http://bit.ly/1c1Tm5u
Newsletter sign up: http://eepurl.com/qjFcz

If you enjoyed TEMPTATION, check out my other books:

A NIGHT OF SOUTHERN COMFORT
HIS SOUTHERN TEMPTATION
SWEET SOUTHERN BETRAYAL
PLAYING THE PART
SEX & THE SINGLE VAMP
SECRET SANTA BABY

ACKNOWLEDGMENTS

When I was growing up in a small Virginia town, I was surrounded by stories. My family (bootleggers and preachers) could spin a tale that would have you laughing and crying in turn. For that heritage, I am so grateful and I hope that I am living up to the very high bar they set for me.

On this journey, I get to walk with the most amazing people and they hold me up, drag me along, or kick my butt when I need it.

Kimberly Kincaid and Avery Flynn—I don't know what I'd do without you.

Debra Hill Hodge, Tina Payne, and Karin Evans – for helping me with the beta read. You guys sizzle!

To my Sizzlemongers – I love you guys!!!

Sara Humphreys, Laura Kaye, Gina L. Maxwell, & Tracy Brogan—Thank you for inspiring me, making me laugh, and showing me how to do this.

Washington Romance Writers, Maryland Romance Writers, Contemporary Romance Writers, the Indie Club, and the Self–Publish loop writers—So much talent shared so generously. Thank you.

To the Main Man, Little Man, and Lulu—I love you all so much. Thank you for supporting me and helping me reach my dream.

Made in the USA
Middletown, DE
16 November 2016